PENGUIN BOOKS

SINNERS atone

Somme Sketcher is an internationally bestselling author of dark and mafia romance.

She is best known for her Sinners Anonymous series and for writing the slowest of the slow burns (for which she is not sorry at all).

Also by Somme Sketcher

Sinners Anonymous
Sinners Condemned
Sinners Consumed

SINNERS
atone

SOMME SKETCHER

PENGUIN BOOKS

PENGUIN BOOKS

UK | USA | Canada | Ireland | Australia
India | New Zealand | South Africa

Penguin Books is part of the Penguin Random House group of companies
whose addresses can be found at global.penguinrandomhouse.com

Penguin Random House UK,
One Embassy Gardens, 8 Viaduct Gardens, London SW1 1 7BW

penguin.co.uk

Published in Penguin Books 2026

001

Copyright © Somme Sketcher, 2025

The moral right of the author has been asserted

Penguin Random House values and supports copyright.
Copyright fuels creativity, encourages diverse voices, promotes freedom
of expression and supports a vibrant culture. Thank you for purchasing
an authorised edition of this book and for respecting intellectual property
laws by not reproducing, scanning or distributing any part of it by any
means without permission. You are supporting authors and enabling
Penguin Random House to continue to publish books for everyone.
No part of this book may be used or reproduced in any manner for the
purpose of training artificial intelligence technologies or systems. In accordance
with Article 4(3) of the DSM Directive 2019/790, Penguin Random House
expressly reserves this work from the text and data mining exception.

Set in 10.86/14pt Fanwood
Typeset by Six Red Marbles UK, Thetford, Norfolk

Printed and bound in Great Britain by Clays Ltd, Elcograf S.p.A.

The authorised representative in the EEA is Penguin Random House Ireland,
Morrison Chambers, 32 Nassau Street, Dublin D02 YH68

A CIP catalogue record for this book is available from the British Library

ISBN: 978–1–911–74665–2

Penguin Random House is committed to a sustainable future
for our business, our readers and our planet. This book is made from
Forest Stewardship Council® certified paper.

A NOTE FROM
Somme

Dear reader,

Thank you for picking up a copy of *Sinners Atone*! I hope you love reading it as much as I loved writing it.

I wanted to remind you that *Sinners Atone* is book one of a duet. It ends on a cliffhanger, and the story concludes with *Sinners Absolve*.

Before you dive in, you should know that this book is a **dark romance.** There are several triggers, including talk of alcoholism, murder, incarceration, violence, and child abuse (not on page). Please read at your own risk.

Love,
Somme x

We can easily forgive a child who is afraid of the dark; the real tragedy of life is when men are afraid of the light.

— UNKNOWN

THREE YEARS
Earlier

My father had these rules.

They were mostly bullshit, hammered together from age-old clichés and Hollywood one-liners, but when he spoke them into existence, they had a nasty habit of hardening into prophecies.

I was born bad because he said I would be. He said I'd withhold my first breath out of spite, and that not even shoving the family's silver in my mouth before I took my second would pacify me.

Now, I'll take my last exactly where he said I would: in the dark that made me The Villain.

My laugh echoes through the forest, deep and bitter, before morphing into a spluttering cough.

Guess death isn't so funny after all.

Wiping my mouth with the back of my hand, I scan the black sky. I learned the first time I died that the long tunnels and the white lights weren't meant for men like me. Hell, after everything I've done, God is more likely to cut his electricity and draw the curtains than signpost me to heaven. I'm looking for a different light, an orange one, and when I spot it filtering through the branches, I bite out a curse.

It isn't growing any fucking closer.

I press my palm against the gash in my side and glare up at it. I'm dying, but I'm not delusional. There's no miracle waiting for me at that streetlamp, but if I reach the lamp, I'm on the main road. Then all I have to do is cross it and I'm at the church. It's my only chance to warn my brothers.

My brothers.

Fuck.

A new kind of pain behind my sternum drives me onward, but as my boot strikes soil, a white-hot heat roars up my leg and explodes in my stomach. I stagger backward and clip something with my heel, and when a whirring noise prickles my ears, my muscles tighten.

I've tripped over that fucking 'play' button.

I knew it was coming because it always comes. It's a myth that the worst part about dying is the pain or the uncertainty of what comes next. It's not. It's the part where your life flashes before your eyes and there's fuck-all you can do about it.

I tried outrunning it once; it only chased me. Tried closing my eyes, but it just projected off the inside of my eyelids.

Knowing I can't spare the energy fighting it, I clench my jaw, steady myself against a tree, and reluctantly wait for the show to start.

The Beginning plays out in Technicolor.

Nine summers spill out from between the trees and swallow the darkness whole. Days roll out along the forest floor; long and lazy; grass-stained, sunburned. Even the October wind warms and thickens, bringing with it the smell of chlorine and that sun-block I hated so much.

A memory of Angelo putting me in a headlock and smothering my face with it dances against the trunk of an oak tree. My mother pretending not to notice while she flips through a magazine by the pool plays out on another.

Amusement rattles my next exhale, and I rub my thumb over a mud-caked knuckle. The first scar I ever got was from the day I was strong enough to twist out of my brother's grip and sucker punch him in the nuts.

Then the days fade to terracotta. Summer nights never got dark in The Beginning. They were always lit by bonfires in the garden and the torch I'd tuck under my chin to tell my brothers ghost stories around them.

Rafe's shrieks rustle between the branches, and a cold snap brushes my cheek as Angelo's laugh chases after it. He was *vicious* long before it solidified into a nickname.

When the next sound echoes in my ears, my smirk fades. All the fresh blood in my mouth congeals and threatens to choke me.

'*Gabriel.*'

Fuck. I'd be an idiot to close my eyes. Being this close to death means there's a good chance they won't open again. But when my mama's voice shoots through the night and pierces my chest like a second stab wound, I squeeze my lids shut and drop my head back against the tree.

Maria Visconti was a woman with many hobbies, but her favorite was believing in bullshit. She believed some chick named Eve ate an apple and caused all the evil in the world, but if she'd just wished on a stray eyelash, everything would have been okay anyway. Every shiver was someone walking over her grave, and every black cat to cross her path was a sure sign she'd soon be lowered into it. The bearded dude in the sky, the fortune teller at the fair. Even the smackhead who hangs outside the Visconti Grand Casino and swaps tourists a lucky penny for a dollar.

She believed everything everyone told her to.

Except her husband and his rules.

'*Gabriel!*'

I grit my teeth and turn away from her voice.

No doubt she'd have believed him at first, back when he was telling her all the shit every mother wanted to hear. That her first child would be born to lead, and her second would take the silver spoon in his mouth and turn it to gold. But when he placed his hand on her swollen belly and declared her third son the Devil, she'd soured into a skeptic.

'*Gabriel . . .*'

I press harder onto my bleeding stomach, letting out an acidic hiss. I was wrong. The worst part of dying isn't watching your life flash before your eyes, it's hearing it ring in your ears. And tonight, not even the sound of sins could drown it out.

A guttural wheeze shoots from my lips, melts into a bleach-white puff, and blows all nine summers out of the clearing.

Nine winters bring silence and a blanket of snow. My retinas burn from the sudden contrast, and I look to the gray fog hanging beneath the forest canopy to escape it. But there's no relief up there, just a familiar face, a familiar expression, and a familiar fucking smirk disappearing behind the faceted crystal of a whiskey glass.

A new voice sears the back of my neck.

'*I told you so, Maria.*'

And then comes the familiar fury.

Alonso Visconti was so certain I'd be bad, so certain of his prophecy that he'd refused to name me after an angel like my brothers. Something about blasphemy and poor taste. But my mama had a way of making spite look pretty, and named me after her favorite angel of all.

'*Oh, Gabriel.*'

The bastard was right from the jump. While my brothers gurgled, laughed, and crawled, I bit, hissed, kicked. One of my earliest memories is stabbing a cousin with a butter knife at

Sunday lunch, and I can't even remember which one because I've tried to kill them all at some point.

I slam my head against the tree, trying to shake my mother's voice out of it. But it's too late, it's already crawled into my brain and made itself at home. *'Gabriel' plays* on a loop over and over and over. All three fucking syllables because she only ever said my full name, and never with a hint of irony. If anyone, including myself, dropped the last two, she'd tut, pick them up, and stitch them back on.

I don't know if she said my name the way she did to try to convince God I was good or just to piss off my father. If the latter was the case, it worked.

For the first nine years, he called me nothing at all.

From the tenth on, he called me The Villain.

My lungs seize, and my next inhale is desperate and wet. When I throw my head back to gulp more air, the darkness eats at the edges of my vision. Right on cue, it swallows all nine winters, all the half-drunk hot cocoas, and the half-built snowmen with wonky carrots for dicks.

When The Beginning ends, the darkness will take everything.

The last pinprick of light swims before my eyes, then disappears, plunging me into the black abyss. Silence doesn't follow, it's just bittersweet memories yelled through a megaphone, and when I can no longer stand it, a roar of frustration lights a path of fire up my throat.

I slide a few inches down rough bark, panting.

My stomach slides south too, and my gaze reluctantly follows.

There's that glow from the streetlamp again, only it's not. It's too small and too low, dancing against the dark at chest height. I give my head a shake, squeeze my eyes shut, and when I open them, the light has fractured and sharpened, taking the shape of fire.

Birthday candles. Ten, striped blue and white.

They flicker in the wind, pushing the darkness from my vision until all I can see is light. They slow my heartbeat, steady my breathing, and for a moment, life isn't leaking out of me from the six-inch gash in my stomach.

The last time I cheated Death, I swore when it found me again and flashed this part before me, I wouldn't hold my breath. Said it the time before that too. Yet here I am, my inhale locked at the base of my throat as if I'm saving it for later.

The backs of my eyes sting. Guess dying makes you a sentimental pussy. It's got me wondering about stupid shit, like alternate realities and butterfly wings and what would have happened if I'd been the first or second child. If I hadn't been born at all.

Seconds pile up into minutes, and I'm still holding my breath, chest convulsing, lungs burning, doing it anyway. The flames turn a darker shade of orange, pulsing in and out of focus. My lips tingle and my head spins. Instinct rises, and before I can squash it, blood and breath splutter from my lips, snuffing out the candles.

Darkness engulfs the forest again. I wipe my mouth and glare out at it. It glares right back and whispers, *What did you expect?*

I huff out a weak laugh. Yeah. Mama could have said all three syllables until she was blue in the face, it would never have made a difference because my father had sealed my fate.

I was born bad, and I'll die in the dark that made me the worst.

Fuck this.

I don't have time for end-of-life hallucinations, I've got shit to do.

I shove myself off the tree, my boots sinking farther into the soil with every step. The Devil's grasping at my ankles, trying to drag me home, but he can't have me, not yet. Not until I've knelt on the concrete steps of the church and carved my message into its doors.

The Middle starts with a honk of a horn.

That *bastard* noise.

The first time I heard it, I made the mistake of looking out of the bedroom window.

The second time, I wished I'd never heard it at all.

And after the third, I learned the consequence of pretending I hadn't.

The sound rips through the dark again, louder and angrier, hitting me in the back like a freight train.

Even after all these years, it still has a way of lurching me forward.

When the brush thickens and scrapes over old scars, I turn my eyes skyward and find the orange glow again.

It's growing closer, but so is my father.

He had the dangerous combination of being a heavyset man with a light tread. I'd know the sound of his gait anywhere – in The Middle, it followed me into these woods every night for eight years. Eight fucking years of torture, games, *lessons*. Eight years, until he followed me up a gravel path, shoved me through iron gates, and left me to fight for my life.

The Middle was dictated by a new set of rules. And like the birthday candles, there were ten, just for me.

His whiskey-tainted breath grazes past my ear.

Rule one: You must become The Villain for your brothers to call you a hero.

I walk faster to get away from The Middle. To get away from him. The next few steps send a molten heat to my groin and buckle my knees, but I grind the pain between my teeth and keep moving.

Finally, the orange glow stretches out its hand. Space expands, branches retract, and soil turns to asphalt.

Though I slow to a stop under the streetlamp to catch what little breath I have left, my gaze goes for a walk. It sweeps over the road, and I wonder when it got so fucking wide. Then it climbs the stones of my father's church on the other side.

That bastard building hurts to look at on my best days, but on my worst, just a glance in its direction burns.

I skim over broken windows and the crumbling spire, looking for relief where the Pacific meets the black sky behind it.

And then I realize what I'm doing, and sour amusement floods my chest.

A dying man always turns his eyes to the sky.

When I was young and invincible, I vowed I'd be the exception. That when Death finally stepped out of my shadow and tapped me on the shoulder, I wouldn't tilt my chin and look for the God I've cursed for a lifetime. Yet here I am, gazing in the opposite direction to where my soul is headed, wondering if he's really up there and if he's taking good care of my mama.

My next inhale rattles around my chest; my next exhale paints a white streak across the night. When the wind rises over the cliffs and sweeps it sideways, I see Him.

He glances down at me and breathes a sigh of relief.

No laughing this time.

Lungs too weak now.

Legs too weak. Arms too weak.

Don't close your eyes.

Don't. Close. Your. Eyes.

I step forward and the world tilts, trying to shake me off it. I push onward against the wind; it drives me back even harder. Its roar is deafening and cold, but when I cock my head, I hear something softer within it.

'Hello?'

Tension leaves my lips in a short breath.

The voice is like cashmere and chocolate. Like a gentle kiss on the cheek, a warm bath on an icy night.

'Hello? Are you okay?'

It's a ray of sunshine through an open window, a cool breeze on a hot day.

I want to die to its soundtrack.

I want to hear it again.

I scan the horizon for its source, and when I find it, my vision jolts.

Under the next streetlamp stands a girl. No – an angel. Not one of those biblically accurate ones they'd draw on the whiteboard to scare the shit out of us in Sunday school, but one from the movies. The human-shaped, heaven-sent kind with outstretched wings and a halo hovering over flowing blonde hair. She's also wearing a fuzzy pink jacket and matching earmuffs, but fuck, who am I to question what angels wear these days?

There's no time for side quests, but getting to the church suddenly feels secondary, and curiosity steers my path.

I take a step toward her; she takes one back, glances at my stomach, throws her hands in the air, and says, 'Um, that's a Halloween costume, right?'

What?

The cogs in my brain whir at half speed, but when they groan into place, I realize I'm a fucking idiot.

It's October thirty-first. Halloween.

Of course I'd die on Halloween.

I'm still too weak to laugh, but the irony is all-consuming, so I do it anyway. It takes the last shred of energy from me, and I fall to my knees.

She's not an angel; she's just a girl dressed like one. Looks like one, sounds like one, even now that she's shouting. She floats toward me like an angel too, out from underneath her lamp and into the light of mine.

Sparkly pink boots and frilly socks pulsate in and out of focus beneath my eye line.

Christ. So much pink.

'Oh my God. What happened?'

Ha.

I blinked, that's what fucking happened.

Rule two: Near enemy, family, or friend, The Villain never blinks.

He'd plucked that one straight out of his ass in a panic after the first time he shot me. He swore he'd done it just to show me what it feels like, but even at eleven, I knew the cunt just had shit aim.

Rule three came just nine hours later as I was waking up under the harsh strip lights of a makeshift operating theater: *The most powerful villains are as unlovable as they are untouchable.*

I'm as unlovable as I am untouchable.

So why the *fuck* is she now touching me?

Delicate fingers sear my shoulder. Violence is a deep-rooted reflex, and I jerk out an arm to shake her off.

'Fuck. Off,' I snarl.

But more fool me, because now the sky is slipping. I'm falling forward, down into the Devil's arms.

The ground catches me, because *not yet*.

With her sweet voice, she calls out to God again. My cheek scrapes gravel, then suddenly I'm on my back, and there she is.

Fuck. Maybe she is an angel. Because I swear, the streetlamp above wasn't as bright until she dropped to her knees beneath it. Now it bends to accommodate the curves of her heart-shaped face and reflects in her wide blue eyes, like sunlight dancing on water. It skates over her golden bangs, sparkles on her eyelids, and carves a straight line from the top of her nose down to the deep groove of her cupid's bow.

No. This isn't how death is supposed to go. I'm meant to die in the dark, not under her light, and the last thing I need is to be seen like this. Remembered like this. Weak and pathetic, lying in the fucking dirt bleeding out.

But the ground is too comfortable and my jaw too heavy to tell her to fuck off again. The best I can do is fight to keep my eyes open and track her every move.

Her gaze fixes on my stomach, wide-eyed and disbelieving. 'Is that *blood*?'

'No, it's ketchup,' I grit.

'It looks painful.'

'No shit.'

She nods solemnly, ignoring my sarcasm. With a hand at her mouth, she bites down on the tip of her middle finger and tugs off her pink glove. 'Don't panic, I'm going to call for help.'

Trying to call anyone is useless, but so is my voice box, so I only watch as she stuffs her hand in her coat pocket and pulls out her cell. Like the rest of her, it's ridiculously pink, as are the half a dozen charms attached to it. They clink and rattle like my mama's wind chimes on the back porch as she furiously taps in her pass code.

'No signal,' I manage to huff out after several attempts. 'Just go.'

She glances at her screen, down to me, and back again. The tiniest crease lines her forehead. 'Dammit. Well, there's a phone booth just there. You got any quarters?'

'It. Doesn't. Work.'

'What?'

Fuck this, I'm wasting too much time. Must cross the road. I feel for the ground beside me and push down on it in an attempt sit up. A sharp stabbing pain shoots through my core, and I collapse back against the asphalt.

'Hey, you need to stay still –'

I bark at her to leave again, but it comes out in a gurgle so guttural it jolts her to her feet.

'Crap, crap, crap,' she whimpers, her composure cracking for a moment. Then she rolls her shoulders back and takes a deep breath. 'Okay, wait right here.'

As if I can go anywhere else. The light follows her to the middle of the road. My eyes tag along too, watching as she paces from left to right and back again, holding her bag on her shoulder with one hand and her cell to the sky with the other.

Pausing for breath, I try to make sense of her.

Maybe God sent her as a cruel joke. A final taunt of what could have been had I been born Angelo or Rafe. But then I dismiss the idea immediately, because He's not stupid enough to send her to a man like me. He wouldn't take the risk.

So if she's not from another world, what the fuck is she doing in this one, walking along a dark road alone in the middle of the night?

Curiosity and a slither of annoyance entwine with my pain, but I ignore it. I don't have the time or energy to dig deeper. She needs to leave, and I need to get moving.

With a hard puff, I roll myself onto my side. I ball my hands into fists and press into the earth, trying to drag myself forward on my knuckles. If I can't walk, then I'll crawl to the church. And if I can't crawl, I'll fucking roll – whatever it takes to warn my brothers.

She jogs over and gives my chest a little kick with the tip of her toe. 'Christ – stop moving! You'll make it worse!'

I glance up to see if she's joking, because how can this get any worse? But I'm distracted by the cell phone pressed flat against her forehead.

What the fuck is she doing?

I guess my glare asked the question for me because she launches into a rambling explanation.

'If you have no signal, you can put your phone to your head and you'll magically get service. Don't ask me how it works, I just saw it on Instagram – oh, *God*.'

There she goes, calling out to God again. But I've collapsed flat onto my back and can see that the sky beyond the lamp is empty.

She doesn't float now, she stomps and jingles, then drops to her knees at my side, muttering empty promises into the wind.

'Okay. You're okay. Let's see, uh . . .' She slips the huge bag off her shoulder and upturns it. Its contents spill out around her, and she combs through the mess. 'Right, we just need something to stem the bleeding, that's all.' She picks up a tube from the pile and holds it up to the light. 'Eyelash glue? No, not strong enough. Okay . . .' Another small package glints under the light. 'I've got Band-Aids, but they're for, like, blisters and cuts, not . . .' Her gaze shifts over my stomach.

'Stab wound,' I grunt.

She freezes, and for a second, fear threads through her perfect features, but when her eyes climb up my torso and lock with mine, her expression changes shape, and I don't fucking like it.

I'm used to being regarded with fear. It's familiar and comforting. The sickest part of me almost enjoys it. But now she's got the same strain of pity in her eyes as my mama had every time she'd watch me limp down the driveway at dawn.

'Who did this to you?' she whispers.

Mama used to ask me that too. And like it did then, my father's voice scratches my inner ear.

Rule four: If it happened in the dark, it didn't happen.

But as with my mama, silence doesn't satisfy her.

'What did he look like?' she presses. 'Or she,' she quickly adds, clamping her hand to her mouth. 'Sorry, that was *so* sexist of me. Would you recognize them if you saw them again? If he – or she! – is still out there, we need to tell the police immediately so they can catch them. Can you describe them to me?'

Irritation rises within me, and it hurts more than the gash splitting me in two. 'Go away,' I mutter. I've never been in the business of asking twice, let alone three fucking times. I'm starting to sound like a broken record.

But she's not even listening, let alone looking as though she's about to fuck off. Instead, she goes back to mumbling to herself, picking up objects, tossing them down. Rinse, repeat.

I grit my teeth and squeeze my eyes shut. The voice that was so sweet just moments ago is now grating.

Guess my father was bang on the money with rule five: *A Villain never dies peacefully in his sleep.*

I always thought it meant I'd be tortured to death, not slowly bleed out in a sea of beauty products under the watchful eye of an annoying angel.

'Hey – don't close your eyes,' she demands. 'You've gotta stay with me, okay?'

I force an eye open to make sure she doesn't touch me again. But it's worse. She pushes up off her heels, sucks in a shaky breath, and slams her hands down on my torso.

The pain is excruciating. It zaps through my body like a lightning strike, shocking every cell, nerve, and muscle. I writhe and shake and groan, trying to buck her off me.

My thoughts are nasty, and they're all pointed at her. If I had even a fraction of my usual strength, I'd snap her fucking wrists, every finger and knuckle too.

But the angrier I get, the more she apologizes and tells me to *just breathe*, as if I'm getting a fucking Brazilian wax or something and it'll all be over in a moment.

Her voice is breathy and restrained as it cuts through the ringing in my ears. 'I've got to apply pressure to the wound, but my hands are too small. I'm going to have to sit on you.'

'No –'

Too late. Pinning her dress to the backs of her thighs, she shifts sideways onto my stomach, like she's sliding into a diner booth.

I'd think I was hallucinating if the pain wasn't so fucking visceral. I can feel its pulse, taste its minerals. But before I can let out the scream to accompany it, it wilts in my throat.

She's touching me again. Skin to skin. The fingers I desperately wanted to snap now rest on the hollows of my cheeks. Her thumb tracks over the same two inches, dipping in and out of my beard in an unfamiliar, soothing, stroking motion.

Her gaze locks with mine, and for a split second, the world dies instead of me. It drains of color and light. Even the wind has stopped breathing.

'That feels better, right?'

The pain returns, but it's dull and misplaced. My torso throbs a little less, but now it hurts where she touches, a slow-moving burn seeping through skin and bone and bloating every cell between.

No, it doesn't feel better. It feels worse than dying.

Rule six, my father warns from the treeline: *the most successful villains aren't the ones who have nothing to lose, but who have* nobody *to lose.*

He didn't just speak that one into existence, he beat it into me with the hard crack of his belt during the summer my balls dropped and I realized blood rushed to my dick every time a pretty girl walked past in a tight dress.

Not that it mattered, of course. Just because I looked, doesn't mean they were brave enough to look back. And even if they were, they never looked at me like this girl is gazing at me now.

She regards me with this wide-eyed concern, as though she's seeing the worst of humanity for the first time and is certain she can fix it. Not an ounce of reservation or fear swims in those ocean-blue eyes. Judging by how she's sitting on top of me, touching me, there's none in her brain either.

Annoyance darkens my edges. She shouldn't be out here, at this hour, looking like . . . *that*. She's an angel with broken wings, and I couldn't count on both blood-stained hands the number of men I know who would snatch her off these streets in half a heartbeat.

'What are you doing out here?' I grunt, rolling my head away from her touch and eyeing the contents of her Mary Poppin's bag. There's a lone flip-flop, a jumbo pack of crackers, and enough lip glosses to stock a beauty store.

'Saving your life, what else?' she replies flippantly, checking her cell for signal again.

My annoyance burns hotter at her smart-ass answer. 'Do you stop and chat to every strange man you meet on a dark road?'

'When they're bleeding like a waterfall, sure.'

'Well, you shouldn't.'

Her gaze falls to mine, sparkling with amusement. 'But aren't you glad I did?'

I study the smugness puckering her lips, and disbelief trickles through me. 'You realize I'm going to die, right?'

She tuts. 'Well, you will with that attitude.'

I let out a frustrated groan. Great. Not only does she not understand the concept of personal safety and personal space, but to top it all off, she's a fucking optimist.

When The Middle began, I soon developed a hatred for all the positivity in the world because I'd seen what the dark side of it looked like. My brothers were oblivious, happy kids, and it never seemed fair they got to wake up every morning and laugh over breakfast while I'd spent the night before in Hell's seventh circle.

I'd tried to show them the dark side too. I'd bring home roadkill with the hope the corpses would haunt their nightmares, and hold their heads underwater until they grew limp, just so they, too, knew what dying felt like.

And when that didn't work, I started carving the dark side into the church doors instead.

Looking up at this girl now, I'm overcome with the same childlike spite I had back then. I want to shake the light out of her. To peg her eyes open and force her to watch my life flash before them too, if only to make her realize the world isn't all sunshine and rainbows and she shouldn't walk around late at night in it.

But I couldn't shake her even if I tried. My arms and legs are growing heavier and melting into the earth.

As though she feels me dissolving beneath her, she rests a light hand on my chest.

'Don't worry, it's nearly dawn.'

'So?'

'So, a car will pass by soon.' She cranes her neck and squints down the long stretch of road ahead. 'You're going to be fine, we just need to get you to the hospital.'

'Yeah. A couple of stitches and a lollipop, and I'll be right as rain.'

'That's the spirit.'

Christ. I really must be the number one player on God's shit list.

We linger in stiff silence for a while, only my wheezing breaths and her little puffs of impatience polluting the air.

She keeps glancing down the road. Then she tugs at the hem of her dress and shifts her weight on me. As she reaches up to smooth down her bangs, she stiffens. Slowly, she turns over her hand and inspects it under the light, as if seeing it for the first time. Then her gaze falls to her coat, dress, legs.

Blood. It's everywhere. Soaking into all her pink, dripping from the tips of her wings, staining her the same shade of black as my soul.

Good. Bitter amusement washes through me as the realization drains all the color from her face. I can practically hear her little bubble of delusion *pop*. Maybe now she'll fuck off and leave me to die in peace.

But seconds scratch by, and she doesn't move. She just stares, blank-faced, at a lone red droplet snaking down her thigh. It dribbles over her knee, along her calf, and disappears into the instep of her boot.

'Blood's a bitch to get out,' I say, only to twist the knife further.

'Only if you don't know how to clean it.' She dabs at the red trail with the cuff of her coat and flashes me a limp smile. 'Nothing hydrogen peroxide, enzyme cleaner, and a little elbow grease can't handle, honey.'

My eyes narrow. What the fuck does she know about getting blood out of clothes? A river of curiosity runs thin beneath my skin, but then common sense gives me a weak kick. My view of the world is so skewed that I'd forgotten normal people clean for cleanliness's sake and not just to hide a body.

Letting out a labored breath, I finally give in to the weight of my eyelids.

Rule seven, my father hisses from between the trees: *The Villain never taps out.*

Yeah, well. Here I am, old man, finally tapping out.

I've fought my whole life, and I'm tired of it. I don't even care to make it to the church anymore; I just want to go home.

There's nothing left to do now, apart from watch The Middle bleed into The End.

I roll my head to the side, and my cheek smacks the 'play' button. The clicking and whirring are weaker this time, the memories on the backs of my eyelids little more than flickering shadows and whispers.

Eighteen, no candles. My father honks his horn outside my window for the last time, and so begins the long drive to hell.

A pile of dead friends. I stacked the bodies high enough to climb on top and claw myself out.

My brothers glancing at me over the dinner table.

My mother crying a year's worth of tears.

'*Where have you been?*'

'*What's wrong with you?*'

'*Gabriel. Gabriel. Gabriel.*'

'Hey.' Warm fingers grip my jaw and tilt my head back to the sky. 'Talk to me.'

'Can't.'

'Then what are you doing right now, silly?' When I don't reply, she pokes me square in the chest, and her huff skitters along my jaw. 'All right. Listen, then.'

Something foreign probes at my ear.

'No –'

'Shh.'

My protest melts under the palm on my cheek. I swear, all the good in the world is behind it. It seeps through my skin and churns my blood into butter. Then it clots at the base of my throat because it's not *right*. It's too soft, too kind.

I've done nothing in this lifetime to deserve it.

I realize the thing in my ear is an earbud when a familiar piano run fissures out of it. Forcing my eyes open, I wait for my vision to sharpen, and find her at the heart of it, grinning.

She adjusts her own earbud. 'It's "Dancing Queen," by ABBA,' she says proudly, as if she wrote the fucking song herself.

'Get it out,' I grunt.

'No, it'll make you feel better.' When met with my glare, she adds, 'Seriously, it's scientifically proven that ABBA songs make you happy. With "Dancing Queen," it's because both Agnetha and Anni-Frid are singing the same key – which literally never happens in a duet, by the way – and at a really high register. When you hear it, your brain signals to your body to produce adrenaline, which, in turn, reduces the feeling of pain.' She glances down at my blood seeping out from beneath her thighs. 'I'd say Google it, but there's no signal. And well, you know . . .'

She gestures down at me as if the sweep of her hand will finish her sentence.

But I'm too busy staring at her mouth to register the nonsense seeping out of it.

'Fuck, you're beautiful.'

I hadn't meant to say that aloud. Guess death softens your insides, and liquid shit is coming out of my mouth too.

Her wings flutter beneath the light as she cocks her head and flashes me a broad smile. It's like looking at the fucking sun.

A bitter amusement filters through me. 'You hear that all the time.'

'Yes, but tell me again.'

My laugh comes out in a weak choke. The chorus in my ear drowns it out, and when her fingers smooth over the curve of my cheek again, I suddenly can't even feel its burn.

She changes path, tracing a line from my brow down to my chin. 'How'd you get this scar?'

I swallow. 'My barber was a drinker.'

Her laugh is warmer than the wind. It'd feel good in a different timeline; tonight, it feels bittersweet. 'How'd you get those wings?'

'Eh, I just bought them off Amazon,' she chirps, eyes holding a sparkle.

I shake my head, humor playing on my lips. I can still see her eyes when I close my own.

With ABBA in my ears and her touch dancing on my skin, an odd sense of calm drifts over me. Turns out, there's peace in purgatory. Never felt it in my life, and I sure as hell won't feel it in the afterworld, either.

So I lay in limbo for a while. The flames of hell brushing my back, the touch of an angel caressing my face. She's heavensent, I'm hell-bound, and here we are, crossing paths in the middle.

When the music cuts out mid-verse, I open my eyes again.

Something in her expression has shifted. A storm shaking the calm in her gaze.

She breathes out on a shaky whisper, 'You're actually going to die, aren't you?'

'I will with that attitude.'

Humor flickers across her face, but it doesn't meet her eyes. They're too full of something else, something dark and heavy. Her hand slides down from my face and fists the fabric of my shirt.

She leans in. So fucking close that she steals one of my last breaths from me. An inch more, and I'd feel those lips on mine and taste the strawberry scent of her gloss. 'Can I tell you a secret?'

What?

My thoughts fizzle and my gut twists. A secret. The mere idea of a secret breathes new life into me, but then my father's voice blows it away.

Rule eight: a secret is The Villain's most powerful weapon.

'No,' I grit out, twisting my head out of her grip. She only tightens her hold and pulls me back. A weak spark lights in my core as her nose brushes mine.

'Please,' she whispers, urgency tugging at her tone. 'You're dying. I just need to tell someone. You'll take it to the grave.'

The darkness rears its ugly head.

If we'd met on a different night, under different circumstances, I'd reach down her throat and yank out her secret with my bare hands. I'd have her researched and studied. I'd find her name, age, address. Her fucking star sign. I'd climb her family tree and shake all the secrets from its branches too.

That's what I do. I take secrets and turn them into weapons.

But for once in my goddamn life, I don't want to know. The moment's too perfect, *she's* too perfect. I ruin everything I fucking touch, and I don't want to ruin her.

I shake my head, but she decides to tell me anyway.

Her secret bobs in her throat and rolls over her tongue. It passes her teeth, then dies on her lips.

Her gaze slides upward, following the sound of a slow-moving roar. It draws closer, ruffling her hair and fluttering her wings.

She leaps to her feet and starts to scream.

For the briefest of moments, I think it's God coming to get her. I glare at the sky and consider the consequences of stealing from Him. Then the chopper cuts across my eye line and amusement bleeds through me.

It's not God. It's Denis.

Fucking *Denis*.

Rule nine: The Villain must learn that trust is a weakness, not an ally.

My father couldn't have been more wrong.

The girl drops to her knees, relief pouring out of her like a sunbeam. 'See! I told you someone would pass by soon.'

The hands that grip me beneath my armpits are strong and familiar. But somehow, the hand curling around my bicep feels more inviting.

'Wait,' she yells, over the whir of the blades. 'I didn't get your name!'

For the first time since Mama died, all three syllables bubble up my throat. 'Gabriel.'

She shields her eyes with her hands and smiles. 'Gabriel, like the angel?'

I laugh. She laughs. 'I'm Wren.'

Wren.

Denis drags me backward, and that familiar piano run bursts into my ear again. This time, at max volume. Wren grows smaller and smaller, the gold aura around her burning away the dark.

I watch her through the window. Even when the doors slam

shut. Even when Denis rips away at the fabric stuck to my torso. Even when the ground disappears beneath us and she becomes a pink speck of light, I can't take my eyes off her.

Wren.

Her name carves into my heart and etches into my skin. I hope the Devil allows keepsakes in hell, because fuck, I'm taking it with me.

We climb above the treetops, and she disappears from view. The earbud crackles with static until 'Dancing Queen' comes to an abrupt stop mid-lyric.

The roar of the wind. The low hum of urgency.

And then my father's voice.

Rule ten: The Villain never ever gets the girl.

CHAPTER One

Wren

The sweet promise of a happy ever after paints the club a perfect shade of pink. It stains my cheeks, colors my mood, chasing me into the elevator and clinging to my coat as I burst out of the entryway and under the veranda.

Then my cell buzzes in my coat pocket, and the night fades back to black.

No.

No, no, no.

I fold in half under a heat lamp. My SOS bag slips off my shoulder as my clutch slides from under my arm, and both drop to the concrete with a heavy thud. Why is the punch to my gut always so violent? It's been three years. Daily, for three years, and I still haven't figured out how to soften the blow.

It takes a few seconds for the sting to die and common sense to take its place. Then I straighten my back, smooth down the faux fur of my coat, and walk to the edge of the veranda, where the lamp's orange glow bleeds into the never-ending night.

An ice-cold inhale soothes my lungs and relaxes my shoulders.

I'm being dramatic. Not to toot my own horn, but I probably

have lots of notifications coming through after being underground in the Devil's Hollow nightclub for hours with no cell service. Messages from all the group chats I'm in, likes and comments on my latest Instagram post, and probably a text or two from Uncle Finn asking how the night's going.

Even if the buzz was an email, maybe it's not *that* email. A bad habit of online shopping and an even worse habit of ticking random boxes at the checkout page means I'm subscribed to a million newsletters, and God knows how many back-in-stock notifications I've signed up for.

It could be anything. It could also not even be midnight. But my phone feels like a rock in my pocket, and I can't bring myself to pull it out and check. Instead, I ball my hands into fists and slide my gaze to the starless sky.

'What time is it, Leah?'

The question leaves my lips in a frosted whisper. When the silence stretches over seconds, I wonder if she heard me, or if she's even out here at all. Then wobbly footsteps strike concrete, and a shadow travels along the walkway to merge with mine.

'Just past ten. Why?'

Ten. It's only ten o'clock.

And just like that, I'm one sentence, five words, and twenty-nine characters, including spaces, lighter. The high hits me so hard I don't care if the relief is only guaranteed for the next two hours.

I do care when Leah takes two steps toward me, because I'm not quick enough to take two steps back before she doubles over and vomits on my boots.

'Ew!'

All thoughts of midnight emails and unfinished sentences leave my head as I jump out of the splash zone and into action. I'd grabbed my SOS bag from the coatroom when I followed Leah out of the club. Even though she said she only needed some fresh air, I'd watched her sink three tequila shots in as many minutes, and I've spent enough time holding back hair and wiping away tears outside of nightclubs to know there's not a girl on this coastline who can do that without consequence.

Leah hurls again. Thankfully, nowhere near my sparkly pink boots this time. I pull out two types of wipes – antibacterial for my heels and cosmetic for Leah's smudged lipstick – and a hair tie.

'Don't worry, it's one of those spiral ones that doesn't leave a crease in your hair,' I reassure her, pulling her long brown locks into a loose bun. She's about to say something, maybe *thank you*, but more vomit comes out instead.

'You're welcome,' I chirp anyway, scrubbing away at my boots as she decorates the deck.

Leah's not the first person to vomit on me, and she won't be the last. And I guess I deserve it, because although I work at The Rusty Anchor in Devil's Dip, where power washing regurgitated beer off the back patio every payday is practically a job requirement, I also volunteer in a lot of places people puke in. Nobody pays me to stand on the Devil's Cove promenade every Saturday night, looking out for worse-for-wear partygoers who need help getting home. Nor for my shifts at the Devil's Hollow hospital, where puke is the bodily fluid I have to worry least about.

Tonight is a rare night when I'm not working or volunteering. This is Rory's bachelorette party, and as her self-appointed party planner, I'll be damned if I spend all night out here.

Time to call Leah a taxi and get back to the party. I toss the wipes in a nearby garbage can and tug out my cell, which is easy now that I know there's no dreaded email waiting for me – yet. I call Coastal Cabs with one hand and rub Leah's back with the other.

Comforting clichés come as easy as always, and I murmur the ones everyone wants to hear when they're bent over outside a super-fancy nightclub spewing their guts up. *We've all been sick at some point. Honestly, no one even saw you leave.*

I want to add that she should have lined her stomach with the sandwiches I laid out instead of sneering at them, but I keep my thoughts to myself. No one likes a Judgmental Judy.

Before I can tell Leah that a taxi is on its way, the nightclub door groans open and slams shut, trapping the sound of 2000s pop classics and drunken laughter between its hinges.

I glance up and meet the steely eyes of a bouncer I don't recognize. He glares at Leah, at the deck, then at me.

I beam up at him. 'Such a chilly night, isn't it? I hope you've got some thick thermals on under that jacket.' Frost crackles under my boot as I shift my weight from one foot to the other. 'Do you think we'll get a White Christmas this year?' Leah's spine arches under my palm as she retches like a cat. My smile widens as I pretend not to notice. 'I suppose it's too early to tell.'

I don't catch what he mutters under his breath as he stomps back inside, but his tone is mean, and because I have skin as thick as one-ply toilet paper, it stings.

'Rude,' I huff out, my face burning under the heat lamp. Rude *and* weird. There's not a single bouncer on this coastline who isn't happy to see me.

He must be new.

'Is he going to kick me out?' Leah gargles, slumping back against the wall.

I tuck a stray strand of hair behind her ear. 'Of course not, honey.'

It isn't a lie, not really. No matter how grumpy the bouncer is, he'll have to grin and bear all the perils of a bachelorette party tonight because the bride is marrying into the Visconti family.

I was eleven when Uncle Finn moved us west out of Seattle to the Devil's Coast. The first thing I learned was that he'd picked the worst out of its three towns to live in. The second thing I learned was the name Visconti. They seem to own everything around here. This club, plus all the other clubs, and the bars, the restaurants, the hotels. Leah could punch the bouncer's mother and he'd likely still let her back into the party.

I, on the other hand, am kicking Leah out. I didn't get up at 6:00 a.m. to bake a hundred cupcakes and blow up double that amount of balloons for Leah to puke all over my hard work.

'I've called you a taxi, okay?'

I think she's going to protest, but instead, her upper arm tenses against mine.

'Wren?'

'Yeah?'

She lets out a stuttered breath. 'Someone's watching us.'

'Huh? Who?'

'I-I don't know.'

I stare at her profile for a few seconds before following her gaze and glaring out at the night. Beyond the reach of the heat lamp, there's nothing but black. Even when I blink a few times, I can't make out the club's gravel parking lot I know to be there or the row of willow trees that separate it from the quiet main road.

I slowly exhale and fold my hands together to keep them warm.

I've never been afraid of the dark, even though cautionary tales and horror movies teach us we should be. From a young age, we're told it's where bad things bloom. Where monsters live, sins multiply, and secrets are buried six feet under soft soil. I'm afraid of a lot of things – dying before I find The One, manmade objects at the bottom of the ocean, Rory when she inspects my recycling efforts – but never darkness.

Only, I can't remember why.

'I can't see anyone?'

Leah sniffs beside me. 'Me neither, but I can *feel* it.'

I'm about to ask whether she's snorted or swallowed anything she shouldn't have, when suddenly, I feel it too. Awareness, like a rough hand, brushes all the hairs on my body in the wrong direction. Stomach clenching, I squint until my eyes burn, scanning the abyss.

Nothing.

'You're being silly,' I whisper, though now I'm conscious of how bright and hot it is under this heat lamp and how dark and cold it is *out there*. I flatten my bangs with my palm and tug at the hem of my coat.

'I can't see anyone?'

'I bet it's the Boogeyman.'

'Okay, now you're definitely being silly.' My laugh shakes with relief. Drunk people say the weirdest things, honestly. Still, there's a sense of unease clinging to my skin, and I can't seem to shake it off. I pluck a lip gloss from my clutch to distract myself. 'You've watched too many horror movies.'

Leah's gaze warms my cheek. 'You've never seen him?'

'The Boogeyman? From that film?' I coat my lips in gloss and smack them together. 'Horror movies aren't my thing. Besides, didn't it get, like, a four on IMBD?'

'Nooo . . .' she slurs back. 'I'm not talking about the film, I'm talking about *him*. The Boogeyman of the Devil's Coast.'

I slowly twist on the cap of my gloss, eyes narrowing on Leah. She's messing with me. I know everyone on the Coast, at least by nickname. Partly because it's only a short coastline with three small towns, and partly because I'm the nosiest person on it.

'Well, what does he look like?'

She tilts her head against mine. Her sour breath makes my nose scrunch. 'Like your worst nightmare.'

Then she doubles over and gives my boots a fresh lick of vomit.

Stifling my sigh, I return to consoling her while silently willing a taxi to swing into the parking lot. She's in no state to converse, but that's okay. I'm good at talking for two. I tell her about the cute out-of-towner who came into The Rusty Anchor last weekend, and the new therapy dogs they've brought into the children's wing of the hospital. I'm halfway through rattling off my Christmas wishlist from my phone's Notes app when headlights filter through the trees and sweep over gravel.

Oh, thank God. I've missed at least three ABBA songs and a party game by now. I sling Leah's arm over my shoulder and help her step off the lit veranda and into the dark toward the waiting car. When I see who steps out of the driver's side, I break into a grin.

Roger Burrows is the type of old man who thinks it's super cool to be grumpy. Grunting is his second language, his beard is his fourth child, and if he isn't complaining about sports, politics, or the state of his neighbors' front lawns, then he's probably taking a nap.

Sometimes, I think he's Coastal Cab's only employee who works outside of a Saturday night, because he's the only one they send every time I call.

'Thought you had the night off?' he grumbles, tucking his hands under his armpits.

'Well, good evening to you too, Roger. I'm having a swell night, thank you for asking,' I chime. 'How's Lou?'

Ignoring both my sarcasm and my question about his wife, he yanks open the back passenger door. He glares at Leah as she crocodile-crawls onto the seat. 'She gonna be sick in my car?'

'Yes,' I say sweetly.

He scowls at me.

I smile back.

Roger likes to play this silly little game where he pretends he doesn't like me, or more specifically, doesn't like me folding drunk girls into the back of his taxi and asking him to take them home for free, *just one more time*. He bitches and moans, but he does it anyway, plus texts me a snippy one-word confirmation when they're safely behind their front door. He's got a heart of gold under his too-tight plaid shirts. Besides, I'm sure he'd want someone to do the same for his daughter.

I know he loves me deep down, anyway. At the very least, he loves the homemade brownies I hand out at the Devil's Cove taxi rank every Saturday night. He always inches down his window just enough to snatch them out of my hand like a starving raccoon.

We stare at each other for a little longer, but staring is one of my talents, so of course, Roger breaks eye contact first. He curses into the wind, slams the door shut on Leah, and leans against it.

'I'm getting sick of being your personal run-around, kid. Ain't it about time you learned to drive? You could waste your own damn time instead of mine.'

Now it's my turn to ignore his question and the way it prickles my cheeks and curdles in my stomach.

I clear my throat and force a tight smile. 'Excuse me, please,' I say, trying to keep the wobble from my voice. I usher him away from the passenger door with a flutter of a fresh antibacterial wipe in my hand, then rap-tap-tap on the window.

When Leah rolls it down, I fish out a water bottle from my SOS bag and drop it on her lap. 'Sip it, don't gulp. When you get home, don't get into bed until you've had two more glasses of water and eaten a slice of dry toast. Oh, and don't forget to take your makeup off. Did you know that every time you don't take your makeup off, you age ten days?' I heard this on TikTok, so it's probably not true, but I've found the threat of it is enough to get most girls to at least drag a wipe over their face before their head hits the pillow. 'Sleep on your left side if you still feel sick. Actually, sleep on your side anyway, because –'

'Enough with that damn monologue,' Roger grunts, rounding the car and yanking the driver's door open. 'I've heard you say it so many times, I could recite it in my sleep.'

I catch his eye over the roof of the car and raise a brow. 'And it shows. I can tell you take your makeup off every night without fail.'

Even though the light from the car's headlights barely touch him, I'm sure I see the corner of his lips lift under his handlebar mustache. Before I can tease him about it, his shoulders pinch. With a tight grip on the doorframe, he twists around and glares out into the night.

Ice-cold silence crackles against the nape of my neck. Holding my breath, I ball the wipe in my fist and stare at the rigid line of his back. It feels like ages before he looks back at me, and when he does, the unease in his gaze makes the breath catch at the back of my throat.

'Don't hang around, kid' is all he says.

That rough hand reaches for me again, and I wonder if it grabbed hold of him too.

With a quick nod, I push away the paranoia and duck my head through Leah's window. I press the wipe in her hand and give her shoulder a sympathetic pat. 'You'll feel better in the morning, I promise.'

She smiles weakly and hiccups. 'You're so nice, Wren. Like, if God held a gun to my head and told me I had to nominate only one person I know to go to heaven, it'd be you.'

And there it is.

My laugh warps with delirium, and suddenly, the December chill has lost its bite and all I can feel is the warmth of her words.

You're so nice, Wren. Like everyone else does on the Devil's Coast, she said it like one would say the grass is green or the sky is blue. Like it's a simple, undeniable fact.

Though I don't take drugs, aside from the occasional Tylenol, I know the high from being called *nice* is comparable. And I don't just dabble in 'nice' either.

I've had a full-blown addiction to it since I was eighteen.

Volunteering at the hospital and peeling drunk partygoers off the Devil's Cove boardwalk is the tip of the iceberg. I do everything – from knitting onesies for premature babies and checking in daily with my elderly neighbors, to holding bake sales for every charity under the sun – and I do it all for my hit of nice.

The Good Samaritan, the Angel in Pink. The fun sponge who writes down the license plates of every punter at the bar she works at, just in case they ignore her makeshift 'no drunk driving' sign. I don't care how the residents of the Devil's Coast call me nice, as long as they call me it.

But it's polite to be modest, so I dismiss Leah's compliment with a flap of my hand. 'Nice is just what I do, honey!'

With a reluctant promise to text me when Leah's home safe, Roger pulls out of the parking lot. I wave them off with a bright smile, but when the headlights simmer, dim, and fade, I find myself alone in the dark with a heart that's sliding south.

Because that's the thing about feeding your addictions: the high is only ever temporary.

Tucking my clutch under one arm and hitching my SOS bag over the other, I close my eyes and suck in a breath so deep the night's frost burns my chest. I'm hoping it'll burn away at the guilt that sits there too, but when it doesn't, I try to turn my attention to other parts of my body. A trick my therapist taught me years ago to deal with my thoughts sliding south. I find the steady beat of my pulse in my neck. I taste the night's moisture on the tip of my tongue and smell its earthy scent. My ears prickle at the sound of tires hissing over the frosted tarmac of the nearby road and the bare trees shivering in the forest beyond it.

Crack.

What the hell was that?

My eyes pop open and scan the darkness. It sounded like a twig crunching underfoot, and it sounded close.

'Hello?' I whisper, clutching my bag strap. 'Who's there?'
Silence.

My stomach clenches as I glare out to the never-ending void. It stares right back, offering me only the trickling sensation of being watched.

Seconds pass, slowed by the weight of tension. I stare until my eyes ache.

Nothing.

A sharp gust of wind skates down my collar, and I shudder enough to shake myself out of my trance.

I've let Leah get into my head with all that nonsense about the 'Boogeyman' of the Devil's Coast. She was so drunk she was probably hallucinating. I'm being silly, and even if I'm not, why am I still standing out here? I might choose a rom-com over a horror any day, but even I know the ditzy blond doing something careless, like hanging out alone in an empty parking lot, always dies in the opening sequence.

Not the type of movie I daydream about starring in, thank you very much.

With a weak chuckle, I turn on my heel. I only make it two steps toward the dimly lit veranda when another noise reaches out from the dark and taps me on the shoulder.

Hiss. Fizz.

My laugh wilts on my tongue. I spin around, and now, at the heart of the dark, there's a flickering flame. A match, little more than a pinprick against the broad black expanse. The flame moves north, and my eyes move with it, transfixed by how it dances at the mercy of the wind. I can't make out most of the objects that shift and contort in its wake. Something patterned. Something metallic. Then something that makes my heart trip over its next beat.

A cigarette.

Which means someone is out there smoking it.

I let out a stunted gasp. The flame comes to a stop beneath its tip, and I almost don't dare drag my gaze up to what it's brought to light. I follow the length of the cigarette, skim over the full lips its tucked between, then trail the sharp, straight line of a scar over a hollowed cheekbone, and come to rest on a heavy brow.

Is he the 'Boogeyman' Leah spoke of?

He sure looks like a monster.

The man's eyes lift from the match and clash with mine. Suddenly, the air drops ten degrees, chilling my blood and slowing my breathing.

And now I'm not breathing at all.

I recognize those eyes – only, I don't. It's a weird, fleeting feeling. A short, sharp tug on a memory I didn't know I had. Perhaps an alternate me has seen them in an alternate universe or in a dream that slipped from my mind the moment I woke up.

That gaze . . . it's glassy. Magnetic. *Certain.*

And then I have this slow, syrup-like feeling it didn't find me by chance.

The realization shoves me backward. One step, two, my heels skating over frosted asphalt. Three steps and I nearly trip over the raised deck of the veranda. Four, and I'm back under the light of the heat lamp, grappling for the nightclub's door handle.

There's a voice screaming at me to get inside. I hear it often, and I'm pretty certain it belongs to my friend Tayce – she has a habit of yelling at me about safety, and I have a habit of rolling my eyes in response. But I guess being the nosiest person on the coast has its pitfalls, one of them being I can never resist the pull of curiosity.

Heart slamming against my ribs, I slowly turn and press my back against the door.

He's still there. Watching me. The flame is fading now, its dying reflection trapped within the walls of his cold gaze. I'm trapped there too, frozen between running inside and staying to find out what will happen when the flame reaches the end of its life.

I don't have to wait long. The flame never kisses the tip of his cigarette. It doesn't burn out, either. The monster kills it with a quick snap of his wrist, plunging him back into the dark.

I blink at the night, straining my ears to find something, anything to latch onto in the silence.

Nothing.

A beat passes as I shift from one sticky boot to the other. He's still watching me; I can *feel it*. Seconds stretch into minutes, and eventually, my heartbeat slows to its regular rhythm. My lungs expand, and when I release my next breath, a laugh tumbles out with it, nervous and light.

I've suddenly remembered why I'm not afraid of the dark.

It's because I know those cautionary tales and horror movies are just fiction.

In real life, monsters don't live in the dark; they live in the light.

They hold your hair back when you're puking.

They bake cakes, make signs, volunteer in hospitals.

And sometimes, they even wear pink.

I stick my tongue out toward the black horizon, turn on my heel, and run back inside.

CHAPTER Two

Wren

Low lighting, even lower ceilings, and air so damp it thickens the lining of your lungs.

The Catacomb Cave Bar in Devil's Hollow is as creepy as its name suggests. Though, I'm proud to say it looks less macabre tonight because I arrived three hours early to give the space some much-needed razzle dazzle. Now, pink fairy lights soften the jagged cave walls, and clusters of rose gold balloons burst out of its darkest corners. I shoved anything ugly-but-movable into the back office, and anything ugly-but-nailed-down has been artfully concealed with table runners and glitter.

The elevator descends into the cave, and when the doors open, I'm pleased to see the night still has a pulse. I shimmy across the dance floor to the tune of a Spice Girls classic, airkissing and giving apologetic one-armed hugs to all the girls I've yet to greet.

In the midst of showing Alessandra that the penis straw in her cocktail actually flashes if you squeeze its balls, a strong grip on my arm tugs me sideways.

'Where the fuck are your shoes?'

I don't even need to turn around to know it's Tayce. I can tell by her potty mouth and the scent of her expensive perfume. She's glaring at my frilly socks, so I wiggle my toes for good measure. Being shoeless wasn't on my agenda for the night, but I used up all my antibacterial wipes scrubbing at my boots and they still stink of tequila-laced vomit. I had no choice but to chuck them into the coatroom and pray they're salvageable. They're pink and sparkly, with a block heel that lets me walk all the way from Devil's Cove to Devil's Dip without so much as a blister, and saving for college on a minimum-wage bar job means I definitely can't afford a new pair.

Holding onto Tayce's shoulder, I tip up on my toes to yell in her ear. 'Leah puked on them.'

Disco lights and disgust pass over her features. 'The girl who works at the Devil's Dip diner?'

'No, silly. That's Libby. Leah's the one who dated –'

'I don't care who Leah dated. I care that you're prancing around barefoot in a nightclub. What if you step on a needle?'

Frowning, I scan the sea of giggling girls waving glow sticks and two-stepping. 'I don't think anyone here is the type to shoot up in the restroom –'

'You have flip-flops in that big bag of yours, right? I'll go and grab them.'

I tug her back by the wrist before she can head toward the elevator. 'Yeah, but I gave my last pair to Rosalie. Her heels are two sizes too small. She said she got them on sale so . . .' I shrug. 'Sacrifices had to be made.'

The music's too loud to hear what curse word Tayce mutters, but her top teeth bite her bottom lip, so I can only assume it begins with a hard *f*.

'You're too nice, Wren.'

Annoyance prickles at my cheeks. I love being called nice, just not by Tayce. She always says it with a side dish of disapproval and at the most inconvenient times. Like now, when the DJ has just started playing Gina G's 'Ooh Aah . . . Just a Little Bit.'

I stare wistfully at the Wren-shaped hole on the dance floor, then drag my gaze back to one of my two best friends.

We met three years ago, shortly after I started volunteering on the Devil's Cove promenade. Well, three years and two months ago if you count all the weekends she spent glaring at me through the glass front of her tattoo parlor before we ever spoke. I'd gawped back awkwardly, partly because she was a new addition to the Coast, and partly because I couldn't help it.

When she finally left her shop and crossed the road, it was with a bat. She swung it around the head of a drunk man trying to yank me into the taxi I'd hailed for him. As he withered on the ground under the sharp point of her stiletto, she asked me if I was a prostitute and if I knew there were safer ways to sell my body.

I told her what I was doing.

She told me I was an idiot.

Then she called me something even worse when I refused her offer to drive me home.

Tayce doesn't look like one of the world's most sought-after tattoo artists. She doesn't have a smidge of ink on her entire body. Instead, she looks like one of those girls on Pinterest – hot and unapproachable. Tonight, she's wearing a gold satin dress, but only because I reminded her it's bad luck to wear black to anything wedding related. Her long midnight hair falls straight to her hip in a sharp middle part, and her full lips are forever painted red.

I once asked her if they're her own or if she paid for them, but she told me to 'Mind my own fucking business.'

I don't dare ask about her boobs.

'Wren!'

My gaze follows the sound of my name and lands on a mass

of blonde curls bobbing over the sea of dancers. Long limbs and a sparkly clutch part the crowd, then a body crashes into me.

'Oops, sorry. I think that girl pushed me,' Rory mumbles, glancing over her shoulder. Tayce glares at the crowd too, though we both know Rory can't stand in heels, let alone walk, after two white wine spritzers.

When she finds her balance, she tugs down the hem of her dress and grins up at me. 'We've been looking for you. Where have you been?'

'Leah was sick on her boots,' Tayce yells in her ear.

Rory frowns, scanning the club. 'The girl from the diner?'

I flutter a dismissive hand. I've been walking my other best friend, Rory, through the six degrees of separation between her and her guests all night. Her fiancé hired the party planner, who booked this huge club, and Rory was too proud to admit she doesn't have enough friends to fill it. Luckily, with all my hobbies, volunteer work, and the fact I'll strike up a conversation with anyone who sits within five seats of me on the bus, I had no trouble rustling up a guest list.

I was going to leave my input at that. After all, I don't like to step on anyone's toes. But then I caught a glimpse of the decor plan, and well, I thought it was best to take over that too. And the music because there wasn't a single crowd-pleaser on the set list, and by that point, it was just easier if I did everything myself. Besides, I don't trust a party planner who would choose a bar named after a cemetery for a bachelorette party *and* schedule it the night before the wedding.

As much as I'd love to say it was my social skills that convinced the girls who don't really know Rory to attend, it's much more likely that the Visconti name was the real draw. No one on this coastline is passing up the opportunity to drink free-flowing champagne and analyze why Aurora Carter managed to snag Devil's Dip's most-eligible bachelor when they couldn't.

And I suppose I wouldn't blame them if they only remember Rory from our school days. She was the weird kid who carried tadpoles around in jam jars. But she was also the only one who would talk to me when I moved here from Seattle in sixth grade. Shy small talk evolved into her teaching me about bird migration and the importance of bees, and when we grew into awkward teenagers, I taught her about leave-in conditioner and the importance of matching your foundation to your skintone.

Looking at her tonight, you'd never know she used to keep injured birds in a shoe box beside her bed. She's every bit the rich businessman's bride: a vision in a white designer mini dress, her long blonde curls tumbling down her back.

I'm so happy for her, I could cry.

Again.

She wobbles backward for no other reasons than her drinks are strong and her heels are high. I steady her before she takes Tayce down with her too.

'Jeez.' She touches her necklace and sweeps the crowd with bewilderment. 'Where did you get these girls from, Wren? Fight school?'

Tayce laughs and grabs both of our hands. 'You're so damn drunk, Rory. You need water; Wren needs shoes. Go and sit down while I figure this shit out.'

I purse my lips, trapping in a comment about the irony of Tayce looking after *me* in a nightclub for a change, and let her lead us to the VIP area before disappearing back into the crowd.

Rory looks down the long table, taking in the sweating ice buckets, penis straws, and half-eaten cupcakes. There's finger foods, games, sparkly confetti. Sashes, pink cowboy hats. Against the back wall, helium balloons spelling out *Bride to Be* bob lazily under recessed lights, and beneath them, a cutout of Angelo Visconti's face is stuck to a dart board. He glares over at me, clearly not amused that we're using his likeness for a cruder version of Pin the Tail on the Donkey.

Rory clamps her hands to her chest. 'Thanks for doing all of this, Wren. If you ever change your mind about going to law school next year, you should consider becoming a party planner for a living.'

Law school.

Sometimes, it feels as though my future is an invisible hand. It likes to roll up its sleeve, shove itself down my throat, and stir up the contents of my stomach.

I gulp down the churning panic and tape over it with a weak smile before sliding into the booth next to Rory.

Law school is future Wren's problem. Current Wren's only problem is making sure her best friend makes it to the altar tomorrow without puking down the aisle.

'Hey, who's been kissing my husband?'

I follow her glare to Angelo's cutout, which is now covered in messy lipstick prints. I laugh and squeeze her knee. 'Relax, you're the only one smooching the real deal, honey.'

A beat of realization passes, then her face stretches into a grin so wide it raises goosebumps along my arms. It's followed by a rush of hot, intense jealousy, which I force out of my body with a loud sigh.

I love their love story; it follows a plot I could only dream of. It started with an explosive meet-cute, jumped right over the dreaded third-act breakup, and now they're waltzing toward the happy ever after.

I rest my chin on my fist and gaze up at Rory, a soppy smile tugging on my lips. 'Tell me the story of how you and Angelo met.'

She shifts in her seat, letting out a light laugh. 'I've told you a million times, Wren. You must be sick of it by now.'

'You could tell me a million more times, and I still wouldn't be sick of it.' I stick out my bottom lip. 'Please?'

She waves a dismissive hand. 'The music's too loud.'

'I can hear you just fine.'

She grabs a cream cheese and cucumber sandwich off a platter and crams the whole thing in her mouth. 'Yeah, but I'm eating,' she mumbles, spraying the glittery tablecloth with crumbs.

Rolling my eyes, I tuck a pink napkin into the neckline of her dress. 'Next time, then.'

'Next time,' she agrees.

Rory doesn't share my love of hyperbolic statements – she probably has told me the story a million times. But I wasn't being dramatic when I said I could hear it a million more either. I'll never tire of hearing how their eyes found each other across a busy bar and the world fell silent. Or how later, they reached for the same champagne flute on a passing tray, and the brush of his thumb against hers made sparks fly.

Their meet-cute isn't even the best part of the story. She'd left the bar without telling Angelo her name, and for the next week, he couldn't rest until he knew it. In the day, he'd scour the length of the coast, trawling sidewalks and knocking on doors, and at night, he'd wait at the bar they met in, in the hope she'd show up again.

Their first date – a moonlit dinner on the beach – was magic. For their second, he whisked her off to New York, where they had their first kiss atop the Empire State Building, the wind roaring in their ears. They made love for the first time under the stars in Paris, then he declared his love for her as they wandered, hand in hand, through the cobbled streets of Rome.

The courting was a whirlwind so strong and intense that I didn't see her for *three whole months*. Only when she breezed into The Rusty Anchor, a handsome Visconti in her shadow, did I get the full story.

As she scarfs down another sandwich, I grab her free hand and rub my thumb over her ring. It's a sweet, sparkly diamond that fits both her finger and personality like a glove. 'You're getting married!'

Her hand curls over mine. 'I'm getting married!' she squeals, treating me to a view of the mushy cucumber in her mouth. Then her gaze snags on something in the crowd, and she stops chewing.

For a split second, the air pulls taut, but then Rory breaks into a grin and clambers to her feet. 'I'm getting married to *that* man!'

I follow the point of her finger, to the imposing figure slicing through the dance floor. With every stride he takes toward us, dancers slow, torsos twist, and jaws drop open.

Although Angelo Visconti hasn't lived on the coast for nearly a decade, he has the same hypnotic hold over the women here as his more well-known brother and cousins do. It'd be naive to pretend a large part of his appeal isn't all the money lining his pockets, but he also benefits from the signature Visconti good looks. He's a tall, dark, and handsome stereotype poured into a bespoke black suit, And I just know that underneath it, he's built like a man who could pick you up with one arm without grunting.

From the moment I looked up, Angelo hasn't taken his eyes off of his fiancée, nor has that satisfied smirk left his lips. As he steps off the dance floor and reaches our booth, my heart skips a beat.

Is this how he looked at her the night they met? Because, sweet Lord, if a man looked at me like that, I'd fall – no, *jump* – off the face of the earth with him for three months too.

'What are you doing here?' Rory laughs, wrapping her arms around his neck.

He slides his hands up her sides, breaking eye contact long enough to drink in her dress. 'We had a meeting nearby.'

'We absolutely did not have a meeting nearby,' a velvet voice drawls.

I turn to find its owner. Raphael Visconti steps out of the crowd, casts an amused glance at the table spread, then winks at me.

Angelo's brother is a stereotype in his own right – he embodies every cliché male lead in the straight-to-TV movies I make Uncle Finn binge-watch with me around this time of year. *Handsome and ridiculously charming billionaire who made his fortune under the bright lights of Las Vegas moves back to his sleepy hometown to help with the family empire. There, he meets . . .*

Well, I don't know who he meets. Lots of women, actually, because every time I see him in Devil's Cove, he has his hand on the small of a different brunette's back, guiding her through the door of a swanky restaurant, then later guiding her into the passenger seat of his car.

Serial dating habits aside, he really is the perfect Hallmark hero. Sharp suit, silver tongue, and he's mastered the type of intense eye contact that makes a girl feel dizzy with importance. He's got that amused half smirk down too. The one they all wear when the heroine does something adorably awkward, like leave the house with a pair of panties wrapped around the heel of her shoe.

Seriously. All he's missing is a cable knit sweater and an English accent.

He presses his lips to my cheek. 'Looking as beautiful as ever, Wren.'

He hasn't so much as glanced south of my eyes, so I doubt he could even tell me what I'm wearing. Still, my face turns as pink as my dress. 'I'm sure you say that to all the girls.'

'I do, but with you, I really mean it.' He tugs a champagne bottle from an ice bucket on the table, winces at the label, and puts it back without pouring himself a glass. 'How are you?'

Before I can answer, his gaze darts left and mine follows, landing on Tayce. She's elbowing her way through the crowd toward us, thunder clapping under her stilettos.

Rafe stretches his arms out. 'Tayce. Looking as beautiful as –'

'Shut it, asshole. You and *him*' – she jabs a finger toward Angelo – 'aren't supposed to be here.'

She yells Angelo's name and snaps her fingers. Patience has never been one of Tayce's virtues though, so when he doesn't immediately stop eating Rory's face, she barks a little louder. When that doesn't work either, she squeezes herself into the tiny gap between them. I've seen her do this many times when a drunken fight spills out of a club and onto the doorstep of her tattoo parlor, but breaking up a couple in love appears to be much harder than diffusing an argument between two steroid-fueled men hell-bent on putting the other in hospital.

Rory unsticks herself from her fiancé long enough to flick Tayce a disinterested look. 'They had a meeting nearby.'

'My ass they did.'

Angelo wipes amusement and secondhand lip gloss off his mouth with the back of his hand. When his gaze drifts from Rory to Tayce, it hardens.

'You've pissed me off. You know that?'

Tayce pauses. 'Uh, is this about the pin-the-dildo-on-Angelo-Visconti's-forehead game? If so, that was all Wren's idea.'

It wasn't my idea. My idea was a singalong Disney marathon and to be in bed by 10:00 p.m. so Rory gets enough sleep for the big day tomorrow. Anything mildly X-rated comes from Tayce's filthy imagination and ridiculously high sex drive.

All eyes come to me, all three pairs flecked with disbelief. I resist the urge to tug on Tayce's hair and instead, gaze up at Angelo with my best wounded-puppy impression.

'Please don't shout at me, I cry easily.'

'So fucking easily,' Tayce mutters.

I bite my tongue, but only because we have this unspoken pact: she pisses people off, and I take the blame. It's a win-win, because not only am I much harder to get mad at, I get to emotionally blackmail her about it for the next month.

'Yeah. Somehow, I don't think the male stripper was Wren's idea.' Angelo wraps a possessive arm around Rory. 'A cop? How original.'

Tayce frowns at him, and in turn, I frown at her. A stripper? First, ew. Second, I made her pinky swear that all the penises making an appearance tonight would be plastic or, at the very least, not have a muscular man with loose hips attached to them.

She licks her lips. 'Uh, a stripping cop?'

'Mm. The one hanging around in the parking lot.' Angelo flexes his fist. 'Yeah. He can't make it anymore.'

Rafe drags a hand over his mouth to hide his smirk.

'I didn't . . .' Tayce turns to me, looking as confused as I feel. 'Did you . . . ?'

'What do you think?' I huff, standing straighter. Jesus, I wouldn't even know what to Google to find one.

Several beats pass. Awkward and dense, out of sync with the bubblegum pop song pumping out from the DJ booth. Rafe locks eyes with his brother, then slowly puts down the pink fluffy handcuffs he was inspecting. A disco light sweeps over a tight muscle in his jaw, then down to his clenched fist, but by the time he looks up, he's all teeth and charm, then I think I imagined it.

He smooths down the placket of his shirt and disarms me with a mega-watt smile. 'If you'll excuse me for a moment, ladies.'

He slips into the crowd.

A fleeting unease skates over me. A feeling that something important has passed me by and I wasn't quick enough to grab it and stay in its loop. I look to Rory for answers, but apparently, she's looking for them too, in the bottom of a champagne flute.

I glance to Angelo instead, but he's now glaring at his cell, its screen lighting up the hard planes of his face.

Weird.

For the second time tonight, Tayce grabs my arm and tugs me sideways.

'Shit.' She glances at the elevator doors closing on Rafe and snatches her purse up off the table. 'Cover for me.'

'Huh?'

'Just while I call him and tell him not to come.'

A second passes before the realization hits me. 'You hired a *stripping cop* ? After you promised me that –'

'Jeez, Wren, could you squeak any louder?' she hisses, stealing a shifty look at Angelo. 'Of course I didn't hire a stripping cop.'

'Oh, thank God.'

'He's a firefighter.' She turns on her heel. 'Be right back.'

As she fights her way through the sea of dancers, irritation washes over me. I love her, dammit, but I sure wish I'd followed through with my earlier intrusive thought of pulling her hair.

Sighing, I turn my attention back to the table and busy myself with tidying. I dab at spilled liquor and smooth out a crease in the tablecloth. As I sweep Rory's sandwich crumbs onto her discarded plate, I remember Tayce never grabbed her that water.

I glance up from rearranging the cupcakes to make sure she's still standing. Though, it's never a good sign when she's not actually standing where I left her. Squinting into the flashing lights, I scan for blonde curls and sequins, and eventually, find her in a dark, quiet corner, trapped between a jagged wall and Angelo's broad silhouette.

My gaze lingers.

Then it sticks.

Her hand squeezes the nape of his neck. His grips the curve of her hip. A fistful of fabric, an arched back, parted lips brushing over a flushed cheek. They flash like stills from a movie under the pulsating light, every *click* burning a bigger hole in my chest.

This is true love, and Christ, how I crave it.

Dangerously so.

A shock of guilt and something darker zigzags through my insides. I catch myself and snatch up my thoughts before they can run away from me. Before they can bolt out of the club, get behind the wheel of a beat-up Chevy, and peel east down the highway.

If my future is a hand, my past is a vise, and it's starting to squeeze my lungs. I scan my surroundings for a distraction. Tayce is nowhere to be seen – she's probably still arguing with the stripper over a last-minute cancellation fee – and even though the DJ is playing the best songs to have ever graced the charts, hardly anyone on the dance floor is dancing, thanks to the magnetic pull of the Visconti in the corner.

I settle for collecting as many empty glasses as I can carry. When I squeeze through the crowd and dump them on the bar, Dan glances up from behind it and rolls his eyes.

'Can you stop doing that already? It's your day off.'

'Someone's got to do it.' I smile at him pointedly and dodge the wrath of his dish cloth as he pretends to whip it at me.

'Where are your shoes?'

'Leah puked on them.'

'Figures. Wanna borrow mine?'

I lean over the bar to get a look at his shoes. He's swapped out his Nikes for smart black loafers tonight – not that I'd be caught dead wearing either, even if they were my size.

'Mm. Don't think they'll match my dress, but thanks for the offer, honey.'

He laughs and twists the cap off a water bottle. 'Here, your friend needs this.' He nods to the shadowy corner where Rory and Angelo are making out. 'She bumped into a bar stool earlier and accused it of trying to start a fight.'

It's my turn to laugh. Dan usually works Friday and Saturday nights with me at The Rusty Anchor, and it's safe to say Rory's drunken antics are far tamer than what we're used to. He's the perfect shift buddy: he doesn't complain when I prop my iPad against the tip jar and watch nineties rom-coms, and he'll always unpack the deliveries off the truck so I don't break a nail.

I prop an elbow on the bar and twist to follow Dan's amused gaze. 'Can we take the white wine out of her white wine spritzers?'

Rory backs up my suggestion by wobbling sideways and knocking into a high-top table nearby. Angelo steadies her with one hand and catches a toppling champagne bottle with the other.

'Yes, but if she notices, it was your idea, not mine. I'd rather not get on the bad side of a woman who fights furniture.'

A reassuring reply is on the tip of my tongue, but it wilts as quickly as it blooms.

Because there's that feeling again. The rough, prickly sensation of being watched. It drags up my spine and grips a hold of my nape. Then it whispers a warning in my ear, and with a sharp tug on my chin, it pulls my attention to the far side of the club.

'Wren?'

Dan's voice is a hollow echo behind me. I want to turn and grab onto it like a life raft, but I can't. Everything is suddenly too heavy and too slow. My limbs, the music, the dancing. Even the strobe light is working in slow motion. It crawls up inked skin, over an angry scar, up to an unwavering stare.

Green.

Dan calls my name again, but he sounds even farther away this time. And he is, because now my bare shoulders are brushing past other shoulders as I move across the dance floor.

Inked skin, angry scar, *green.*

Inked skin, angry scar, *green*.

The light sweeps over this trifecta on a lethargic loop. I've seen it before, only illuminated by different lighting. Lit by the lone match in the parking lot earlier, but also –

Hands meet my waist, green spins into sparkles and a slur of metallic pink. I'm facing the direction of the bar again, only this time, I'm not looking at Dan but Rafe.

He pins me with a look of mock disapproval, then brings his hand to his chest. 'Are you trying to break my heart, Wren?'

I blink at him, disorientated. 'Huh?'

'*The* Wren Harlow dancing alone to an ABBA song? I've never seen such a sorry sight.'

He tugs me into the thick of the dance floor. Blood rushes back to my brain, and the world picks up its regular place.

ABBA. Rafe Visconti. Right.

I breathe out a dry, shaky laugh, and force my body to move to the beat of 'Waterloo.'

'Did you know ABBA won the Eurovision song contest with this song in 1974?' I yell in his ear, a little too loud, gripping his upper arm a little too tight. 'It was originally titled "Honey Pie," but that just doesn't have the same ring to it, does it?'

Rafe glances down at me in amusement before spinning me in a full circle.

Ink. Scar. Green.

My socks slide on the mirrored floor, and I crash into Rafe's chest, but he's quick to steady me. 'Whoa, easy there.' His gaze darts south, and he frowns. 'Where are your shoes?'

'Do you know that man?'

I didn't mean to say that. I meant to say, *Leah puked on them* like I've been saying all night. But the spin loosened my tongue, and the question flew off it, desperate and breathy.

Rafe looks over my shoulder and cocks a brow. 'Who, Gabe?'

Gabe.

The synapses in my brain crackle and pop, bridging neurons and hammering disjointed puzzle pieces into place.

Gabriel, like the angel?

It can't be.

'Wren –'

'Who is he?' I blurt out.

We're no longer dancing. We're standing still, staring at each other, him with an expression somewhere between concern and confusion, and me with a heavy chest and a throbbing pulse.

My eyes drop to his lips. I don't want to miss a single syllable of his answer.

'He's my brother.'

My ears ring.

Ink, scar, *green*.

I'm not religious, but in this moment, I thank God.

I thank God he's alive.

And then I thank God I didn't tell him my secret.

Because I didn't know there was another Visconti brother.

But I do know that man.

CHAPTER
Three

Wren

He's alive.

Relief crashes over me in a wave. I'm swimming in it – drowning in it – until Rafe tilts my chin and pulls me up for air.

'Has your lemonade been spiked?' he asks, amused.

It feels like it. 'I didn't know you had another brother,' I murmur.

'Really?' He sounds surprised. 'You've never met Gabe?'

My mouth opens, then closes again.

Even in the throb of confusion, I know I don't tell lies. Even those in the lightest shade of white get stuck in the base of my throat, and I have a hard time choking them out. But the truth is now stuck there too, because if Rafe doesn't know we've met, it means Gabriel hasn't told him either.

Which means he doesn't know about that night.

I shake my head.

Rafe laughs in disbelief and lets go of my chin. 'Yeah, well, Gabe keeps himself to himself.'

You know, perhaps we're not talking about the same person. Maybe he's talking about another man, one I haven't spotted yet, who happens to have a similar name. Maybe someone over at the bar or surrounded by that group of girls in the corner. A man who fits the Visconti mold, with a sharp suit and an air of importance like the rest of them.

Perhaps there's not a man in the shadows. It's just the darkness playing tricks on me.

Anticipation grips my neck as I slowly look over my shoulder. I find the strobe light and track its path over stilettos, discarded penis straws, and pools of spilled liquor.

It inches up the wall.

Ink.

Scar.

A green gaze clashing with mine.

In a short, sharp breath, he's gone again, reclaimed by the shadow.

Rafe's eyes warm my cheek. 'He's not as scary as he looks, I promise.'

My body is throbbing, and I swallow thickly. 'Does he live on the coast?'

'Sometimes.'

'And he works for the family business too?'

His smile pulls taut. 'Mm-hm.'

From what I've seen of him, even under the dimmest of lighting, I can't imagine him sitting behind a desk tapping away on a keyboard. 'Doing *what*?'

He pauses. 'Security.'

My heartbeat slows a little. Well, I suppose that makes sense. The Viscontis are probably worth a fortune, and I'm sure both their family name and bank accounts bring all sorts of criminals out of the woodworks.

It would also explain why I haven't seen him around and why he was lurking in the shadows of the parking lot. Being covert is likely part of his job description.

But it doesn't explain what he was doing that night.

ABBA fades, and the DJ rambles something incoherent over the microphone. A loud cheer ripples through the crowd in response.

Rafe puts his hand on my shoulder and flashes a brilliant smile. 'It was a pleasure, Wren, but it's about time that I . . .' He tugs back the cuff of his shirt and glances at his bare wrist. A look of contempt flickers through his expression. 'Get a new watch,' he mutters, then kisses the back of my hand. If he notices it's shaky, he doesn't mention it. 'Save a dance for me tomorrow, okay?'

With a wink, he's gone, parting the crowd with his mere presence.

Now what?

I'm too jittery to dance or make small talk. Shuffling from one foot to the other, I run my sweaty palms down the side of my dress and peer around. Tayce is still AWOL, and Rory and Angelo are still attached by at least two limbs and a mouth.

Rory. I bet she still hasn't had any damn water. I take a step toward the bar but stop myself. My legs are like jelly – but *why* ? Why am I so nervous? I should be happy – he's alive! – and I am happy. In fact, I should bounce on over to him, throw my arms around him, and tell him so. Then we'll gush over how it's such a small world and how we can't believe his brother is marrying my best friend, then we'll marvel about how we've never bumped into each other before this.

I'm sure he'll thank me. And then . . .

A cold sweat drifts through me.

And then he'll ask me to tell him my secret.

There it is, the source of restlessness humming under my skin.

My mind drifts back to that night. The ghost of the October chill caresses my nape, and those words dance on the tip of my tongue. I blow them out in a long, hard breath, letting them dissipate between dancing bodies, never to be uttered aloud.

Another cheer rises up from behind me, and a plucky base fissures out of the speakers. Someone shouts my name over a rising beat. When I spin around, two lines have formed on the dance floor.

Well, then. The day I don't dance to the 'Macarena' is the day I'm dead.

Usually, I'd elbow my way into a space front and center, but tonight, the black hole in the back corner has a gravitational pull. So I squeeze through a gap in the first row and join the far end of the second, turning to face the front before the strobe light can reveal the man at the heart of it.

Shyness is a foreign concept to me, and it's not the reason I can't bring myself to turn around and break the ice. Or even just melt it a little with a smile and a wave. It's something more unsettling. It crackles out of the darkness, prickling my back like a low hum of an electric fence warning me not to touch it. It glues my socks to the floor and rolls my head to the right, forcing me to make pleasantries with Priti, a girl who used to sit in front of me in math class.

She ignores my compliment about her cute shirt. 'So, you and Rafe Visconti, hmm?' She wiggles her eyebrows, just in case the insinuation dripping from her tone wasn't obvious enough. 'We all saw you dancing.'

I roll my eyes. 'I dance with all my friends.'

'Uh-huh, sure.'

'I'm dancing with you now, aren't I?'

The dance floor shudders as twenty girls in heels jump to face the right wall. We put our hands out front and turn our palms up.

'You look cute together,' Priti shouts over her shoulder.

Whatever. Even if my thoughts weren't too busy probing around in the shadows, I wouldn't bother defending myself.

Because if I had a crush on Rafe Visconti, Lord knows the world and its wife would know about it.

We wiggle. We jump. Now we're facing the back wall, and the nerves in my chest drop to my stomach and hum in anticipation.

Hands out front. Palms face up. The strobe light sweeps, and there he is, glaring at me again.

From this angle, the light frames his whole face. It's only a fraction of a second, and I'd have missed it if I'd blinked. But I didn't, and now it's stamped onto my retinas as though I've been blinded by a too-bright camera flash.

Shock and something colder freezes me in place. I scan the darkness he's disappeared back into, trying to commit the image to memory and reconcile it with *that* night.

But I can't. There's nothing familiar, nothing to grab a hold of for comfort.

Survival instinct stiffens my muscles, but it's kicked in three years too late. I jump to the right, half a chorus too early, seeking relief.

Hands out. Palms down. No – palms across chest.

Wait. What am I doing again?

My cheeks burn and my pulse throbs as I struggle to claw back my rhythm. When we jump to face the front again, Priti's smirk bores into my cheek. 'I still can't believe he's Rafe and Angelo's brother.'

My eyes slide sideways. 'You know him?'

'You don't?'

There's no room in my brain for annoyance, so it slithers under my skin instead. How on earth does Priti know of this mysterious, terrifying third Visconti brother and I don't? I've got that feeling again, the one where I can't quite jump into the loop, and I *don't like it*.

And my expression must show it because she swaps out her smirk for a frown. 'Seriously? You don't know the Boogeyman?'

Boogeyman. There's that damn word again.

Wiggle.

Jump.

I'm dancing on muscle memory alone now, staring at the back of Priti's head as she thrashes out the moves half a beat behind the music.

She glances over her shoulder. 'Come on, Wren. You've never heard the legend about avoiding the Reserve after dark on a full moon? They say it's when the Boogeyman comes out of his underground lair.' Her eyes widen in mock horror. 'And he doesn't like people being on his turf.'

Dread slows my pulse.

The Devil's Coast is littered with lore. The Pacific winds spread myths and legends as fast as gossip along these cliffs, and they pique my interest just as much. They even make up the bulk of my small talk with any out-of-towner who stumbles into The Rusty Anchor on a quiet night. Of course, I'm partial to the self-serving tales. With elbows resting on the splintered bartop, I'll whisper the warning of Grim Reaper Road to those with cars in the parking lot: drive too fast around the bend connecting Devil's Hollow with Devil's Cove, and Death himself will step out into the path of your headlights.

If I'm feeling particularly romantic, or if said out-of-towner happens to be good-looking, perhaps I'll suggest he take a walk on the eastern side of the Devil's Reserve, turn left at the felled oak tree, and stroll half a mile to the Bleeding Falls. There, if he closes his eyes and listens, the blood-red cascade will whisper the name of your one true love – and would you know it, whoosh sounds like 'Wren' if you concentrate hard enough.

But the Boogeyman roaming the forest during a full moon? Underground lair? The mere mention of it prickles my skin with unease. It was a full moon *that* night.

Death brushes past my shoulder, and I shiver.

My throat itches with the need to ask questions. Though, I have a sinking feeling I don't want to know the answers.

We jump. The floor pushes back in protest. Palms down, palms up, palms across chest. My body aches with awareness, and this time I'm not brave enough to follow the light's path.

Jump. Hands jut out with a tremble. Palms glisten with sweat under the disco lighting. Up, no, across – oh, to hell with this.

I'm not a skeptic, but I have common sense. He's not some mythical monster, he's a Visconti, not to mention, my best friend's soon-to-be brother-in-law. I survived that night unscathed, didn't I? That's proof enough that it's all bull.

I break out of the routine, spinning around to face the back wall, and slip into a clumsy two-step and stare into the void, waiting.

When the strobe light frames his cold gaze again, I'm shaky but ready.

I smile and wave.

He glares back.

Hmm. Okay, well, he obviously didn't see that. The light is probably shining right in his eyes. But jeez, I'm too antsy to wait for the chance to try again, so screw the 'Macarena.'

'Wren, are you insane –'

Priti's protests are swallowed by the rapid Spanish verse as I step out of line and to the edge of the dance floor.

'Hi!' I yell, cupping my hand to my brow as if doing so will give me night vision.

Nothing.

Well, I guess the music is pretty loud.

I step off the dance floor. 'Hey! Remember me?'

No answer.

Blame it on being an only child, but I loathe being ignored. A spark of annoyance lights a flame under me and drives me forward.

With the stomp of my fluffy socks, darkness brushes over my toes.

Another, and it swallows me whole.

I'm immediately uneasy. The air feels different in this corner of the club. A few degrees warmer, a few inches thicker. I hover, pulled thin between wanting to turn around and seek safety in numbers and wanting to stay and find out more.

Before I can decide, the strobe light circles back around, and now I'm the one in its path. When it brushes my spine and stretches my shadow up the jagged wall, my heart sinks to my stomach.

The shadow next to mine is all-consuming.

It's huge in contrast, in both height and width. The type of shadow that doesn't trigger your fight-or-flight response but paralyzes it. My gaze feels as heavy as my limbs as it reluctantly follows the path of light to the left.

'Hey.'

A flash of green; no response. Well, I practically squeaked that greeting, so of course he didn't hear me. I clear my throat, clench my fists, and try again. 'Hi! Remember me?'

Nothing.

Is he . . . *okay*?

And then it suddenly dawns on me. The blood, the gurgle in his breaths. Yes, he survived that night, but at what cost? It doesn't mean he made a full recovery.

Fear is only a short road to morbid curiosity, and I cross it with a small step forward. Well, I try to. My sock skids on something wet, then I'm falling. Forward, deeper and deeper and deeper into the abyss, like Alice plummeting down the rabbit hole. I reach out to grab something, anything, to steady myself, and my fingers brush over something hard and *hot*, but before they find purchase, I'm spinning.

My back slams against something solid and knocks the air from my lungs. *What the hell?*

We've traded places. Him with his back now to the dance

floor, mine pressed against the wall. I glance down at my socks as if they're the culprit here, but the ghost of a too-tight grip on my shoulder tells me otherwise.

I look from my feet to his. Now backlit by the disco lights, his outline is sharper, and I can make out the shape of combat boots. Weird choice for a nightclub, but okay. At least he's committed to the look with the black cargo pants. I skim up the side of his bulging quads and drink in the broad lines straining against his matching long-sleeve crew neck.

The first inch of visible skin starts at the trunk of his throat, which is wrapped in intricate tattoos I can't make out the details of. They spread across a wide jaw and disappear under a thick, dark beard.

I lift my gaze to meet his.

I wish I hadn't.

Those eyes. They're not green up close, they're black. Black and bottomless, as if they swallow the light instead of reflect it. All my pulse points throb out of sync as I scan his other features for a part of him I recognize from that night.

But his mouth, his nose. The hollows of his cheekbones and the depth of his scar. They're all wrong. He's all angles and no soft edges. Deep crevices and dangerous terrain. There's something strikingly inhuman about him, as though he's clawed his way out from the underworld.

Time has a way of distorting memories, sure, but I'm certain of two things – those eyes would have never softened at my cheesy, badly timed jokes, and they belong to a man I should have never been on a dark road with.

I seek relief by turning my attention to his mouth. As I'm wondering what the hell will come out of mine, his lips move.

My gaze flicks back up. 'What?'

Despite the heavy baseline and the blood roaring in my ears, I heard him. Each word was deep, slow, and unmistakable.

And his wavering stare tells me he meant every syllable.

It's not often I'm lost for words, so my mouth opens on instinct, but I clamp it shut when he steps toward me.

Crap, he's close. Fibers-of-his-shirt-grazing-my-chest kind of close. My bare skin tingles from the heat, and I swim in the hot, dizzy feeling it gives me.

He stoops to meet my ear. I hold my breath and palm the wall behind me, anticipating the scrunch of his beard against my cheek, but it never comes.

'If you stick your tongue out at me again, I'll cut it out of your head.'

What?

Shock freezes me in place. I'd heard him the first time and, of course, thought he was joking. Not everyone was blessed with a good sense of humor. But there's no lightness in his tone; it's flatline, factual. He could be reciting Pi to the tenth decimal point.

As the strobe light touches our corner of the club again, I follow its path. It reveals his fist clenched tightly at his side, and the letters on his knuckles dance with the movement. I track it up his neck and tilt my chin to meet his eyes. Maybe that's where the humor lies. But he's too close and so damn tall that all looking up does is brush my nose over his beard, bringing me the scent of charred firewood and well-worn leather.

The dizziness heightens.

Then as quickly as he closed the gap between us, he backs off. Fists still clenched, he steps to the side and glances tightly over his shoulder. It feels like a dismissal, and Christ, he doesn't have to dismiss me twice.

Cheeks burning and legs shaking, I resist the urge to break into a run. Instead, I walk stiffly onto the dance floor, where it's warm and bubbly and the sound of bad singing soothes me. Each sweaty shoulder that brushes against mine thaws me a little, and by the time I've reached the other side of the club, the shock has melted, giving way to something else: irritation.

Did he really just *threaten* me? For something as innocent as sticking my tongue out at him?

Oh, I know his type. They're a dime a dozen on the Devil's Cove promenade: bouncers and security guards drunk on the dribble of power they possess. He guards the keys to the Visconti kingdom instead of the entrance to a nightclub, but the attitude is still the same.

Irritation fizzles into anger. He's not the Boogeyman of Devil's Coast, he's the local bully.

And there's only one way to deal with bullies.

When I reach the far side of the dance floor, I spin back around on my heel. I catch his eye just as the strobe light hits him and stick out my tongue again.

I'm tempted to stick my middle finger up too, but that'd be rude.

And Wren Harlow is *never* rude.

CHAPTER
Four

Wren

I was right: Angelo Visconti can pick you up with one arm without grunting.

'Water,' I announce as he wraps an arm around my waist, hauls me to his side, and lifts me a few inches from the ground. I lean back against his forearm to stare up at him. Gotta make sure he's listening. 'Lots and lots of water. Do you have electrolyte packets? If not, salt will do.' I poke the top button of his shirt. 'Just a pinch though, otherwise she might have a puffy face for tomorrow.'

He checks his watch. 'That would be a travesty.'

'Oh, God. Don't even put it out into the universe.' His shoulder connects with the nightclub door, and we spill out into the icy night. I pull my knees up to avoid my socks touching the veranda's wet concrete. 'She has silk pillows, right? Make sure she piles her hair up into a loose ponytail – emphasis on *loose* – and that she sleeps on her back.'

Glancing to where Rory is sliding into his car, Angelo dips his free hand into the pocket of his pants and pulls out his cell.

Then he lazily checks his messages before putting it away again. 'Silk ponytail. Got it.'

My frosted sigh grazes his cheekbone. He's not paying attention. 'You know what, maybe I should just stay over tonight. Rory's lax with her skincare routine at the best of times, let alone when she's –'

'Wren.' Angelo comes to a stop under the heat lamp, his eyes humming with quiet amusement. 'You're welcome at our house anytime. Anytime, but not tonight.'

There's a stiff second before the penny drops. When it does, the shells of my ears grow hot. 'Oh,' I mumble, fiddling with the shoulder strap of my SOS bag. 'Yes, of course. Well, um, just make sure she's hydrated.'

'Yes, boss.'

I rake my fingers through my bangs, then wiggle down the hemline of my dress. Though always polite and pleasant, Angelo is a man of few words, and I bite back the urge to fill the comfortable silence with a barrage of vapid questions. *Am I heavy? Cute suit, where's it from? Sooo, are you nervous about tomorrow?*

Instead, I readjust my position on his hip and squint out into the depths of the parking lot, looking for my uncle.

Taxis arrive in a slow-moving conveyor belt, then peel off into the night with slumped silhouettes pressed up against their windows. A few feet from the veranda, a group of girls nurse empty champagne flutes and puff on cigarettes, desperate to stretch the night out a little longer.

I look beyond it all to the tree branches rustling against the black sky. A gust of wind brings the *hiss* of a striking match past my ear, and I shiver.

'You're cold. Rory's got my jacket. I'll get you another.' Angelo glances to the left and gives a curt chin jerk to someone in the shadows.

'No need.'

Despite my bare legs and the fact the heat lamps switched off a while ago, I'm far from cold. I'm hot, itchy, antsy, and riled up by the exchange I had earlier with Angelo's rude-ass brother. For a moment, I consider telling him about it. I wouldn't have to mention our previous encounter, just that I tried to introduce myself and was immediately threatened. But that feels like snitching, and besides, I don't want to cause any family drama the night before his big day.

When Angelo jerks his chin again, it's at Uncle Finn.

He strides through the parking lot toward us, two fingers looped into the heels of a pair of pink sneakers. His gaze drops to my socks and fills with disapproval.

'You're too nice, Wren.'

My jaw tightens. He sounds like Tayce. But I keep my mouth shut. He's done me a solid by bringing me vomit-free footwear at this time of night. I grip onto Angelo's arm for balance, and stuff my feet into my running shoes. He makes pleasantries with Uncle Finn above my head before touching me lightly on the shoulder.

'You know I'm going to ask.'

My smile wobbles. 'And you know I will politely decline. Thanks for the offer though.'

In the few months he's lived on the coast, I can't count how many times he's offered me a ride.

My answer is always the same.

He nods and wishes us a good evening. We wish him good luck for tomorrow, then he strides toward a waiting car on the far side of the parking lot.

Uncle Finn's eyes burn into the side of my cheek.

I know what's coming. It always comes.

'Next September is going to come around quicker than you think, you know.'

Of course I know. How can I *not* know? This September

hit me like a lightning-speed slap, and so did the one before it. These next ten months will peel away like steamed wallpaper, and I've run out of excuses.

Now I'm hot and itchy for a different reason, so time for a change of subject.

'You look nice.' I pass him my SOS bag, now weighed down by my smelly boots, and cast an eye over his wool coat. His shoulders tense, then he tightens the scarf around his neck.

But it's too late. I've already seen the cashmere sweater underneath.

'Hmm. You look *really* nice,' I say, eyes narrowing. I lean in, sniffing him like a curious dog. 'You smell nice too. Where have you been?'

'Don't change the subject. When are you going to start driving again?'

We fall in step to cut across the parking lot. 'Don't change the subject by telling *me* not to change the subject. Where have you been?'

He side-eyes me over the rim of his designer spectacles. 'In my workshop, measuring up some biscuit joints for my latest commission. Passing the time until my favorite niece finishes partying, because she *insists* on risking her life by walking the forty-five-minute journey home down a dark, scary road instead of driving.'

I laugh, not because I'm his *only* niece, but because he's lying. He's been at the Devil's Hollow Country Club playing chess and eating caviar on fancy little crackers.

Finnegan Harlow is often mistaken for my father, and not just because he scolds me like one. We share the same sun-yellow hair, deep-blue eyes, and wide smile – although you wouldn't know he was capable of smiling most of the time. Even with the perma-frown denting his brow, he looks nowhere near his forty-eight years, which I guess is why he gets away with telling anyone who asks that he's forty-two.

He's a carpenter. Well, he cosplays as one, spending hours in his workshop and buying ridiculously expensive tools. In his previous life, he was one of Seattle's highest-paid lawyers, with a reputation for representing the discriminated, the framed, and the justified. Poverty-stricken teens in the wrong place at the wrong time, housewives who couldn't take another beating. That kind of thing.

He was the people's lawyer.

I was eleven when he scrawled his signature on my adoption papers and took me out of Seattle. He said we weren't leaving the city because of the men with cameras hiding in the bushes on the front lawn, but because a slower pace of life would be healthier for us. His husband, Oliver Harlow, had dropped dead of a stress-induced heart attack some months before, and he suspected it was the chaos of the city that did him in.

Finn had driven us west with a locked jaw. I had my feet propped up on the dash, humming along to ABBA's greatest hits on the stereo and flipping through his copy of *Country Living* magazine. Devil's Dip was the first place we came across that looked like the pictures within its glossy pages. By the time he'd realized the town was more rusty than rustic and that had we'd stuck to the highway for a few more minutes we'd have hit a town far more palatable, it was too late. He'd already bought ten acres of farmland, enrolled me in a local school, and committed to a carpentry course.

I fell in love with Devil's Dip's wonky charm, but Finn has never let go of his big-city thinking and luxury habits, though he's far too stubborn to admit it.

And so for the last ten years, we've played pretend. We pretend like I don't know there's a wine cellar behind a false wall in his workshop, or that he spends most of his days in Devil's Hollow schmoozing with the likes of Castiel Visconti at the country club. As for the whole carpenter shtick, I've never seen him build anything with my own eyes, aside from the bookshelf he put up for me a few years ago.

It collapsed the moment I placed a hardback on it.

Finn tugs back his coat sleeve to check the time on his Rolex. 'Your insistence to walk is cutting into my sleep schedule, you know. I have to be up at the crack of dawn.'

I frown. 'To do what?'

He tuts. 'Chores on the farm. Have to be done before I fly over to Colorado for my carpentry course tomorrow.'

'What chores on the farm?'

'Farm-y things.'

'Like what?'

'Oh, you know. The usual.'

I bite my lip, choosing to focus on his shiny timepiece instead of picking apart his crappy agricultural knowledge. 'I thought you only wear that thing for birthdays and weddings?'

He pauses, then his eyes warm behind his glasses. 'Nothing gets past you, Wren. You're going to make an excellent lawyer.'

My smile flickers, as though the wiring in my brain is faulty. I don't bite; I never do. So it sits like a wedge between us, solid and heavy, as we turn onto the main road that leads us home.

It's a long, lonely road, and the only one connecting all three towns on the coast. A crumbling slab of asphalt less than twenty feet wide that separates the edge of the National Reserve and the rocky cliff face.

Uncle Finn hates this road, and not just because the potholes have blown out his tires countless times. On one side, there's the Pacific Ocean and its unrelenting wind, steep drops, and no guard rails. On the other, the streetlamps, strangled by vines escaping the border of the woods, are few and far between, leaving large stretches of darkness when the sun goes down.

More than anything, he hates that I walk it all the way

from Cove to Dip if I miss the last bus home after my nights volunteering.

And I get it. A cute girl walking along a dark, quiet road at midnight all alone? I've watched the news. I might as well wear a flashing sign saying *Kidnap Me*! But not only do I know every twist, jut, rise, and dip of this route, I know the towns it runs through.

The Devil's Coast is safe. Leave-your-car-unlocked, offer-a-ride-to-a-stranger kind of safe. Unlike Seattle or other big towns, there's no crime, no gangs, no mysterious murderer with a sinister nickname on the loose. The proof's in the pudding: I've been walking this route nearly every weekend, and nothing bad has ever happened.

The closest I've ever come to danger is *that* night.

As we pass, my eyes lift to the flickering streetlamp, then to the looming silhouette of the church across the road from it. Spires softened by shadows, the broken stained glass casting watery colors on the gravestones below.

And suddenly, I see him again, cloaked in black and bloodied, crawling away from the light of the streetlamp, fists scraping gravel, with ragged breaths barely audible over the sound of crashing waves and blistering winds.

My name touches the back of my neck. Then comes a grip on my elbow.

'Wren?'

I blink and meet my uncle's concerned gaze. When I look back down at the road, it's empty. Christ, I must be tired.

I take a deep breath and exhale a nervous laugh. 'Thought I saw a bear,' I mutter.

Pathetic, I know, but Finn tuts, mutters something about bears being *yet another* reason I need to get a car, and follows me as I turn off onto the trail that leads to our land.

Unlike the main road, the one up to Strawberry Farm is well-lit and well-maintained. Fairy lights wrap around the fir trees flanking either side, and you can't walk more than three feet without stepping into the glow of one of the many Victorian-style lamps. At the end sits a white gate, with a painted wooden sign on it. Underneath, there's an even larger sign warning trespassers that they'll be shot, though I doubt Uncle Finn has ever held a gun, let alone pulled a trigger.

I don't live with Finn anymore. My house sits at the edge of the land, a cozy two-story cottage with white board and batten and a pink front door. It was his eighteenth birthday gift to me, and allegedly, his most ambitious project to date. I never questioned how he built it so quickly, or why I've seen the exact same house being transported in two parts on the freeway, I was just so happy to have my own place to decorate how I want and to call my own.

Finn walks me down the gravel path, climbs three steps to the porch, and flips on the Bat Signal – a single pink bulb dangling above the front door, visible from any rear-facing window in his farmhouse opposite, that he installed after one too many nights of me forgetting to text him when I got home.

He slides his hands into his pockets, nudging the swinging love seat with his knee so it creaks back and forth. 'I hope you have a great time tomorrow. I'll be sad to miss it.'

'Uh-huh. I'm not sure your carpentry course is worth missing the wedding of the century, but I'm sure it'll be very educational.' I search his eyes for a flicker of dishonesty, but he just nods solemnly. Lawyers really do make the biggest liars. 'I'll be sure to take lots of photos,' I add, tucking my clutch under my arm and slipping my SOS bag off his shoulder and onto mine. 'Unless I meet The One, of course, then I'll be far too busy for that. Did you know, studies show that twenty-two percent of women meet the love of their life at –'

The short vibration in my clutch cuts me off. My vision warps, and there's a familiar punch to my gut, hard and violent.

No.

My shaky exhale floats off the porch and into the dark. I wish it'd just take me with it. Somewhere, *anywhere*, as long as unfinished sentences and rejection emails can't hurt me.

I choke out the question, though I already know the answer. 'What time is it?'

Finn tugs back the sleeve of his coat and checks that stupidly expensive timepiece supposedly reserved for birthdays and weddings. When he glances up at me, his jaw is tight.

His voice is even tighter. 'You promised to stop doing this, Wren.'

The back of my eyes start to burn. How can I stop when it's all I think about? When that one sentence – five words, twenty-nine characters, including spaces – dictates every single second of my life?

A hot fat tear rolls down my cold cheek, my rapid blinking doing nothing to stop it from falling. Finn tracks it with a look of disapproval, then turns his attention out to the night, seeking relief from the discomfort my emotions always bring him.

'If you went to law school when you said you would, this would have all gone away by now,' he mutters.

Guess lawyers make the biggest jerks too.

I wipe my wet cheek with the back of my hand and turn on my heel before the rest of my tears can come.

'Good night, Uncle Finn.'

Though, I don't wish him a good night at all.

CHAPTER
Five

Wren

Dear User3569,
  Your edit has been rejected.
  Reason: Bias.
  If you feel your edit was rejected in error, you can appeal the decision via the Helpdesk. Live support is available between 9am-5pm, Monday-Friday. Appeals sent after these hours will be replied to the next working day.
  Regards,
  Damien Cross

With my fists clenched on either side of my laptop, I glare at the name at the bottom of my email until my eyes burn and the pixels separate.

I'm not one for name-calling, but Damien Cross is an asshole. There're only two people on this earth I loathe, and though the most I know about him is that he has a grainy profile picture on a private *Instagram* account, this man is one of them.

My blowup chair squeaks under me as I flop against its backrest and sigh. Adrenaline and a stupid flicker of hope drove me up the stairs two at a time to read the email on a screen bigger than my cellphone, *just in case*. I haven't even taken off my coat or sneakers yet.

Why I expected any different, I don't know. No matter what I say, how many news articles I send in, how many new accounts I make, or what device I create them from, the midnight email is always the same.

I hover the cursor over the link to the Helpdesk, a strongly worded appeal itching in the tips of my fingers. But there's no point. It'll just have me anxiously waiting for yet *another* email, a stock reply telling me to submit more evidence, so I slam the laptop shut and slide it across my pink shag pile rug so hard it disappears under the bed.

I guess I'll just try again tomorrow.

Groaning, I clamber to my feet, peel off my clothes, and replace them with a silk nightgown and fluffy slippers. Then I do what I always do when the anger and desperation feel like they'll spiral downward into something darker: drown out and distract.

Spotify open. ABBA on. Walk from room to room, lighting every candle on every surface and flicking on every set of fairy lights until my pink and cream walls glow with warmth and it smells like a Bath & Body Works.

Skincare. A ten-step routine – well, twelve now that I've been crying. I smooth on my undereye strips in the glow of the vanity lights of my bathroom mirror, and by the time the beat drops on 'Gimme! Gimme! Gimme!,' my shoulders have dropped a few inches and my heart isn't so heavy.

Screw Damien Cross. My best friend is getting married tomorrow, and I'll be damned if I let him and his stupid website darken the day.

Once a hot shower has washed off the remnants of the bachelorette party and my rollers are firmly in place, my lids are heavy. Tapping my cell screen, I realize it's nearly 2:00 a.m.

Jeez. Time really does fly when you're getting cute.

After tightening the sash of my nightgown around my waist, I begin my nightly wind-down routine of working my way through the house and blowing out candles. I start in the bathroom first, then move to the bedrooms before heading into the kitchen and finishing in the living room.

Something's not right.

There are three candles on the mantelpiece, and none are lit. For a moment, I think perhaps I forgot to light them, but then the smell of burned wick drifts over, and slow-moving coils of smoke rise into the path of the moonlight cutting across the wall.

My spine goes rigid, but I ignore the prickle of unease on the back of my neck and glance over to the window. It's closed, so there must be a draft coming from somewhere. That's a future-Wren problem, because shuffling around trying to find it tonight will only cut further into my beauty sleep.

I shake it off, making a mental note to tell Uncle Finn when he's back from his 'carpentry course,' and lean over the coffee table to blow out the last candle.

Then I feel it. An awful, heavy sense of doom drags all the blood in my body down to my feet. A feeling of imminent danger in the darkness, and I'm too late, too slow, and too helpless to do anything about it.

The armchair lets out a lazy groan, and a face emerges from the shadows.

Ink.

Scar.

Green.

I've spent enough time on the sidelines of fear to know what it sounds like – blood-curling screams and final pleas of mercy. Though now, I realize I've been lucky enough to never actually feel it. Not this heart-stopping, icy kind that trembles deep within the marrow of your bones and wipes your brain clean of thought.

Christ, I know how *they* felt now.

With Gabriel Visconti in my living room, spilling out of my floral accent chair, and nothing but three feet of table and a cinnamon-scented candle between us, this must be what it feels like.

He shifts, resting his forearms on his thighs, and traps me with an expressionless stare.

'You always leave your front door unlocked for anyone to walk in?'

His voice is a rough drawl, unhurried and certain. I pick apart the calmness within it, and nausea turns my stomach. It's the voice of a man who believes he has every right to be here, in my living room, at 2:00 a.m.

Though I doubt breaking and entering is a new hobby for him, I realize he's right. My door, I slammed it shut behind me in my haste to get away from Uncle Finn and upstairs to my laptop and didn't lock it.

Somehow, that makes this all feel worse.

My throat won't work, so I stare back, watching the glow of the flame dance beneath his beard. It flickers only briefly over the curve of his mouth and contrasts the darkness in the space under his cheekbones.

Even the light is too scared to touch him.

Anticipation crackles like static over the coffee table, and I realize he's actually waiting for an answer.

I shake my head.

This seems good enough for him. His eyes release mine and carve a path down the front of my robe as steady and slow as his tone. My skin tingles underneath the thin fabric with every inch he covers, and it suddenly dawns on me that there's a fate worse than death.

My brain kicks back in, bursting with vivid snapshots. Me being pinned to my cream carpet by a wall of muscle. A tattooed hand muffling my sobs. Everything I've been saving for The One, from my first kiss to my first time, ripped away from me by this monster.

A noise escapes my lips, strangled and guttural. He glances up, disinterested, before laying something wrapped in black leather on the table before him.

With a flick of his wrist, it unrolls, revealing slithers of silver that wink in the light of the candle. Different shapes and sizes. All with sharp edges.

A set of knives.

Now would be a good time for my body to work, even just part of it. My feet, my voice, or my common sense.

'Choose one.'

My eyes snap back up to his.

'W-what?'

'I warned you.'

My pulse aches from throbbing as I remember his earlier warning. *Stick your tongue out at me again, and I'll cut it out of your head.*

Oh my God. It wasn't an empty threat.

We stare at each other. Me looking for any hint of the man I met three years ago, him looking for an answer.

The clock in the hall scratches out each tense second. Somewhere upstairs, ABBA has moved onto 'Dancing Queen.' It's my favorite song, and now it sounds like some sort of sick joke.

Irritation flashes in his gaze, then without breaking eye contact, he leans closer to the candle.

Then he blows.

The room plunges into darkness, and somewhere within it, I find my will to live. I turn on my heel and run, losing a hair roller somewhere near the television set, and a slipper at the bottom of the staircase. The entryway stretches out in front of me, but the pink glow of the porch light coming through the window isn't growing any closer, no matter how fast I move.

Time slows down, matching the leisurely thump of footsteps behind me. He's not in a hurry.

He knows I can't escape him.

As his shadow stretches up the doorframe, I consider turning around and begging for my life. Deep down, I always knew I'd die a horrible death. Something drawn-out and violent because it'd only be right. The good deeds came too late, and bubblegum pink and a chirpy disposition can't hide the rotting within me. I should have known karma always keeps score, and it always comes back for those who deserve its wrath.

My fingers grapple with the door handle. When I wrench it open, the ice-cold wind brings the taste of freedom through the crack, but a gloved hand reaches over my head and shuts it again with a soft *click*.

No.

Another hand clamps over my mouth.

Please, God, no.

I gasp into warm leather. Though I know from the sheer size of him that fighting will be fruitless, I flail my limbs anyway, trying to wriggle and wrestle out of his grasp. My elbow connects with hard muscle; the heel of my foot strikes a shin.

His strength is sickening.

So are my thoughts.

Despite staring death in the face, all I can focus on is what's happening behind me. The heat of his torso seeping through the thin fabric of my gown, the cold, hard metal of his belt digging into my lower back. My heart pounds and my chest heaves, and for a brief, ironic moment, I feel alive.

It's impossible to think sensibly when this close to dying, but I always knew it'd be impossible for me to think rationally this close to a man too. Even the one who will kill me.

His hand slides off the door, and a heavy arm wraps around my waist, crushing me against him. Electricity crackles along the length of his bulging forearm, humming inside of me in places it shouldn't even touch. When his other hand inches south of my mouth, the current surges and sparks.

He grips my jaw and squeezes.

My mouth pops open on command, filling the entryway with my damp, ragged breaths.

Oh, God, he's really going to do it. The Boogeyman is going to kill me.

Any flicker of optimism flew out of the window the moment those knives winked up at me from the coffee table. This isn't a Disney movie or an episode of *Grey's Anatomy*. He's going to *cut out my tongue*, and I won't survive it. I won't become the mysterious mute with a sad backstory, I'll be *dead*. I'll fall to my knees and bleed out on my 'Thank You for the Music – And For Wiping Your Feet!' doormat. I'll be an episode of a true crime podcast, or one of those *Netflix* docuseries everyone talks about on *Twitter*. They'll say I got straight A's in school, and that I lit up every room I walked into.

And worst of all, it'll ruin Rory's wedding.

Oh my God, the wedding.

Gabriel's arm slides across my stomach and lingers on my hip before dropping off.

Metal clanks against metal.

Metal glides along my bottom lip.

It sizzles like rain on hot concrete. I couldn't move even if I wasn't locked in this monster's vise.

They say your life flashes before your eyes when you're about to die, but when my gaze finds the black sky beyond the pink porch light, all I see is one sentence. Five words, twenty-nine characters, including spaces.

A bitter thought, tinged with irony, drifts through the space between my ears.

At least it'll finally be complete.

He slips the metal between the part of my lips and pushes it down on the flat of my tongue. I close my eyes and tense, waiting for the pain.

It doesn't come.

Instead, smooth leather glides down to my throat. He pushes two fingers against my clavicle, then the top of my head slams against his collarbone.

The roughness of his beard grazes my earlobe, and his hot breath skitters over my pulse.

'Lock your fucking doors,' he growls.

I stand there, frozen, open-mouthed and panting. Even when his shadow shifts around mine and the wind bites my chest. Even when he slams the door behind him so hard the house vibrates.

Even when his silhouette melts into the darkness beyond my garden path, I stand there not daring to believe it.

The clock behind me starts ticking again, seconds turning into minutes, maybe hours. ABBA floats down the stairs again, belting out track after track, oblivious.

Only when the taste of metal fills my entire mouth to where it burns and I fear it'll choke me, do I spit it out into my palm.

It's my house key.

I lock the door and sink – down, down, down, like a deflating balloon.

And that's where I stay until daylight comes.

CHAPTER

Six

Gabe

The only time I ever have my back to a room is when I'm more concerned with what's happening outside of it.

There's chaos on the front lawn. A line of cars wait behind the gates at a makeshift checkpoint. Alek is running plates, and Maxim is ripping apart the interiors.

A distant uncle is palming the hood of his car while Yemi pats him down for weapons, then over on the circle drive, the wedding planner teeters across the gravel path with a stack of boxes sealed with the red tape that lets me know they've been checked. She stumbles onto the grass, the cement truck backing up to the dirt pit narrowly missing her.

'Benny fucked our third cousin at the Mirales wedding last weekend.'

'Fuck off. How was I supposed to know? The broad had a different last name.'

'You'll know in nine months when she turns up on your doorstep holding a kid with three eyes.'

Gruff laughter fills the room. In the reflection of the window, I see my cousin Benny sucker punch his brother Nico in the gut.

Running a hand over my buzz cut, I let out a hiss through gritted teeth.

If outside is chaos, inside is delusion in its most maddening form. Rafe's opening a third bottle of whiskey, and Cas is bent over the humidor, talking smack about the cigar collection. And for some reason, I've got some cunt with a measuring tape around his neck fiddling with the hem of my pants.

I keep having to resist the itch to give him a swift kick to the jaw.

Rafe appears beside me, bottle angled to my glass. 'Need a top up?' He frowns when he realizes my whiskey remains untouched. 'What, are you hungover or something?'

Of course not. Alcohol isn't my vice of choice when I need to dull my thoughts.

Besides, how can I drink at a time like this?

But the lack of a watch on his wrist and the sloppy signatures on the documents I took from his desk and burned this morning tell me he is.

Rough Arabic comes through my earpiece: *This is Emile for Commander. Over.*

Scanning the grounds, I find Emile beside the truck, staring up at me expectantly, and nod. He nods back, slaps the cab door twice, and the drum on the back groans to life.

Rafe watches in disgust as the cement splutters out of the chute. 'Of all the days to work on the lawn.'

'Of all the days to have a fucking wedding,' I grunt back.

He smirks and straightens my bow tie for the third time this morning. 'Take the day off, brother. You know what Dante's like. He couldn't organize an orgy in a brothel.'

A sour taste brews at the back of my tongue.

My brothers are, well, my brothers, but fuck, they're ignorant at times.

Raphael Visconti did exactly what our father said he was

born to do: take the silver spoon in his mouth and turn it gold. Now he spends his days in a diamond-clad bubble, where the sun always shines, his casinos are always profitable, and his biggest worry is the one-inch scratch on his car from driving like an asshole.

He's too busy with boardrooms and women to realize that if I ever took a day off, he'd be dead ten times over. Of all times to *take a day* off, today definitely wouldn't be the day. Not when Angelo decided to pop a cap in Uncle Alberto's ass and marry his fiancée a few weeks later.

My annoyance shifts from Rafe to Angelo, our oldest brother and Capo of the Devil's Dip outfit. He was born to lead, and turns out, born to be a pain in my ass too.

He could have delayed the wedding. He could have done it behind closed doors or over Zoom for all I care. But no, he wanted a grand affair with champagne, cigars, and whiskey. In the middle of the damn National Reserve, where there're over forty blind spots and sixteen entrances to secure, with a guest list including every extended family member we're on speaking terms with. He wanted plus-ones, an orchestra, and an eight-course meal by a chef flown in from Italy, all of whom needed to be surveyed, searched, and swept.

It's a logistical nightmare.

But neither Angelo nor Rafe have thought about that.

It's not what they were born to do.

'What are you doing down there, anyway?'

Irritation flares up behind my ribs. Rafe loves a shit joke. They make up every other line of his wedding speech, but I can tell by his blank stare that this isn't one of them.

I glance down at the tailor, who flashes me a nervous smile, then glare at Rafe. This is why his pool boy ended up hog-tied in the trunk of my car. He has no problem running his mouth around staff, then he wonders why they keep on disappearing.

'Top secret.'

'Ah,' he murmurs against the rim of his tumbler. 'Gabe Visconti and his chamber of secrets.'

I'd laugh at how close to home his comment hits, but that gene skipped me. Even if it hadn't, war is coming. And there's nothing funny about that.

Rafe slaps me on the back, mutters something sarcastic about it being a good chat, then strolls over to Cas, who's now sprawled in an armchair, running his nose along the length of a Cuban.

I crack my neck, but it does little to release the tension knotting it. I'm wound tight and burning beneath the surface, and not because I'm waiting for gunfire to ring out at any moment – that's background noise at this point.

It's *Her*.

'You know what I need? A table plan.' Benny yanks at the stopper of a whiskey decanter. 'With big green check marks next to the names of all the chicks we're not related to.'

No, what Benny needs is to finish his course of antibiotics. He has the clap for the second time this year, and with eighteen of his prior conquests on the wedding guest list, it'll soon be a third.

'Yeah, and big red crosses next to all the *chicks* with restraining orders against you,' Rafe drawls.

Cas lets out a booming laugh, though he'll be swallowing it come Monday morning when his Russian fiancée slaps him with a restraining order of his own. Her brothers aren't stupid enough to interfere with an arranged marriage to a Visconti, and her four-day hunger strike didn't work, so she's trying her luck with the American legal system instead.

I look down. 'You done?'

The tailor slips the needle into the crook of his mouth and shuffles around to my other leg. 'Uh, nearly, sir. I just need to let out a little more fabric, and then I'll be out of your way.' I tug my pant leg up an inch. His gaze falls on the blade strapped to my ankle, and the blood drains from his face. 'Never mind. All done,' he says before scurrying off somewhere safer.

Smart man.

Between Rafe chewing my ear off and this dick buzzing around my feet, I'm behind on my checks. I scan the perimeters, making sure none of my men have broken rank. There're four cars at the checkpoint now, all of which I recognize as low risk. All boxes being carried to and from the house have the red seal of approval, and a quick glance at my watch tells me Fez has eyes on Angelo and Rory in the rear garden.

Good.

I grip my nape and release a tense breath. Rafe's right, Dante couldn't tell his right hand from his left. Now that Uncle Alberto is dead, he's been forced to step into his shoes as the head of the Devil's Cove outfit two decades too early. He's under prepared and overwhelmed, and even if he wasn't, he doesn't have the balls to be a Capo. The guy can't even pull a trigger without asking for permission, let alone order someone else to pull one. He barely has enough men to secure the perimeters of Devil's Cove anyway. He'd be an idiot to feed them to my wolves this early on.

Besides, retaliating today, of all days, would be predictable.

And I learned a long time ago that Dante Visconti can be anything but.

My chest starts to burn and my vision flickers. It's been three years, but the memory of that night still blinds me with rage. Swallowing, I force it to the pit of my stomach and continue my sweep.

As my gaze moves along the wrought-iron railings, it snags on the pedestrian entrance, then narrows on the familiar blonde beside it.

Speaking of that night.

She hands over a little bag to Arben for inspection. It's the size of a postage stamp and obnoxiously pink, like the rest of her. Pink hair rollers. Pink turtleneck sweater spilling out the collar of a pink coat. Pink knee-high boots. Even under the cold gray sky, I can tell the garment bag slung over her forearm is a pale shade of pink, and I'd bet my entire arsenal that whatever is inside of it is too.

Pink. Pink. Pink.

Christ. I never thought it'd be possible to hate a fucking color so much.

Palming my jaw, I let out a hard exhale through my nose and move on to my other checks.

I last all of ten seconds before I'm glaring at her again.

I knew she'd be at the wedding, she's Rory's bridesmaid, but after putting the fear of God into her last night, I didn't think she'd be so fucking chipper about it.

I don't make a habit of terrorizing young girls, but I knew the moment she stuck her fucking tongue out at me from across the Catacomb parking lot that I needed to nip this shit in the bud if we're to coexist on the same coastline. That it'd only be a matter of time before she recognized me. Spoke to me.

Touched me.

Annoyance burns hot under my collar, and I yank at the stupid bowtie around my neck for relief.

The threat to cut out her tongue didn't work, so I had to double down. But more fool me, because I'd turned up at her house in an attempt to teach her about the age-old adage of fucking around and finding out, but instead, I fucked around and found out what her heavy breaths feel like against my palm, and how her hair smells when it's freshly washed.

The heat in my chest slides south, and I expel it from my body with a gritted hiss before it can reach my groin, irritated that it was there in the first place. I hate my father for a million reasons but beating the ability to lust out of me isn't one of them.

Women make you weak. You let them run their hands over your body, and they'll find every hairline fracture and fissure, claw them open until they're canyon-deep, then have the nerve to look you dead in the eye and call it love.

It's best not to let them touch you to begin with.

I shake her fingerprints off of my jaw and, glare back down at her again.

I don't know what's pissing me off more, the fact she didn't know danger when it crossed her path three years ago, or the fact she hasn't learned to recognize it in the years since. Why the fuck was her door unlocked, and why did she just stand there – slack-jawed and wide-eyed, in the thinnest robe on the planet – instead of running for her life?

My gaze narrows on her with reluctant curiosity. She got her bag back, so why is she still standing there, laughing?

It sounds like sunshine and helium, light and loud enough to float over the lawn, penetrate the bulletproof window, and land on my sternum like a weak punch.

She's laughing at Arben, of all fucking people. As if he's even funny. As if he doesn't have a Glock in his waistband, a taser in his pocket, and the strongest chokehold I've ever seen.

My temples throb, and an intrusive thought passes through me, burrowing deeper and worming its way back in time.

She touched me then too. It was soft. So was her voice. As was her breath when it grazed my top lip.

'Can I tell you a secret?'

Something in my sternum twists, and I pick up the whiskey glass and sink its contents in one gulp in an attempt untangle it.

The Good Samaritan and her little secret.

Running my tongue over my teeth, I glare at her and Arben

over the rim of the glass. He's laughing now too. Head tilted back, gummy smile on show, revealing the consequence of the last time he pissed me off.

There must have been something in that drink, because before common sense can stop me, I tap his channel on my watch and bring it to my mouth.

'Share the joke, Arben. I could use a good laugh today.'

He jolts and touches his earpiece as though it's given him an electric shock. Probably because I switched to English. His sheepish gaze finds me instantly, but hers roves over the front of the house, trying to figure out what's startled him.

When she spots me, she freezes. Realization washes all the light away, and black floods the blue.

Instead of glancing away like I expect her to, she doubles down and steels her chin. The longer she stares, the hotter her anger burns and the harder my heart beats. For a moment, I think she's going to stick her tongue out at me again.

Adrenaline floods through me as the deep-rooted sickness in me hopes she does. There would be no bluffing this time; I'd carve it out slowly with a dessert spoon, then, depending on how much she fought, I'd shove it down her throat to muffle her screams.

She glares at me.

The glass cracks in my fist.

She turns away.

Though the last thing I have time for is paying her another visit, disappointment taints the faint satisfaction I feel. I've always enjoyed cutting out tongues. If you avoid the lingual artery and keep them in an upright position, it'll take three-to-four days for them to bleed out.

She pulls something up on her phone and shows Arben, and my muscles twitch, preparing my body to do something it shouldn't. Not to her, but to him. I don't need to hear the girl running her mouth to know whatever she said isn't the reason he's tickled.

My men are as carefully curated as her sunny personality. They're the best in the business, and I've trained, tortured, and traumatized them to be even better.

Unfortunately, they still have dicks and the animalistic urge to stick them into pretty things.

He didn't laugh because he thought she was funny, no, he saw the blonde hair, the heart-shaped face, and the way her button nose scrunches when she smiles. He saw the wide eyes and wondered if he could corrupt the innocence within them. And when she touched him, he thought he stood a chance of finding out if what's underneath that bright-pink raincoat is as tight as her silhouette would suggest.

He'll lose the rest of his teeth tonight.

And I'll lose my fucking mind over her secret.

The faint sound of footsteps tugs me back into the room. I cock my head, listening. Heavy strides, decisive steps. A slight lean on the left heel.

Even before the door flies open, I know it's Angelo.

He's agitated too.

'Listen and listen good because this is your one and only warning. No fighting, no fucking, no stepping out of line. Today is my wedding day, and if any of you idiots fuck it up, you'll be dead before you can squeal out an apology. Got it? Good. Now get out.'

Amusement flutters through the room, peppered with a sarcastic 'Yes, Boss' from Benny.

It flutters through me too because my brother rarely makes threats. Usually, he skips straight to the good part in a blind fit of rage, then calls me to sort the cleanup.

Angelo Visconti was born to lead. He was born to look good in a suit too, which is why he got away with cosplaying as a law-abiding citizen for so long. After our parents died, he stepped on a plane to London instead of into our father's shoes and tried to shake the made man out of his bones.

I always knew he'd come back to the *Cosa Nostra* long before his eyes locked onto our uncle's fiancée.

You can't run from what you were born to do.

He shuts the door with a swift kick, then sinks into the chair behind his desk.

Rafe brings him a whiskey, letting out a low whistle. 'Looking suave, brother. Nervous?'

'No. Paranoid,' he grits back, smoothing down the front of his tux.

'Of Rory not turning up?'

He huffs out a dry laugh, his eyes drifting to the photo of her smiling beside his laptop. 'I'd drag her down the aisle by her curls if I had to.'

'How romantic.'

'Mm.' Angelo sinks his drink in two gulps, slams it down, and jerks his chin at me. 'We set?'

I nod.

'Good. Now tell me why the fuck you're digging up my front lawn on my wedding day.'

'It's a secret, apparently,' Rafe says with a smirk, sliding onto the edge of the desk.

My gaze drifts down to Emile smoothing over concrete with the back of a shovel.

Secrets. The Villain's most powerful weapon.

Our father needn't have wasted his breath speaking rule eight into existence. He'd led by example.

When he and his two brothers arrived on the coast from Sicily, they'd decided to divide and conquer. Uncle Alberto built Devil's Cove up into the sky, Uncle Alfredo buried his riches beneath the cobbled streets of Devil's Hollow, but our father saw the state of Devil's Dip and thought it best to build outward into the Pacific.

He knocked up a port in its raging waters. Bought the church looming on the cliffs above it and established himself as it's God-fearing Deacon.

The worst thing the locals ever did was trust him to pass on their confessions onto the big man upstairs.

Another laugh rings out by the gates and chafes my skin.

And the worst thing She did was nearly tell me hers.

Behind me, Rafe grinds out an Italian curse. 'I don't have my fucking watch. What's the time? We need to leave soon, right?'

He's spinning his poker chip a mile a minute, wearing out the carpet as he paces from the bookshelf to the door and back again.

I suspect his sudden change in demeanor has something to do with red hair and a smart mouth.

Sliding my hand into my pocket, I pull out a fistful of cold metal and dangle it between us.

He stops dead and stares at it. 'Is that my Omega Seamaster?'

I toss it at him in response.

'Where the fuck did you get this?' he mutters, turning it over in disbelief.

'Where do you think?'

It takes a moment for the realization to dent his brow. 'You know the code to my safe?'

Angelo smirks into his knuckles, earning himself a glare from me too.

'I don't know why you're laughing. Because if you kill another cop, I'll have to dig the backyard up too.'

Ignoring the mutterings behind me, I turn back to the window with a locked jaw.

Secrets are my most powerful weapon but also my darkest obsession.

I bury them. I dig them up. I listen to them. Feast on them.

I make it my job to know every secret up and down this coastline, and beyond.

My attention goes back to the girl in pink.

I know every secret.

Every secret, except Hers.

CHAPTER
Seven

Wren

I've always thought it ironic that the thing that makes the world go round is the thing that hurts most.

It hurts when you have it but also when you don't. Whether you're searching for it or running from it.

When it ends, it's devastating.

But when it's unrequited, it's flat-out dangerous.

My chest aches as though my heart is missing. A tightly packed ball of emotion clogs my throat, swollen with joy and heavy with the worst part of me: hot, bitter jealousy.

One day, it'll break me.

'Babe.' An elbow connects with my rib. 'Stop crying.'

I glance sideways at Tayce and pat my cheeks. 'It's okay, I've got a new mascara,' I whisper. 'Totally waterproof.'

She rolls her eyes. 'No, you're just being *so* loud.'

Oh.

With a sniff, I swallow hard and muffle my next sob with a tissue. How can I *not* cry on a day like this? The scene is set for tears. From the sunlight piercing through the clouds and shimmering on the lake, to the flowers and fairy lights wrapped around the arbor. Underneath it, a moment so pure and true that even time has stopped to witness it.

In one frosted breath, my best friend utters the two words that'll tie her to The One forever.

Love hurts. And in this moment, I know with every fiber of my being, it's worth the pain.

Rory's lashes flutter as Angelo seals his fate too. When he brushes a gentle thumb over her cheekbone, another sob escapes me, twice as loud as the last.

'Sorry,' I mutter to no one in particular.

The tissue in my palm is soaked through. As I rummage in my purse for another, my heart decides to make a reappearance. It beats like a warning, sending a throb of dread through my veins and raising the hairs on my skin.

I must be a sucker for reliving trauma because I lift my chin and look across the aisle to find the threat.

My lungs squeeze out my next breath.

Everything is scarier in the dark. Everything except Gabriel Visconti. Under the pale winter sun, there's no trick of the light to cast doubt about his expression, nor shadows to conceal the true breadth of his frame.

It's been impossible not to look at him today, and not for my lack of trying, and it's not because me being a bridesmaid and he a groomsman means we're standing across the aisle from each other. Or that, after last night, I'm viciously aware of his every move.

He's just hard to miss.

He's the type of man you'd spot first in a crowded room, and decide to walk back out the way you came in. He's huge – six-foot-five, a conservative guess – spends all day lifting heavy things and has to have his clothes tailor-made kind of huge.

If one was brave enough to look at him closely, only then would they realize he's related to Angelo and Rafe. He has the same green eyes, sharp bone structure, and dark features. He's *beautiful*, in the most objective sense. Look a little harder, and you can see what I should have seen three years ago.

The evil.

There's so much darkness inside of him it bleeds through his pores and sits on his skin. It's in the fading initials on each of his busted knuckles, in the cross etched onto the side of his neck. I see it in the angles of his skull under his buzzcut and in the thickness of his beard. It's in the hard lines of his face too, from the permanent scowl to the violent scar that cuts across it.

I'm not usually one to judge a book by its cover, but since that book made himself at home in my living room and threatened me, well, I think have every right to assume what that book is about.

Gabriel Visconti is as terrifying as he looks.

Even more terrifying now that he's staring right at me.

His gaze is filled with cold disdain. As if *I'm* the one who broke into *his* house and he's stewing over the fact I got away with it. The irony twists inside of me like a hot dish rag, but I rather like having a tongue, so I look away.

I stare down at my heels and curse myself with all the letters of the alphabet. My body is humming from lack of sleep and an unwavering sense of fear. I've done stupid things in my time, but not turning on my heel and running when he crossed my path that night is up there with the worst. Sticking my tongue out at him and not locking my damn front door, battle for second place.

As my new pink peep-toes sink slowly into the muddy grass, injustice flares up my spine.

He won't get away with what he did last night. A man like him belongs in a cell – probably a padded one – and not on the streets of the coast. I don't want to wish Rory's big day away, but the moment it's all over, I'm marching straight to the Devil's Dip police station and telling them everything.

A strangled noise comes from my right. 'Okay.' Tayce sniffs, ripping the fresh tissue out of my clenched fist. 'What mascara are you using?'

I glance up at her. She's turned a rashy shade of pink, and a wet black line dribbles from her eye to her chin. 'Are you crying?' I whisper. 'Christ, I didn't even know you had tear ducts.'

'I'm *not* crying,' she hisses, dabbing at her cheeks with a shaky hand. 'It's hay fever. From all the trees and shit.'

I'd usually revel in the chance to point out it's December and in the years I've known her, she's never complained about allergies once, but here I am, staring at Gabriel again.

I'm more subtle this time. I face the arbor and only move my eyes to find him. I'm looking so far to the right that my retinas ache, but even from this angle, I can see he's not listening to a word of the officiant's impassioned speech.

It's crazy to think he'd smiled that night. Though, now I'm sure it was the dark playing tricks on me. I could have sworn he'd laughed too, but it must have been a moan distorted by the wind and the passing of time. Because as he slowly scans the horizon, his expression is stone, and I can't imagine him being capable of anything else.

Rafe stands beside him, dabbing the corner of his eye, his lips stretched into a small smile as he watches the wedding unfold. Gabriel looks as though he's been dragged kicking and screaming to a distant relative's funeral by his mother. How can he look so bored on the happiest day of his brother's life?

It suddenly dawns on me like a new day: he's not a creepy local legend, the man's a psychopath.

He has to be.

My mind races as I recall the last therapy session I had before Uncle Finn and I moved out of Seattle.

Camilla was a glam woman with a constant-perfect blowout and a soft voice. She listened more than she talked. After thirty minutes of nodding at my every word, she'd slid a laminated infographic over the table and tapped at the title with a long French tip: *Signs of psychopathy*.

Each characteristic was its own bullet point, with bolded keywords and cartoon diagrams. I squeeze my eyes shut and try to remember what they were.

Antisocial behavior. Well, duh. Check.

Impulsiveness. I'm no expert, but breezing into my home with a bunch of knives less than three hours after I pissed him off, sounds pretty impulsive to me. Check.

Lack of empathy. Psychopaths don't feel fear or guilt, and considering he hasn't gone on the run or fallen to my feet with a groveling apology – which I absolutely would *not* accept anyway – makes for a definite double check.

Being charming.

Okay, that one doesn't make sense. I've given sponge baths to patients in comas with more charisma than Gabriel Visconti.

Hmm.

He takes a small step to the left, and my eyes move with him. A muscle puckers in his jaw as he glares into the treeline on the other side of the lake, then lifts his beefy fist to his mouth. He mutters something so quietly even Rafe doesn't notice.

What else?

Well, back in Seattle when the nights were long and loud, I never slept. I'd bury my head under the covers and watch an endless stream of *YouTube* videos on my iPad at full volume. Usually makeup tutorials and Sephora hauls, but since my mother wasn't the type to care about silly little things like parental controls, I once happened across a true crime documentary. It was about this serial killer: a fat, smelly trucker who got his kicks from picking up prostitutes and strangling them in the back of his cab. The host interviewed a sex worker who narrowly missed his wrath, and it was all because she'd learned how to spot a psychopath with one simple trick.

She'd yawned.

He hadn't yawned back.

Apparently, normal people will yawn in response to being yawned at because they have empathy, so a true, cold-blooded psychopath won't.

Gabriel shifts his attention from the treeline to the vast open space between Tayce and me. His shoulders tense and his gaze slowly drops to meet mine.

Panic steamrolls over my lungs and stomach. Survival instinct tells me to look away again, but the simmering irritation in his eyes is paralyzing.

Maybe I should smile.

No, definitely not. He'll probably cut my lips off.

Before I can stop myself, I open my mouth wide, and a long, silent yawn stretches the back of my throat. It comes easier than expected since I'm so damn tired.

'Jesus, Wren, that's so fucking rude,' Tayce hisses beside me, but she sounds a million miles away, and Gabriel just scowls at me. He doesn't yawn back.

He. Doesn't. Yawn. Back.

Oh my God, he really is a psychopath.

The world spins clockwise, and my brain turns in the other direction. The wind blows hot, burning my face like the brush of death. I've stared it in the face on a dark road, stuck my tongue out at it across a club, and pleaded with it in the reflection of my front door window. Now, it stands across the aisle from me, and I can't breathe.

'Tayce,' I bite out, blindly reaching out to grab her arm. 'Tayce, there's something I need to tell you –'

'Shhh, they're exchanging rings!'

'But it can't wait, we need to warn Rory –'

'*Wren.*' The sharpness of Tayce's tone slices through my panic, so I turn my head and stare at Angelo and Rory. My vision swims and diamond rings glint. I slip my hand into Tayce's and squeeze it like a lifeline.

This will be a long day.

CHAPTER
Eight

Wren

The day has faded into a star-filled night, and love warms the air. It's electric, with fizzes in champagne flutes, echoes in laughter, and clicks under designer heels and shiny loafers. My skin is alight with its magic, my heartbeat dictated by the brass band floating in the candle-lit lake.

Sigh.

I *love*, love. Even more so when it looks like one of my Pinterest boards. I'm high on it, drunk on it, and despite my earlier meltdown, not even the black hole looming by the bar can sober me up.

The band breaks into a Whitney song, and though I always 'Wanna Dance with Somebody,' I need a respite. Not breaking in these heels before the wedding was a rookie mistake.

I spot Matt at an empty table, hobble over, and flop down on a chair opposite.

'Are you still sulking?'

He sinks a shot, then slams it on the table so hard the other empty shot glasses shake.

All seven of them.

'I'm not sulking. I'm thinking.'

'About what?'

'About walking out onto the freeway during rush hour and taking a nap.' His gaze shifts over my shoulder and hardens into a scowl. I glance behind me to find Anna, his crush of the week, at another table laughing with her friends.

'Don't say such things.' I reach between the half-eaten desserts to pat his hand. 'You're far too good for her anyway.'

I know that's what you're supposed to say to a friend when they've been rejected, but I mean it. Matt's a delight. A happy-go-lucky guy whose job as an ice-skating coach at the boarding school in Devil's Hollow keeps him in decent shape. Sure, you can't see it under those baggy skater clothes he usually wears, and he could do with a good haircut, but he has a heart of gold and a fun sense of humor.

I throw in another cliché for good measure. 'Any girl would be lucky to have you.' He snorts into another shot. 'I'm serious,' I say, picking up the disposable camera off the table and dragging my thumb over the winder. 'You'll make the right girl very happy someday.'

He mutters something about redownloading Tinder while my gaze sweeps across the dance floor. It snags on Rory and Angelo moving to their own beat. It's a slow, lust-filled one only they can hear, and that familiar jealousy threatens to jump up into my throat. As the glow from a nearby tiki torch flickers upon Rory's grin, I bring the disposable camera to my eye and *click*.

'Bartender, karaoke extraordinaire, professional-figure skater,' Matt mutters, eyeing me over the candle centerpiece. 'Now budding photographer. Is there anything Wren Harlow can't do?'

I smile at him. 'Don't let my Instagram selfies fool you, honey. I'm only making a scrapbook.' He winces at the flash as I sneak a candid shot of him, though I don't even need to get the photos developed to know it won't make the final cut. 'I've put disposables on every table so everyone can take their own photos for Angelo and Rory. I saw it on a wedding blog – cute, right?'

'So cute,' he says in the tone of a man scorned. 'And how's that going?'

I glance up at Benny at the edge of the dance floor. He holds a camera in one hand and fastens his belt with the other. I sigh. 'So far, it'll be a scrapbook dedicated to Benny's balls.'

Matt isn't listening. He's too busy staring at Anna again, so I sweep the forest for other photo opportunities. Tayce has found tonight's prey; she's gazing up at a beefcake in a gray suit while running her fingers along the length of his bicep. *Click.*

Castiel Visconti and his younger brother, Nico, are sharing a joke over a high cocktail table – *click.*

I squint at the bar behind them to see if I recognize the redhead Rafe is talking to. Oh, it's Penny Price. She used to live down the road from me. *Click.* Matt has brought her as his plus-one, though he'll tell any girl who listens it's purely platonic. I'm about to ask him what she's doing back on the coast, but he cuts me off.

'Wait – speaking of Instagram. Anna follows you on there, right?'

My eyes fall to meet his. 'I think so?'

'Great.' With newfound enthusiasm, he lunges for the camera in my hand and shuffles across the seats until he's beside me. With an arm around my waist, he presses his temple against mine and angles the camera toward us. 'If we get a really hot photo together, you can post it, and she might get jealous and realize what she's missing.'

'Uh, I don't think that's how it works –'

The flash burns bright, killing my protest. It leaves a white stain on my vision that doesn't fade with rapid blinking. I'm suddenly disorientated, and maybe that's why the question slips out from my subconscious and through my lips.

'What do you know about Gabriel Visconti?'

As Matt's outline sharpens, I'm met with a glare. 'Oh, for fuck's sake, Wren. Not you too.' He huffs, tossing the camera onto a crumb-caked plate. 'What's every girl's obsession with the Viscontis? Sure, they're all hot, and like, make more money than that dude who owns Facebook. But Christ, can't a normal guy get a look in around here?'

I dig him in the ribs. 'Don't be so dramatic. I'm just asking.'

'Yeah, well. You're far too good for him anyway,' he mocks in a high voice I suppose is meant to mimic mine. 'Any boy would be lucky to have you, blah, blah, blah ...' He eyes Gabriel at the bar. My eyes follow. Although there's a large crowd waiting to be served, they huddle with their backs to him, as if they've decided there's safety in numbers. He's half dipped in shadow, barely visible, and the stillness vibrates off him like a tremor of a slow-moving earthquake.

Matt must feel it too because a shudder rolls through him. 'Is he really your type? It'd explain why you've never dated.'

I'd laugh if my throat wasn't closing. Gabriel Visconti being my type is obscene, and that's before I even found him sprawled over my favorite armchair in the middle of the night. He's someone's type, sure. Not mine, though. I'm looking for smiles and laughter, not scowls and scars. Everyone knows you never get your happy ever after with a bad boy. Besides, I'm certain anyone brave enough to go on a date with a man known as the Boogeyman will likely end up on the back of a milk carton.

'Of course not.'

Matt runs a hand through his hair and lets out a frosted breath. 'Good, because the rumors are true, you know.'

Unease presses down on my shoulders. I shouldn't ask. I should stuff my mouth with cake or bite through the blisters and dance again. Anything but ruin my manicure by peeling back the layers of a question I don't really want to know the answer to.

But, as always, my curiosity rears its ugly head. 'What rumors?'

'That he's feral. Like, lives-in-a-cave-beneath-the-National-Reserve kind of feral.'

I give a weak tut. 'Don't be ridiculous.'

'He does. I've seen him.' He shifts in his seat, getting closer. 'Well, kinda. I was driving home one night from yet another failed date sometime after midnight. I took that sharp turn onto Grim Reaper Road, and my headlights flooded the forest. And there he was, between the trees, staring at me.'

It's a story too similar to my own, and something inside me wants to deflect it, to make it not true. 'Can a man not go for an evening walk without being accused of living in a cave?'

He flashes me a look of disbelief. 'That's not all, though. He was topless.'

'Maybe he runs hot.'

'And he was covered in *blood*.'

My vision swims, and my pulse throbs in my mouth. The panic I felt during the ceremony is creeping back to get me. Now there's a pattern. The woods, the blood.

And where do the similarities end? How many people has he terrorized in their own home too?

Matt slices through the silence with a dry laugh. He picks up a shot glass, and puts it down again, disappointed that it's empty. 'No wonder they call him the Boogeyman.'

The Boogeyman. Cave-dweller. The Devil works hard but the Devil's Coast's rumor mill works harder, and now the lines are blurring between fact and fiction.

A wave of nausea rolls through my stomach, churning the remnants of an eight-course dinner. Darkness claws at my chest.

For once, I was too nice, and to the worst person possible. Though his blood was on my hands, it wasn't on my conscience. Thank God, because it's heavy enough. Yes, it was a selfish idea, trying to shift the weight of my secret from my soul to his, but he was meant to die.

He was meant to take it to his grave, and me, I was meant to feel lighter.

But he's alive. Here. On the coast, at Rory's wedding, forever in my peripheral. So instead of confessing to a dead man, I've given a thread to a living one. He's had three years to pull on it, to rip back the stitches of my perfectly curated life and reveal the darkness beneath.

I can only hope he wants to avoid me as much as I do him.

'Anyway. Lay off the Viscontis, Wren. There are so many dudes on the coast who have the hots for you, why can't you go for one of them instead?'

His words are a fast-acting antidote to my panic. My ears prickle, and I sit up straight. 'Really?'

'Sure.' He flags down a passing waiter and orders drinks. A lemonade for me, and another three tequilas for himself.

'Like who?'

'What?'

'Who likes me?'

'Oh' – he flutters a dismissive hand – 'everyone.'

'Matt, the vagueness simply won't do.' I grab a napkin and retrieve my eyeliner from my clutch, then put both in front of him and tap the table. 'I need names, honey.'

With a groan, he begrudgingly gets to work, fisting my eyeliner like a moody toddler with a crayon. A few moments later, he tosses the napkin on my lap.

Defrosting with excitement, I bring it closer to the candlelight and start scanning the names. There's Rico, the quiet guy whose family owns the local butchers, and Elliot, the idiot cab driver who looks at me like I've hung the moon every time I fold a passenger into the back of his car. Tom – he's sweet, though I'm sure he moonlights as a small-time drug dealer. Each name injects a shot of disappointment into my heart until it finally pops under the pressure.

None of these guys are The One.

Folding the napkin into my clutch, I flop back in the chair and find Tayce through the crowd, deflated. Despite the blistering cold, she's somehow managed to get Beefcake to take his jacket and shirt off, and now she's inspecting a tattoo on his abs with the flashlight on her phone.

We have polar opposite views on love. Tayce is a pessimist, always telling me that meet-cutes, the moment in the movies where two people destined to fall in love meet for the first time, are reserved for rom-coms starring Mandy Moore or Julia Roberts. And that in real life, people meet through mutual friends or on dating apps. She's a bitter believer that the head-spinning, heart-exploding love I'm holding out for doesn't exist. She says that, at best, love is a padded lining that softens the blow of your partner's annoying habits.

She's wrong – Rory's proved it. They have the type of love I *need*, and I need it in its most violent form. It's the only option for me. Not just the earth-shattering meet-cute, but all the clichés that follow. Pebbles hitting my bedroom window at midnight, the yawn-and-reach at the back of a movie theater. Rose petals and candlelight and stolen kisses in doorways while walking home in the rain.

I've saved everything for it. Every first, from my first date to my first kiss, and beyond, for it. I can't simply *date* – there's no maybe-so's, no settling, and definitely no friends with benefits.

It's not in my DNA.

As the band slows the tempo with a Luther Vandross song, couples slip into each other's arms, and a lethargy sweeps over the forest. Everyone's drugged on love's tranquilizing abilities, but now I'm stone-cold sober, sitting forever in its waiting room. Next to Matt and all his empty shot glasses.

He groans and slumps his head on the table when the plucky intro to 'You're the One That I Want' from my fourth favorite musical, Grease, starts to play.

Benny is still pelvic thrusting, looking for his next victim, and as I point the camera in Rory's direction again, the flash catches Benny's eye, and he beckons me with the curl of his finger.

I laugh and don't resist when he pulls me up from my seat with a smooth twirl. As he spins me away from him and back again, I catch the scent of cologne and whiskey, and can't help but wonder how many women on the coast have woken up to that smell lingering on their pillow.

He pushes me away with the jab of his finger and swaggers toward me in time with the music. I push back and chase his retreat. When the chorus hits, he drops to the floor and slides on his knees. Before his hands can start roaming up the sides of my thighs, a tight grip on my arm yanks me out of his reach.

'Oh my God,' Tayce yells in my ear, spinning me around and folding me into a protective hug. 'What's the golden rule?'

'But he knows the whole dance –'

'What's the golden rule, Wren?'

I sink back into my chair and let out a dramatic sigh. 'I know, I know. We don't dance with Benny.'

'We *never* dance with Benny.'

'Cockblock!' Benny yells.

Tayce flips him off over her shoulder, then looms over me with folded arms.

'Anyway, back to me. On a scale of one to ten, how hot is the guy I'm talking to?'

'Um.' He's looking around like a lost puppy. I'm not sure if it's a trick question, so I opt for a pragmatic response. 'A solid ten, if he makes you happy.'

'Mmm.' Her eyes find him, and she blows him a sloppy kiss. 'He has just enough brain cells that I don't feel like I'm taking advantage of him, but on the other hand, his tattoos look like graffiti on a school desk.' She shrugs. 'Meh. I'll fuck him with the lights off. Come on.' She offers me her hand. 'You're dancing with Gabe.'

I stare at her ring-clad fingers. 'What?'

'The bridesmaids and groomsmen dance is about to start.'

My eyes snap up to meet hers. My mouth grows dry, and a dull ache forms at the base of my skull. 'That's not a thing.'

'It is in Italy, apparently.' She wiggles her fingers impatiently. 'Come on.'

But I don't move. Can't. 'Why can't I dance with Rafe?'

'Because I'm dancing with Rafe.'

'No,' I whisper. 'My feet hurt.'

'You were dancing with Benny just fine.'

'Yes, but now I'm tired.'

'That's what espressos are for, sweetie.'

'But . . .' I look around, panic scrambling my brain. My gaze drops to Matt snoozing on the table, then I fish out the next excuse to rise to the surface. 'Matt needs me.'

She glances down at him, amused. 'By the looks of it, he'll still be here when you get back.'

'But –'

'Wren!'

'Tayce!'

I meet her irritated stare and return it with one of desperation. Hot tears swell behind my eyes. I can't dance with Gabriel. I *can't*. He's a psychopath, *the Boogeyman*, the dark shadow who broke into my house just because he could. But I can't tell her that, not right now. Neither subtlety nor self-restraint are Tayce's fortés; if I told her what he did, she'd pop a stiletto off her foot and drive the tip into his skull or something, and ruin what's left of Rory's day.

'Please.' My plea is as thin as water, and my face is about to be just as wet.

Her expression changes, flickering with confusion, then softens. 'He's not as scary as he looks, I promise.'

He's not as scary as he looks. That's what Rafe said. Castiel said it to me earlier too when he caught me staring. It's as though all the Viscontis are reading from the same script and feeding the lie out to the rest of the coast like some sort of propaganda machine.

Out of the corner of my eye, Gabriel steps into the light of the dance floor. He's a storm cloud, black and turbulent. A face like thunder. When Rafe mutters something in his ear, his lightning-bolt glare finds me and strikes.

My muscles seize up. He *is* as scary as he looks – he's proved it. And judging by his expression, he wants to dance with me as much as I want to dance with him.

Tayce takes advantage of the distraction and hauls me to my feet with a sharp tug on my hand.

No.

The ground is moving underneath me. Dresses and suits pass in a blur, then fade into the corners. My heels scrape across the floor, Tayce's hair swishes with determination, and now he's in front of me.

'Dance,' Tayce commands.

She pats me on the shoulder.

Then she leaves me alone with the Boogeyman.

Though you could park a car in the gap between us, his presence scorches me like a black flame. Every cell in my body is hyperaware of him, of what he might do and what he's already done. Cave-dwelling monster or not, men don't find themselves bleeding out at midnight on a lonely road by being nice.

Seeking relief, I stare at my shoes, wondering if I click my heels three times, maybe I'll suddenly teleport back home. I swear I'll lock the door this time. Wedge every bit of furniture against it too.

The band descends into song. It's 'I'm in the Mood for Dancing,' and the lively beat warps into something sinister in the space between my ears. The heat in front of me grows hotter. A cold sweat pools at the back of my collar, and I smooth my bangs with a trembling hand.

With a strangled breath, I drag my gaze upward.

It trails up the sharp crease of his pants, then the buttons of his shirt. The irony twists my gut; he doesn't fool me. A well-cut suit could never make this man a gentleman. It's as though he's wearing another man's skin, and I wouldn't be surprised if he'd ripped it from his bones with his bare hands.

A shiver ghosts through me, and I can't bring myself to look any higher. I seek relief by scouting for Rory and Angelo instead, but they're nowhere to be seen. So I look to Tayce and Rafe across the dance floor. They're both dancing for someone else: Tayce is eye-fucking her mark on the sidelines, and Rafe, well, I don't know who he's looking for. His face is sullen and taut, and he's scanning the treeline obsessively.

Tayce catches my eye over his shoulder and mouths, *Dance*.

Ugh. I'm going to hold this over her head for at least a week.

Gritting my teeth, I turn back around to Gabriel and meet his glare. Cold, expressionless. How can someone look so bored and so terrifying at the same time?

He's not dancing, of course. He's not even moving. He just shifts his gaze to a space above my head, and with a clenched jaw, scans the space between the trees.

Okay. Deep breath. The average song is only a couple of minutes long. Around the same time it takes to brush my teeth or fill in my eyebrows. I can do that. Resting my gaze on his thick neck and the loose bowtie around it, I force my feet into a tight two-step and pray the band isn't playing some extended-cut version.

One step, two. One, two.

By the first chorus, my mind drifts from the count, and irritation nibbles the edges of my fear. Why is he just standing there looking at everything but me? Sure, it's not the rudest thing he's done, but with me being so *nice*, I'm not used to *rude*, and my brain can't figure out how to process it.

Maybe he's one of those sadists who gets off on making girls uncomfortable. Like the trench coat flasher who hangs around in the alleyways of Main Street. He wouldn't do this to a man his own size – if those men even exist.

My steps become stomps, and my fist tightens around the strap of my clutch. That irritation burns into anger and bubbles up the trunk of my throat.

My eyes snap upward. 'You know, I try to see the best in people, but with you, I really have to squint.'

'Don't squint too hard. I'll take your eyeballs too.'

His reply is a reflex; it's easy and even and doesn't miss a beat or interrupt his scanning of our surroundings.

My jaw drops open, and I stop the two-stepping. How can I dance at a time like this, with a man like this? He's unrecognizable. He's not the man I comforted as his blood ruined my dress. Not the man who used one of his last breaths to laugh, or to call me beautiful.

Suddenly, the missing puzzle piece slots into place. There's only one explanation for his rudeness: he's forgotten.

'Remember the time I saved your life?'

The air around him shifts. Lines tighten, muscles clench. It's so subtle, I wouldn't have noticed if I wasn't staring at him so intently.

Slowly, his eyes sink south and latch onto mine. There's boredom, terror, and now there's something else. Something flickering behind the green, inflamed and unreadable. My brain can't decipher it, but my body recognizes *danger*, so I take a shaky step back.

It happens so fast.

A blinding light washes out his features. The sky flashes from black to orange and back again.

And the sound. It's pressure-fueled, loud, and nasty.

The world goes boom.

Like it does in the movies.

CHAPTER
Nine

Wren

Rory and I share a similar talent. She can identify any bird by its call.

Me, I can identify any emotion by a scream.

Within a millisecond, I recognize all the screams around me as ones of collective terror. The guttural and blood-curdling kind, a chorus so loud the ground grumbles beneath my feet.

Gabriel lunges toward me with such speed I don't even have time to flinch, and now my feet aren't touching the ground at all. His forearm pins me to his torso as he drives me backward through a blur of chaos. Sequins glint, glasses smash. The band is no longer singing to The Nolans.

The dance floor grows smaller behind Gabriel's shoulder. Branches scratch at my own. When the wedding disappears behind a veil of trees, I realize we're in the forest. I crane my neck to look up to the canopy; tendrils of smoke swirl between the leaves, and the smell of things that shouldn't be burned thickens the air.

What is going on?

And more importantly, where are Rory and Tayce?

My labored breaths thrum in my ears as I twist in Gabriel's grip to scan the crowd running past. I pick apart stumbling silhouettes, looking for the pale pink of Tayce's bridesmaid dress and the white of Rory's.

When I can't see them anywhere, my body stiffens, and finally, the shock gives way to dread.

'Where are they?' I yell. He doesn't reply. 'What's happening?'

His expression is thunderous, pulled so taut that his cheekbones bulge from beneath his skin. He's laser-focused on the view behind me. Though his mouth is set in a hard line, his lips are twitching. For a moment, I think he's muttering to himself, but then I notice his fist beneath his beard at an odd angle.

He's talking into his watch, like he's Inspector Gadget or something.

I block out the mayhem around us and zone in on his voice. His hot breath grazes the side of my neck, and his chest vibrates against my own, but I can't pick out any buzzwords that explain why the night has descended into madness. In fact, I can't pick out any words at all, then I realize he's not even speaking in Italian, let alone in English.

It's all too surreal, and I can do nothing but stare at him with misplaced fascination. The cold composure, the smooth stride. The determination behind his eyes. He's otherworldly. An unmovable mountain in the storm, and the irony is not lost on me: less than twenty-four hours ago, the arm holding me was the same arm preventing me from leaving my home, and yet I somehow know that clinging to his body is the safest place to be.

I grip him tighter.

Seconds drag out into minutes; he doesn't glance at me once. Christ, if Angelo could pick me up without grunting, well, Gabriel seems to have picked me up and forgotten he's done so.

When we reach the main road, I don't have time to take in my surroundings before my back slams against something hard, new arms wrap around my waist, and distance stretches between Gabriel and me.

He flicks a casual look over my head. 'Take this one.'

Then he stalks back toward the trees without so much as a glance back.

'Take this one.' As if he's a port worker and I'm cargo, some inanimate object that needs hauling from one place to the other before he's allowed to clock out for the night.

Christ, Wren. Rory's wedding is ruined, and I'm over here with these self-absorbed thoughts. Now I feel guilty for being insulted. I'm unable to dwell on it because these new arms are carrying me across the road. I look out to sea over a car roof, and my gut twists.

The port beneath the cliffs is ablaze. Destruction in its rawest form ravishes through buildings, lorries, crates. Fires spit out debris into the raging sea, and the angry waves drag it under. The screams rising from the smoke and ash are chilling. They're deeper, louder, more desperate than they are up here.

Devastation rips a hole through my core. Those screams don't belong to nameless faces on the news, they belong to people I know. Men who prop up the bar at The Rusty Anchor nightly, whose daughters and sons I count as friends. Innocent lives ruined, maybe even lost.

How?

My only guess is some sort of freak accident.

A hand leaves my waist, and I glance down in time to see it yank on a door handle. I was so consumed by the scene below I hadn't noticed that the random man Gabriel passed me on to was carrying me toward a waiting car.

The back door swings open.

A car he's trying to put me in to.

No.

No, no, no.

The hole in my stomach grows wider. Here come those self-absorbed thoughts again, and my hands fly out to grip onto the frame.

A gruff voice scrapes my nape. 'Get in the car.'

I balk at the hard shove on my lower back.

Absolutely not. I drive my weight through my palms and lock my elbows, kicking my feet to find the ground. I find a shin instead, and the man holding me lets out a sharp hiss. When he drops me, I twist around and duck under his arm to escape.

'Get in the car!' he roars, lunging toward me.

I can barely see him, with the huge black void behind him opening wider and wider, threatening to swallow me whole. I can't get in the car. I *can't*. Every bone in my body trembles, every thought in my brain screams in protest.

The man grips my arm and tugs me forward. I dig my heels into the asphalt, not a thought for my brand-new peep-toes nor for the manicure I definitely couldn't afford, as my nails claw at any flesh they can find. I'll do anything – kick, bite, scream. Cry, plea, beg. I'll walk a thousand miles and back if it means not getting in a car ever again.

As the open door grows closer, my desperation burns hotter. I swing a fist; none of my punches land. A familiar voice is yelling my name from somewhere – it's Rory, I know it, but I can't see her through my tears.

'Let her go.' The command slices through my conscience like a hot butter knife. It's calm, almost bored, but the voice holds weight. It belongs to someone who's never had to raise his voice in his life, because he's yet to meet someone who's stupid enough to disobey him.

He drops me in an instant, and I stagger backward, finding my footing as he mutters under his breath in a foreign language. The car door slams shut behind him. Tires screech and kick up dust, covering the hem of my dress.

'Wren!'

It's Rory's voice again. I spin to find her through all the screaming and spot her hanging out the passenger-side window of a slow-moving black sedan. Her curls are ruffled, and her face is flushed red. My gaze shifts to the back seat, where Tayce is hammering against the glass, mouthing my name.

'Go with Gabe!' Rory yells, desperation warping her tone. Her big brown eyes are pleading with me. She shouts it again and again, until the car speeds up and carries her out of earshot.

Standing in the road, I watch the car disappear around the bend. The chaos has left too, and an eerie silence settles among the discarded purses, heels, and handkerchiefs littered on the ground.

It's like a scene from a zombie apocalypse. Everyone's gone. There's only one threat to life now, and its shadow bleeds into the glow of a nearby streetlamp.

My chest fills with despair as I strain my eyes sideways and stare down at the shadow. It isn't moving, and maybe, if I walk real slow and keep real quiet, he'll let me leave without a fuss.

My house is less than a ten-minute walk away. Eight, if I kick off these heels once I'm out of his line of sight. Gravel crunches underfoot as I take a tentative step. Then another. Before my third footstep finds purchase, a deep command paralyzes my spine.

'Get in the car.'

I let out a sigh – a silent one, obviously. Mostly because I'm scared he'll hear me, but also because I'm exhausted. I'm running on fumes, and now this terrifying turn of events has taken the last bit of fight from me.

Resigned, I turn around. A few feet away, Gabriel cuts a haunting figure. I don't know what makes me more uneasy, being alone with him on an empty road again or how comfortable he looks among the destruction behind him. It's as though he's woven into its fabric – his black suit an extension of the black smoke, his molten glare the brightest of the embers dancing under the night's sky.

Even if he *wasn't* the Boogeyman, he could fool the world with his eyes alone.

He jerks his chin to the left. I follow it to a lone black car parked on the verge, half illuminated by a streetlamp.

'Get in the car,' he repeats, with ice-cold restraint.

I roll my shoulders back and meet his eye with restraint of my own. 'Thank you for the offer, but I don't need a ride. I'm more than happy to walk home.'

Irritation tightens his gaze. 'You get in the front or you go in the trunk.'

Holy crap.

Ice threads through my veins. I know little about this man, but I know his threats are never empty. Without waiting for a response, he doubles down by sliding his fist into his pocket. A quiet beep sounds, followed by a double blink of headlights. The hood of the trunk rises open with a chilling hiss.

My heart pounds in my chest, a cocktail of frustration and indignation stretching it tight. I don't know how I'm getting out of this mess, but I sure as hell know it won't be on four wheels.

I glance over my shoulder toward my house, scrambling for a plan. Despite my yearly fun runs for charity, I don't have the speed nor stamina to make a break for it. I wouldn't be able to outrun him based on the width of his stride alone, even if I had my sneakers on.

And any attempt to fight him off would be laughable. A man half his size just dragged me around like a rag doll – Gabriel would rip me open like one, and the only thing left of me would be buttons and stuffing.

Well, then. I suppose I'll try a good old-fashioned refusal.

'No.'

It sounded stronger in my head but came out a pathetic whisper, wobbly and without weight. I consider clearing my throat and trying again, but then he steps toward me.

'I'll scream.'

His eyes flash black. 'Good.'

He's closing in on my clumsy retreat. A few more steps and he's within touching distance – grabbing distance, judging by the angry blaze in his eyes – so I do the only thing I can think of.

With my mother's words echoing in my ears, I drop to the ground.

Damp seeps through the back of my thighs. Pebbles dig between my shoulder blades. I try not to think of the damage I've done to this cute dress, and squeeze my eyes shut, forcing every muscle in my body to relax.

His footsteps stop for less than a heartbeat. Then they start up again, as lazy and heavy as they were when following me down my hallway. It seems he's never in a hurry to eat his prey.

When the tip of his shoes graze my hip and his shadow darkens the inside of my eyelids, I stop breathing.

'What the fuck are you doing?' he growls.

'Playing dead,' I whisper.

Christ. Why did I tell him that? It was an instinct, a flinch to the sharp edge of his question, rooted in fear that silence or a lie would only anger him more.

Dead bodies are heavier. They're limp and floppy and are much harder to move than a living being. Flattening myself against the asphalt felt like a great idea ten seconds ago, but now that I'm sinking into the dirt and growing colder by the second, I can't help but feel foolish.

My gaze snags on his fist as it clenches and flexes. 'Don't make me do this,' he murmurs.

'Do what?'

With a rough grip on my thigh, and another on my hip, I'm levitating. He slings me over his shoulder like a sack of potatoes, and when I open my eyes, I'm staring down the length of his back.

Great. Now what? Politely declining and playing dead didn't work. I guess I'll have to give the whole fighting thing a go.

I kick my legs against his chest; he pins them in place with his forearm. I beat my fists on his back; he doesn't even flinch. He just keeps his leisurely pace as he strides toward the car, as though he fireman carries unwilling participants around every day of the week.

God, forgive me – it's not ladylike to bite, but given the circumstances, I'm sure he'll give me a hall pass. I twist my head in an attempt to sink my teeth into his neck, but my gaze snags on the open car trunk, and my jaw grows slack.

Is that?

Surely not.

Oh, my God. It is.

Under the dim light of the streetlamp, I can just about make out what's in the trunk – rope, a roll of trash bags, and some sort of ominous duffel bursting at the seams.

That's a murder kit, isn't it? A crime scene waiting to happen. All it's missing is the victim. *Me*.

'Stop!' I squeak, trying to wriggle off his shoulder and onto the ground. 'I'll go in the front! I'll go in the front!'

Like hell I will, but I'll say anything for him to put me down, then I can try my luck with the last option – outrunning him, broken ankles be damned. It's still a better alternative than being bundled into the back of Gabriel Visconti's murder wagon.

He's impervious to my pleas. They turn from screams to yelps to flat-out begging once my calves press against the cold rear bumper, and all of them fall on deaf ears.

'Please,' I whimper.

His hands slide from my thigh to my hips.

'I'll do anything!'

He tugs me down until my chest is flush with his.

My hands fly out to grab his face. His beard scratches my

palms as my fingers dig into his cheekbones. 'But I saved your life!' I yell.

Something about those five words has an effect on him, and the world stops turning. Gabriel freezes under my touch, and the weight of a bad decision seizes my muscles. My hands slide back down to my side, and I stare, petrified, at the ink between his spread collar.

I don't dare look up. If his expression is anything like what it was when I said those words earlier, I'm too close to him now to survive it.

As the suspense expands and contracts around us, I become aware of all the places my body touches his. Warmth bleeds from his torso to mine; the hard clasp of his watch digs into the small of my back. He's hot where I'm cold, breaths steady between my ragged pants. Our heartbeats, they're out of sync. Clashing against one another's chest, his tempo slow and strong, mine skittish and tripping over itself.

Feeling his pulse does nothing to humanize him. It only brings a sour taste to my mouth, because for the second time in as many minutes, my thoughts turn to my mother.

Heartbeats always remind me of her.

All thoughts *pop* like soap bubbles when his forearms loosen around my waist, and my body grates against his. Every button of his shirt snags on my satin dress on the way down, until my feet finally find purchase.

He retreats, leaving me just enough room to breathe. I steal a tentative glance up at him from beneath my lashes. He rubs a hand over his jaw, as if my touch was dirty, and his gaze floods with a look of loathing. Under this orange lighting, I can't tell if it's for me or for himself, but it's a look so venomous it could kill.

But no look in the world is as sickening as his next command.

'*Walk.*'

CHAPTER
Ten

Wren

The blood doesn't even return to my toes before I'm fidgeting from one foot to the other.

Scraping a fleck of mud from my cheek, I squint up at him. I'm optimistic to the point of delusion, but even I don't know why I'm still searching for any trace of kindness or humor in his face. Because, surprise, there isn't any. It's the same hardened irritation, interrupted only by that menacing scar.

'Walk *where*?'

He gives a curt nod to the treeline.

'But why?'

His reply is filtered through gritted teeth. 'Because I said so.'

My stomach sinks. There's no way Rory and Tayce are in there. They're probably back at Angelo and Rory's manor, heels off, defrosting by the fire and trying to figure out how the night ended like this.

It's dark between the trees. Like, can't-see-the-tip-of-your-nose kind of dark. And if that's not where my friends are, there's only one reason a man known coast wide as the Boogeyman would want to march me into the forest, and it sure as hell isn't for a teddy bear picnic.

With an odd sense of calmness trickling from my scalp, I stuff my frozen hands into the pockets of my coat and rest my gaze on the bulging vein ticking at Gabriel's temple.

Tic, tic, tic.

'My name is Wren Harlow,' I whisper. 'I'm twenty-one years old, and I work as a bartender at The Rusty Anchor.' I glance to the haze on the horizon. 'Well, I did. I'm not sure it's still standing. I live at Number 1, Strawberry Farm, which is owned by my uncle Finn – he's best friends with your cousin Castiel. You've probably seen him around; he's the blond man with the glasses who pretends to be a carpenter.' The vein keeps ticking to an even beat. 'I like fashion and makeup and ABBA. And helping people, of course. I help drunk people get home safely in Devil's Cove on the weekends, and twice a week, I'm a candy striper at the Devil's Hollow hospital. Um . . .' I scratch my nose, racking my brain for the rest of my redeeming qualities. 'I'm going to school to study pre-law next September. You know,' I add, stealing a quick look at him, 'because of the whole liking to help people thing.'

The vein in his temple has graduated from ticking to throbbing. Somehow, I don't think my monologue is working.

I heard a similar one when I was younger, from my hiding place under the kitchen table. A man on his knees, calmly reciting his life story. Even at nine years old, I realized what he was doing: he was attempting to humanize himself, to appeal to the compassion that lives deep within even the most evil of people, in the hope it would change his fate.

It didn't.

My gaze is drawn to his acidic expression. He runs his tongue over his teeth, and the light shifts over the sharp planes of his face as he tilts his chin up.

'*Walk.*'

It's a decibel above a whisper, but as hard as a full stop: end of conversation.

Okay. So maybe compassion doesn't live in everyone.

I let out a heavy sigh. So *this* is how I actually die. Not tongueless on my ABBA-themed doormat, but by being frog marched into the woods by a man whose life I saved.

Turns out, Tayce was right all along: being nice is thankless work. I'm sure she'll be disappointed that I won't be alive long enough to hear her say 'I told you so.'

Gabriel steps aside, and jelly legs carry me from asphalt to soil. Running is so far off the cards now, it's not even in the same deck, but I guess dying on my own two feet beats being folded into a trunk like a pretzel.

He falls in line behind me, his presence crackling like static down my back. Each of my steps are slow and tentative, seeking all the gnarled roots and ditches I can't see in the dark.

If I have the patience of a saint, clearly, Gabriel has the temper of the Devil. He lasts all of ten feet before a cold growl touches my nape and he dips to lift me up again.

He doesn't carry me like a surfboard this time, but sideways and at arm's length, like I'm a sack of toxic waste he needs to dispose of as quickly as possible. Tension tightens where his forearms meet my shoulder blades and the backs of my knees, and I, too, grow rigid as my gaze lifts to his profile. Even in the dark, I can make out the hard set of his jaw beneath his beard. And even if I couldn't, the disdain radiates off his body in a silent shockwave.

Without so much as a sideways glance, he dumps something into my lap.

It's my clutch – I must have dropped it in the struggle. I'm surprised he bothered to pick it back up – a dead girl doesn't need her lip gloss or her cellphone.

My cellphone.

The tiniest spark of hope ignites in my chest. I rummage among the discarded tissues to find it.

Gabriel steps over a fallen tree trunk. 'No signal.'

A tap on my screen confirms it.

Frustration blows out that tiny ember of hope, and I resign to my fate. I flop against my kidnapper's arms, my limbs bobbing and my hair swaying to the beat of his quick strides.

He navigates the forest with surprising ease, even while carrying me and my heavy heart. He dips under low-hanging branches, jumps over stumps, as though he's committed every inch of terrain to memory. Like he knows the Reserve better than Rory, so maybe the rumors are true – he *does* live in a cave somewhere within it.

Gah, Rory. I'll never see her or Tayce again. Or anyone else, for that matter. I wonder if Rory will ever find out her psycho brother-in-law killed me.

A loud sigh leaves my lips in a curl of frost, and Gabriel's chest tenses against my elbow.

'Stop,' he grits out.

'Stop what?'

'Breathing.'

Oh.

Having learned his commands hold weight, I hold my next breath at the base of my throat. When it starts to burn, I let it out in a shallow puff.

He mutters something under his breath. 'Do you just do anything any man tells you to?'

I blink up at him. He's still staring straight ahead, a fresh sheet of annoyance cloaking his features.

'Um, when they're carrying me like a purse, yeah?'

He drags his teeth over his bottom lip but doesn't reply.

We move through the forest for what seems like miles.

Through clearings, over a stream, twisting and turning until the canopy above us is so dense that not even the moonlight touches the forest floor. Each step adds another brick of impending doom to my shoulders until the weight is too heavy to bear.

'Are you going to kill me?'

'Don't have the time,' he grinds out each word, sounding almost regretful, as if he'd love nothing more than to put a bullet in my skull and drop me in a shallow grave. His tone nor reasoning plug the burst of relief flooding through me.

'You won't?' I try to sit up in his arms, but he fists the back of my jacket with a hot hiss, pulling me flat again. 'Do you promise?'

Again, no reply, but I don't care. There's hope now, real, tangible hope, and I'll cling onto it like a life raft until he gives me reason to let go.

We stew in silence. Shivering branches, crunching leaves underfoot, and contrasting heartbeats knit together into a steady soundtrack. In different arms, under different circumstances, and if I actually knew where I was going, I'd be almost comfortable.

After a while, Gabriel lifts the arm under my knee to check his watch, and an icy breeze skitters up my thigh.

The movement slid the hem of my dress up. I move to adjust it, but when Gabriel's head tilts down, something stops me. It's too dark to see, but I don't need to, because the strip of exposed skin tingles where his eyes touch. A slow-moving heat grazes over goosebumps, up the inseam of my thigh, and settles on the pink silk pooling in my lap. My breath catches at the shiver chasing after it. It's warm, weird, and unwarranted, invading my core and tightening my nipples.

Fuck, you're beautiful.

Suddenly, the night doesn't feel so bitterly cold anymore.

In the absence of light, my other senses prickle. I tune into the warm masculine scent of his neck, hear the strong throb of his heart and the slowing of his footsteps. I can feel the bulge of his muscles propping up my body, and when he curls an arm upward, sliding a rough hand over my bare thigh, I feel what it's like to be touched by him too.

He yanks down my dress with a quick tug. It's a simple, almost reluctant move, as though he didn't want to touch me at all. It's gone as quickly as it arrives, but the heat of it lingers. A small puff of air leaves my lips, and now I'm wondering about irrelevant things, like if he has a wife or girlfriend. If he's this cold around her too, or if she's as scary as he is.

For some reason, the thought rubs until it chafes.

A calloused drawl reaches out from the dark and pulls me back to the forest. 'Do you believe everyone who tells you they won't kill you?'

His words linger longer than his touch. They trickle into my pores, slow and thick, and twist my stomach. With them, comes the realization that he's referring to his earlier promise not to kill me.

And like that, I slip off the life raft, his question a brick tied to my ankle. This time, annoyance and a flurry of bitter memories propel me to the surface.

He's playing mind games with me. Dangling hope, only to snatch it away and give it back again.

I've seen it played out before, in another lifetime, orchestrated by a different psychopath. I've seen grown men cower, then cry with relief. Rinse, repeat, repeat again until they're dizzy and weak and desperate. There're no rules and no chance of winning: the outcome is always the same.

I'm tired of swimming in this man's threats and drowning in his shadow. I won't dance for the Devil or beg for my life simply for his own entertainment.

I tilt my chin up and glare at him. 'You can stop with the psychological torture, you're not going to kill me.'

'No?'

'Nope. Too many people saw you with me, including your sister-in-law. Who, by the way, will be wondering where I am.'

As we cross through a slither of moonlight filtering through the forest canopy, I'm sure I see his lips tilt. In amusement or annoyance, I don't know, but the silence that follows holds me at knife point, leaving me with bated breath and an ever-expanding lump in my throat as I wait for his reply.

It finally comes. A murmur, deep and ominous. 'If it happens in the dark, it didn't happen.'

The words leave his mouth in a tight coil of condensation. I watch it dance and dissipate, and a trickle of cold unease washes the heat of my annoyance away.

What the hell does that mean? It sounds like another cryptic threat, but this one has an unnerving undercurrent. Something softer, more bitter, as though pulled from somewhere deeper.

My brain ticks over for a few more minutes, until my thoughts grow slower and slower and finally stop.

I've run out of steam. I'm so *tired*. My limbs are heavy against Gabriel's grasp, as if my body is letting gravity take over in preparation for being six feet under soon.

When he finally comes to a stop, I realize my lids have grown heavy too. Awareness wakes me like a knee-jerk reaction, and I bolt upright in his arms.

Through bleary eyes, I scan our surroundings. The sky is lighter now, and for a moment, I think dawn has arrived. But it hasn't, it's just streetlamps, their soft glow washing over a large gravel parking lot.

I scrunch my eyes and recalibrate. We're at the entrance to The Whiskey Under the Rocks, a fancy bar in Devil's Hollow. Cars similar to the one Rory and Tayce were whisked away in are parked around the perimeter, and when I glance to the front door, a faint hum of activity drifts out from behind it.

Gabriel's grip loosens around me, and my feet touch ground.

Confused, I blink up at him. He towers over me, the glow from the streetlamp above us catching the high planes of his cheeks, casting the rest of him and the whole of me, in shadow.

His eyes glint with black disdain when they touch me. 'Go.'

My retreat is shaky. I walk backward, not daring to take my eyes off him, in case this is another mind game. I'm weary of everything: the clench of his fists, the hard bob of his Adam's apple, the stillness of his stance, and the way his eyes track my movements like a laser beam.

I thought increasing the distance between us would bring me relief. It doesn't. I'm still tethered to him by a thread, woven with the words of his earlier ominous statement: *If it happens in the dark, it didn't happen.*

It's not even close to the craziest thing he's said tonight, but it stuck. Not just because it's a creepy thing to say, but because of the way he said it. It held a different weight to his other threats, like it wasn't even a threat at all.

I don't know. I'm tired. I should let it go, run inside, hug my friends, and thank the Lord I made it from one side of the woods to the other without being murdered by Gabriel Visconti. But every step backward only pulls the thread tighter, and when he turns and steps out of the light, disappearing from view, it snaps.

'Wait,' I blurt out. The thud of his heavy steps comes to an abrupt stop, and I take a deep breath. For some reason, I need to say it. Whether it's to remind him or myself, I don't know. 'Whatever is done in the dark, always comes to light, you know?'

An uncomfortable silence trickles out of the dark and across the parking lot. Just when I think he won't reply, his words reach out of the dark and fissure through my coat, seeping beneath my skin and disturbing every cell they touch.

'Not if you stick to the shadows.'

CHAPTER
Eleven

Gabe

A slither of moonlight cuts through the window, narrowly avoiding my dark corner of the room. Way beyond the glass, waves roar and crash as they meet the cliffs. Down the hall, a clock ticks, and from behind the bathroom door, the muffled sound of water rains down on marble.

How is the shower *still* fucking running?

Patience thinning, I settle back into the armchair and drive the heels of my muddied boots across the rug, squeezing the lone earbud in my fist.

Darkness is my friend, but silence is the enemy.

Can't fucking stand it. Even more so since I followed Angelo back to the coast, because now my life doesn't just flash before my eyes when I'm dying but in these pockets of silence too. Memories bounce from month to year to decade, running in spirals and zigzags.

And when they grow tired, they run back to Her.

Her.

My hand twitches to put the earbud back in my ear, to drown out her voice with the soothing sounds of sin.

But no. I must stay alert tonight.

I'll roll a cigarette instead.

I balance a rolling paper on my knee and pepper tobacco into its crease. By the time I run my tongue along the gum line, I'm already thinking about her again.

Fuck. I've spent the last three years thinking about her. Obsessing over all the things I know and battling with all the things I don't.

Can you keep a secret?

'Stop,' I mutter, throwing myself forward. Resting my elbows on my knees, I glare down at the blood dripping from my knuckles and onto the rug. I count nine slow *splats*, then start over. Again and again and again until her voice fractures and fades into the dark corners of the room.

When my pulse returns to normal, I light the roll-your-own and take a deep drag. Then I grind the charred match into the rug under the heel of my boot.

Tonight, she told me everything but her fucking star sign unprompted and walked into the dark woods with me just because I told her to.

I could have been anyone.

Could have done anything to her.

Why did I even walk her into the woods in the first place, instead of stuffing her into my trunk and saving an hour of my time? It's not like I didn't have anything better to do.

I know why, of course, but no good ever comes from thinking about it.

'Just stop,' I hiss to nobody but my demons, scrubbing at my jaw. There's something seriously wrong with me, aside from the obvious. I have far more important shit to be annoyed about than some ditzy chick with no survival instinct I met three years ago. Like Dante's attack or the stupid schoolyard plan Rafe has plucked out of his ass to counter it, and the fact Angelo has cosigned the idea.

Yet, here I am, thinking about her. Again. Asking myself questions I swore I wouldn't dig up the answers to. Like why she doesn't drink liquor, why she panicked at the idea of getting into a car.

Why she wears so much fucking pink.

Finally, the shower switches off, and relief comes in the form of rattling glass and the thump of footsteps, lighting a spark of excitement in my chest.

The bathroom door opens, a triangle of light spills out onto the floor, and within it, a familiar shadow.

I take a final drag on the cigarette, then stub it out on the armrest. 'It sure takes you a long time to shave your pussy.'

The footsteps come to an abrupt halt. A whispered Italian curse fissures through the bedroom, and when I glance up, Dante emerges from a cloud of steam.

Cue the same old dance. He slams his palm on the light switch, flooding the room with a yellow glow. Then his eyes dart to all the usual places; the pillows on the bed, the night-stand drawer. Over to the safe in the corner, which has a pass-code set to his birthday. Then his gaze falls to the coffee table, where all three of his guns lay in a neat row, chambers emptied.

He tightens the towel around his waist, eyes narrowing on me. 'What do you want?'

Slipping the earbud into my breast pocket, I let out a tired sigh. He always fucking asks. It's a stupid question at the best of times, but given the circumstances, it's full-on moronic.

Though I'm enjoying the tension lining his shoulders too much to answer, so I pull out another rolling paper and take my time packing it with tobacco. His eyes burn into my lap, and I relish the petty satisfaction it gives me. Much to his disdain, I've been smoking in his bedroom at least once a week for three years. Stubbing out my cigarettes on his armchair too.

He stopped bothering to replace it a while ago, around the same time he finally accepted he wasn't smart enough to keep me out.

My gaze tracks his bare feet as he pads over to his liquor cabinet. He pours a whiskey with a steady hand and moves to the window.

When he spots the bodies slumped on his front lawn, his jaw locks. 'How many men?'

'Three.' I cast a careless look at my bloodied knuckles 'Want some advice?'

'No.'

I give it to him anyway. 'I know nobody wants to work for you but stop hiring your men off Craigslist. They couldn't throw a party, let alone a punch.'

'I don't –' He rolls his shoulders back and slowly turns to pin me with his signature sneer. I swear, he popped out of his mother with that fucking expression, and I couldn't count on both hands how many times my fists wiped it off his face during our childhood. 'Perhaps I should take a leaf from your book,' he says, back to his usual, quiet drawl, 'and pick up a few feral dogs from the local pound. Quite the pack of strays you have, *cugino*. They killed twelve of my men tonight.'

With a bitter smirk, he raises his glass in a mock toast before sinking half of its contents with a hard gulp.

A white-hot heat rushes from the base of my spine to the top. It's a protective instinct, wrapped around the innermost layer of my core. He's right, all my men are strays. Rescued from all four corners of the world, nurtured back to health, put to work.

Angelo hates them, Rafe even more so. But they don't understand – they weren't born to have the misfortune to understand – the thread that ties us together.

I strike a match and light the cigarette, mainly to give my hands something else to do other than reach for my gun. Taking a long, deep drag, I make a point of billowing the smoke in Dante's direction.

The cunt got to me once, and I vowed I'd never let him again.

'You really fucked up this time. You know that?'

His glare burns through the dissipating smoke. 'You want to talk about fuckups? Because holding a wedding so soon after your brother blew my father's head off for that gold-digging whore is pretty up there.'

A sour taste brews at the back of my tongue. It's not often Dante Visconti can say he's right twice in one day.

I must have been silent for a beat too long because he rests against the windowsill, swirls the whiskey around the glass, and flashes me that fucking smirk again, as though he suddenly has the upper hand.

'You're not going to kill me.'

My thoughts briefly boomerang back to Her, and how she said the same thing just hours earlier. She was right – though I don't like how she took my fucking word as gospel. Dante, however, is not.

Still, I give him the same answer. 'No?'

'No. It's not in Angelo's grand plan.' He huffs out a quiet laugh over his drink. 'I can picture it perfectly. The Dip brothers huddled around a table, plotting revenge on their mean older cousin.' He crooks a brow, pondering. 'You would have wanted to blow my head off immediately, of course. But Rafe would have sat there, twirling his little poker chip, dreaming up something more exciting. A game, perhaps. And Angelo . . .' His gaze falls to mine, glinting with amusement. 'Well, Angelo always goes along with Rafe's plans, doesn't he? He's the smarter brother, after all. And you, the Dips' lackey, have to grit your teeth and do their dirty work.'

Well, would you look at that. The bastard's on a roll.

He's right again, about Rafe at least. I don't know what that fuck wit was high on earlier as he sat in Cas's office flicking chess pieces off a playing board and talking some shit about taking Dante's men out one by one until he's the only one left standing.

Because what the fuck does he know?

The only game he's ever come up with that doesn't make me want to suck on the end of a loaded gun is the Sinners Anonymous hotline.

Though games are his thing, war is mine. And while I'll nod and agree and spout whatever bullshit my brothers want to hear to keep them out of my way, I live by a mix of my father's rules and my own to keep them alive.

'Well, this has been fun, but I've got more interesting things to do,' I drawl, twisting the cigarette butt into the armrest and flicking the remains onto the rug for good measure.

When I rise to my feet, Dante stands straighter, tracking each step as I close the gap between us. My shadow creeps up over his torso, and amusement bleeds into my chest. This idiot is so predictable.

Except for when he isn't.

His gaze probes mine as I stand toe-to-toe with him. His jaw is locked and ready, but the flicker of fear in his eyes betrays him. It burns brighter when I slip my hand into my pocket and press the tip of his own knife into the tender flesh beneath his chin.

I let out a slow, wistful sigh, dragging the blade lightly over his skin. 'Your day is coming,' I whisper. 'But it's not today.'

His chest caves when I drop the knife back into my pocket.

Then I drive my knee up into his balls.

A humorless smirk touches my lips as I shut his bedroom door on his screams with a quiet click.

That was for calling Rory a gold-digging whore.

CHAPTER
Twelve

Wren

Every Christmas, Devil's Cove transforms into a snow globe. Nightly, at 6:00 p.m., God gives it a good shake, and the town bursts into a spectacle of festivities.

Thousands of lights zigzag above the promenade, shimmering down on frost-kissed walkways. Christmas classics and laughter bubble out of the bars and restaurants lining it, and in about an hour, so will the locals and tourists as they move on to the nightclubs.

Usually, Cove during the party season never fails to put a little pep in my step, but tonight, the electricity in the air has me on edge. Everybody is celebrating, blissfully unaware – or willfully ignorant – of the disaster playing out just outside of its dome.

It's sickening. It's been five days since the Devil's Dip port explosion cut Rory's wedding short, which means five days of working double shifts at the hospital and five nights of helping out with the cleanup mission too. Three workers were pronounced dead at the scene; another dozen are still fighting for their lives, and yet, the coast's famous party town spins madly on.

What's even worse, the rest of the world doesn't care

either. The explosion barely made local news, let alone hit mainstream media. Everything I've learned of its cause is from the rumor mill and passing conversations not meant for my ears. All explanations, both reasonable and farfetched, point in the same direction: it was someone with a vendetta against the Viscontis.

I chew on my bottom lip, wondering if I should go home, as a gaggle of girls staggers past in matching sexy Santa outfits. Every cheer and clinking of glasses feel like an insult, and here I am, standing in the midst of it.

Then I think of all the girls who will need me tonight. The ones with blisters and boyfriend problems, no cellphone battery, and mascara-stained cheeks.

The thought alone is enough to straighten my spine.

I guess the show must go on.

Leaving my pop-up stand, with my SOS bag under a red-and-white striped streetlamp, I step into the middle of the road, adjust my pink elf diddly boppers, and snap a selfie in front of the twinkling 'Happy Holidays!' sign strung from one telephone pole to another. After some subtle editing and a few filters, I tug off a glove to tap out a caption.

The Ho-Ho-Helpful Elf is back, and she's ready for some (safe) festive fun! I write, along with some cute Christmassy emojis. *Too much eggnog? Holiday heels hurting? Come and find me on the corner of the Visconti Grand Hotel. I've got your back! #HolidayHero #DrinkResponsibly*

As I press upload, a high-pitched whine pierces through the air and puts me on high alert. It's coming from a girl on the other side of the road, wobbling past the champagne bar.

I grab my bag and break into a jog over to her.

'Are you okay, honey?' I place a hand on her bare shoulder and tap the name tag pinned to my pink hi-vis vest. 'I'm Wren, and I'm here to help!'

A slurred response comes through her lipstick-smeared mouth. Luckily, I'm fluent in drunk and realize she's lost her friends somewhere between a restaurant and a cocktail bar.

Usually, I'd take her into Tayce's tattoo parlor to warm up with a hot cocoa, but she's shut up shop for her yearly vacation, so I sit her down on the entryway step instead.

'Here.' I tug a foil blanket from my tote, wrap it over her shoulders, and press a bottle of water into her hand. There's no point dealing with her tear-stained makeup or messy hair; she definitely needs to call it a night. 'Where are you staying?'

'Hotel.' She hiccups.

How very useful. As I rifle through her purse for a key card, I hit her with my usual monologue. 'Sip the water, don't gulp. When you get back to your hotel, drink two more glasses of water, and eat these.' I drop a pack of crackers into her purse. 'And don't forget to take your makeup off.' I find a card for the Hilton at the end of the strip, then get to my feet to wave to the taxi rank across the road. The first cab in the line flashes its headlights and crawls down the street toward us, patiently waiting for the gaggle of partygoers to pass by.

I sit back down and rub the girl's back. 'Make sure you charge your phone, okay? And sleep on your left side, it'll help you feel less sick . . .' A white light snags the corner of my eye. She's wiggled her cell out of her bra and is now clumsily scrolling through the contacts. I squint over her shoulder; she's typing something out to a boy's name with a broken heart emoji next to it.

'Is that your boyfriend?'

'No –' She hiccups. 'I wish.'

I pry the device from her hands. 'Absolutely no drunk texting boys unless your keys unlock the same front door,' I scold. Fiddling with the contact settings, I change his name to Dentist, slip her cell into her purse, and hope she doesn't figure out what I've done until she sobers up tomorrow.

The taxi pulls up to the sidewalk, and the window rolls down, revealing a glare from under bushy eyebrows.

'Are you shitting me? It's not even nine p.m.'

'Hello, Roger,' I chime, helping the girl to her feet. 'Have I ever told you that you're my favorite taxi driver?'

'Several times. I'm still not taking her for free.'

'And I wouldn't expect you to, honey.' I fish through my tote for a Ziploc bag of candy and toss it through the window. 'The macaroons are homemade.' While he mutters and grunts about having a mortgage to pay, I fold the girl into his back seat before he can protest. 'To the Hilton, please.'

'Aw, come off it, Wren. That's only a ten-minute walk.'

'Does she look like she can walk? Besides, I'm too busy to take her.'

'Fine,' he grunts. As he starts the engine, he nods behind me with a smirk. 'Isn't that your friend's shop?'

I turn to find a man in the doorway of Tayce's shop, a stream of pee running from between his legs and splattering the step.

'Ew! That is *not* a public restroom,' I shriek, reaching for the whistle around my neck and giving it a hard blow. 'Shoo!'

The night only gets busier. It passes in a blur of Band-Aids, hand holding, and consoling. I've chipped a nail trying to break up a cat fight between two girls who stepped out wearing the same dress, patched up bloodied knees, treated sprained ankles, reassured worried parents over the phone. By the time the last nightclub slams its doors shut, my SOS bag is nearly empty and I'm exhausted.

Leaning against the streetlamp, I chomp through the last of my crackers, watching the final few strays stumble out of late-night food joints and into waiting cars.

Crumpling the empty pack in my hand, my weary sigh floats down the bare promenade. The last bus back to Devil's Dip left over an hour ago, and my bones groan thinking about the long, cold walk home ahead of me.

It's times like this I wish more than anything that guilt didn't riddle me like a disease. That I could slide into the warmth of a taxi without muscle memory twitching my hands, and the anger, betrayal, and *injustice* flooding my vision red. That I could leave the memory of what I did about it under the dust sheet in Uncle Finn's workshop, like I did with the weapon, or bury it six feet under like I did with the consequences.

But my heart is pounding and my knees are trembling at the mere thought of it.

I gather up my stuff and start walking.

It's only taken a few hours for the strip to transform from a winter wonderland to a deathly obstacle course. My boots crunch over broken beer bottles, and I tread carefully around the ice patches and puddles of vomit.

I'm stooped to check if there's any ID in an abandoned Gucci purse when a prickle of awareness skates over my shoulders.

I glance up. Farther down the road, there's a blond-haired man with an unsteady gait making his way toward me.

'Are you okay?' I shout. 'Do you need help?'

His laugh rolls down the promenade, booming and slightly unsettling. 'Hey, you're the girl who works at the dive bar!'

As he passes under the light of a streetlamp, I study his brown eyes, slender frame, and button-down shirt, waiting for a spark of recognition, but I draw a blank. He's not a local, and out-of-towners in The Rusty Anchor are so few and far between that they always stick in my mind.

I've never seen this man in my life.

But then he trips over a fast-food carton, and my unease turns into concern. 'You didn't drive here, did you?'

He laughs again. 'Of course not. But, uh, I do need some help.'

The knots in my shoulders loosen. 'Sure, that's what I'm here for,' I say brightly. 'Have you lost your friends?'

'Yes, and for the life of me, I can't remember where we're staying. All these hotels' – he staggers backward as he sweeps an arm over the horizon – 'they all look the fucking same.'

'Do you have a room card?'

He pats his pockets and sighs. 'Lost it.'

'Bummer. Can you call a friend?'

'Phone's dead.'

I tut. 'You should never go on a night out without full charge. But not to worry, you can use mine.'

His gaze burns down on me as I rifle through my bag for my cell. I tap the screen, and nothing happens. Frowning, I hold down the on button, only for an empty battery sign to appear on the screen.

'Lllooks like you ssshould take your own advice.'

Dammit.

When I look up, he's a step closer. Too close. Drunk people rarely have any sense of spatial awareness, but there's something about his hot breath grazing my cheek and the way he towers over me that drags a thread of discomfort down my spine.

I glance over at Tayce's shop on instinct, suddenly feeling the void of her constant glare through the window, then I shake off the discomfort, paint on a smile, and step back.

'There's a telephone booth down the road, you can call from that.'

Our lonely footsteps echo along the empty street, our shadows distorting as we pass under pulsating lights. When we reach the phone booth, I tug open the door and step aside to let him in.

Instead, he leans against the frame and studies me for a moment too long. There's something off about his gaze – it's dark and murky, darting around too fast for comfort.

'I'm so drunk I can barely see straight,' he whispers. 'Could you dial the number for me?'

My gaze drifts into the phone booth, to the naked bulb

swaying from the roof and all the corners its light doesn't touch. A shiver vibrates down my spine.

Suddenly, Gabriel's haunting words graze my ear like a whisper in an empty room. *'If it happens in the dark, it didn't happen.'*

It's sat like an itch beneath my skin all week. I can't stop scratching it, wondering why it's there, and why it won't go away.

Sensing my hesitation, he lays a heavy hand on my shoulder. 'Please? You'll be so much quicker than me. I'm so drunk I'm seeing double.'

Well, he's right about me being quicker. I'm cold, tired, and hungry, and the sooner I can get home, the better.

The small voice at the base of my skull whispers a warning, but the call of my bed is louder, so reluctantly, I step inside.

As soon as I cross the threshold, the hairs on the back of my neck rise. The air is thick with regret and the stench of urine, and when I grab the phone receiver, it's ice cold to the touch. With a trembling hand, I dig around in my pocket for some quarters, then drop them in the slot with a hollow *click*.

'W-what's the number?'

The dull *thud* of the door closing reverberates through my bones, and the sudden warmth brushes my back.

Deep down, I knew it was coming, yet I still stepped inside.

Christ, Wren. Why did you step inside?

Movements heavy with dread, I grip the receiver tighter and turn around to face the man caging me in.

Hindsight is everything; mine tuts in my ears and calls me an idiot. The bulb overhead casts him in a new light, illuminating all the things I should have noticed before: the steady gaze, the bad acting. The lack of liquor on his breath.

Swallowing a lump of panic, I slide my gaze up to his.

'What's the number?' I repeat as steadily as my nerves allow.

A cruel smirk twists his thin lips. He reaches up, and I flinch as his palm grazes my bauble earrings, and settles, damp and hot, on my jaw.

There's not enough space to twist out of his reach. Or enough oxygen in here to scream, and even if there was, it's not like anyone would hear me.

My stomach twists when his fingers slide south, down the curve of my neck to my thumping heart, carving a slimy path to the cup of my bra.

'Please don't,' I whimper.

It's not my pathetic plea that stops the roaming hand but a sudden flurry of wind. It ruffles my hair and jangles my earrings, bringing icy air and an inked fist, which wraps around the man's throat and yanks him backward out of the phone booth.

My gaze darts from where he falls, to the large boot stopping the door from closing again.

I don't need to look up to know who it belongs to.

CHAPTER Thirteen

Wren

In what sick world do I live in, where I'm relieved to see the man who threatened to cut out my tongue?

It's a fleeting feeling, replaced with a dizzying foreboding as my gaze drifts up from his boots, over black-clad muscle, and locks with his.

Rage simmers out of him like a slow-burning fire. He's scarily still, and for a moment, I wonder if he's a figment of my imagination, some kind of anti-angel my brain has summoned under duress. Then his eyes spark with a look of disgust marred with annoyance, and the low tremor of his voice filling the booth feels very, very real.

'Close your eyes and count to ten.'

Gabriel slams the door shut, trapping me in with the ghost of his growl.

Growing numb, I try to do what he tells me, but I don't make it past the count of five. There's a sickening *crack* and a scream so guttural it can only be wrenched from the deepest part of one's soul, and it makes my heart lurch skyward.

Oh my God. He's going to kill him.

I haven't witnessed a murder in a long time, but muscle memory and self-preservation are a powerful combination. They want to drag me down to the floor and under the kitchen table. To pull my knees up to my chest and take my brain away to my happy place. It's a house in the suburbs with a white picket fence and a manicured lawn. Where Sundays are for board games and no one goes to bed angry, and no matter how many times the radio plays Mom and Dad's wedding song, they always stop what they're doing, push the living room furniture to the walls, and dance.

But I can't just curl up on the floor. Not just because I'm not a child anymore, but also because I'm pretty sure someone peed in here, and I'm not ruining yet *another* dress.

Another scream launches me into action, and I spin around, desperately searching for anything in the booth that can help. A number to call.

I scan the business cards tacked above the phone. Under the dim glow, I look at ads for escorts, an emergency locksmith, and a local fortune teller. All useless. Then a slither of gold glints under the dim light, and I snatch the black card from the wall.

The Sinners Anonymous hotline.

Wait – what the hell am I doing? Why aren't I calling the police?

As I grapple for the phone receiver and hover a finger over the number nine, a gust of wind blows through the booth.

Then a wall of black bricks it out.

This shadow is larger than the last. It makes me feel even more vulnerable and on edge, and it takes everything in me not to close my eyes and wait for it to disappear.

With a lump in my throat, I turn around. My gaze snags on the blood splatter on the glass panels, then beyond it to a man dragging a body toward a waiting car.

Then finally up to him.

With a sinking feeling, I realize I've jumped from the frying pan and into the flames of hell. Gabriel Visconti is terrifying at the best of times, but under the naked light bulb, he's a nightmare personified. It brings out the red of his scar and the black of his fury. Casts the planes of his face in a demonic glow.

Every nerve ending prickles under his glare as it slides down my body. Down my arm, and to my hand, where it narrows into a sharp point.

'Something to confess?'

What?

With not a single thought in my brain to latch onto, I dumbly follow his eye line to the Sinners Anonymous card in my hand, then grow cold.

Legend has it, these cards started mysteriously popping up years ago, long before I moved to the coast. Tacked above public telephones, at the bottom of tip jars, wedged into the frame of bathroom mirrors in nightclubs. They're matte black and thick, with nothing else but a number printed along the bottom in gold. If you call it, it takes you to an automated voicemail message, encouraging you to confess your wrongdoings.

It's probably some sort of new-wave religious cult or whimsy art school project. Even if it wasn't, I've never been tempted to call.

The only time I've ever been tempted to confess was *that* night, and to him. Only because I was certain he'd die.

The silence grows hot and begins to itch. I suppose I'd hoped he was too delirious, too close to death, to even register, let alone care, what I was asking of him.

'Ha. Of course not.' I crumple the card in my pocket and clear my throat. 'I've never done anything worth confessing,' I mutter, staring at the broad expanse of his chest. My eyes dart across to his arms bulging beneath his short-sleeve T-shirt. No jacket in winter? How is this man not cold?

Silence hangs heavy, then hardens into tension. When it takes up too much of the space between us, I reluctantly slide my gaze up over his tattooed neck, thick beard, and search his expression.

As expected, it's stone-cold and still. Annoyance pulsates behind his eyes and throbs at the side of his jaw. Christ, his stare is so intense, I imagine this is how it feels to stare down the barrel of a gun. It's like he's waiting for something, and suddenly, I remember my manners.

'Thank you,' I say sheepishly. 'For, you know, stopping that creep from –'

He cuts me off. 'Do you always follow men you don't know into dark spaces?'

Feeling as small as child being scolded, I shake my head.

Though his eyes flash dark, his tone is eerily calm. 'What would you have done?'

'What?'

'What would you have done,' he repeats slowly, irritation tugging at his words, 'if I wasn't here?'

Oh. I shift under the weight of his heavy breaths and scan the empty road beyond the blood-smeared glass. 'Well, I don't know, actually. I guess someone would have walked by eventually.'

His nostrils flare at my answer. He looks up to the roof and swallows thickly, composing himself. 'And if they didn't?' he grits out.

'Um. I'd have screamed for help?'

'Are you asking me or telling me?'

'What are you *talking* about?'

Regret arrives quickly, and it sounds like a single heavy footstep and the thud of a closing door.

I hadn't appreciated the space between us, and now it's gone, snatched away by my stupidity and replaced with the heat of his body brushing mine.

What little air is left in the booth wilts and dies, creating a vacuum, and suddenly, I'm hyperaware of every sound and sensation within this eight-by-four box. How his hard torso contracts, then expands, grazing my stomach between the opening of my coat. How it blooms a strange heat beneath my skirt. How his heavy exhales steam the glass and cling to my clammy skin. The bob of his inked throat. Every bulge and vein snaking along his bare arm. I can hear the *drip, drip, drip* of something warm and wet falling from his busted hand pressed against the wall by my head, and onto my shoulder.

I glance down at the dark stain on my pink hi-vis and let out a slow, shaky breath. Electricity sparks from somewhere deep within me. It's a familiar feeling, one I've worked so hard to never ignite again.

He punched that man for me.

Me.

'What would you have done?' he repeats.

His question tugs me out of the murky depths of my thoughts and back into the phonebooth. The thump of my heartbeat fills the silence while I consider my answer carefully. This man is scary, and I don't want to get it wrong.

Truth is, I don't know what I would have done. Sure, I've had a few near misses in my time volunteering in Cove, but it's never been more than a roaming hand, a drunk trying his luck. Nothing that a swift slap and a blow of my whistle haven't deterred.

I drop my head against the back wall and let out a tense breath. 'I don't know. Someone would have seen me in here.'

A gruff growl ruffles my bangs. His bicep bulges as he lifts his arm above his head and wraps a large hand around the light bulb.

He twists it loose, plunging us into darkness.

I blink, trying to adjust my vision, but when I realize I can see nothing but black, a dull weight forms at the base of my spine, then a prickle of panic fissures out from it. Seconds scratch by and morph into minutes. Frozen, I stare into the void and strain my ears, trying to catch any sound of movement seeping out of it.

Only the tremble of my heartbeat and the ghost of Gabriel's cryptic words fill the space.

'If it happens in the dark, it didn't happen.'

And suddenly, I realize why I haven't been able to stop those words from playing on a constant loop in my head. Darkness has never scared me, but the freedom it brings is terrifying. In the dark, I could be anyone.

Even my real self.

And if whatever I did didn't happen . . .

Christ.

The metal wall of the booth is ice cold against my back, but Gabriel's slow-burning heat is closing in. If I inched forward, his body would be flush with mine, and the mere thought of it sends a dizzying high through me.

I can't even make out his silhouette, let alone his expression. Which means he can't see mine either. I could stick my tongue out and him not even know it. I'd taste the tension in the tiny gap between us and taste his leather and tobacco scent too.

I could do *anything*.

'Now what?' he murmurs, almost softly.

My heart is pounding. The lack of oxygen is turning me insane. 'I'd fight,' I whisper back.

'Then fight me,' he says, his breath crackling on my earlobe.

'What?'

'I've cornered you in here, there's no light. Nobody can see you. Nobody is coming to rescue you. Fight. Me.'

My nerve endings spark. 'I-I can't.'

'Why?'

Because I can't breathe. Can't feel my face, or my hands, or my feet. Because I have pulses pounding in places they shouldn't, and they're beating to a different rhythm than my brain.

I manage to choke out a more sensible version of the truth. 'I don't know how.'

He moves closer, and I push my palm into his stomach. I don't know why I do it. Maybe to stop him from getting any closer, or maybe, I'm flirting with the freedom darkness brings. I've never touched a man in this way, let alone one built like *this*. Wouldn't dare to do such a thing in the light, either. He feels as hard as I expected, and I swear, he hardens even more under my touch.

A beat passes, then another. I swallow hard, and I can't be thinking straight, otherwise, I wouldn't curl my hand into a fist so slowly. I wouldn't graze my fingers down his torso, tracking every ridge and dip. I wouldn't ball the fabric of his shirt into my palm.

Suddenly, he slams a hand against the wall by my head so hard the whole booth rattles. The vibration rumbles from my scalp to my toes, snapping me out of my trance.

I bring my forearms to my face, bracing for impact.

Instead, the door flies open.

'*Walk.*'

I grab my bags and shoot past him into the night, faster than a bullet from a gun.

The icy air kisses my sweaty nape and fills my lungs. It does absolutely nothing to calm me. I'm buzzing – part adrenaline, part disgust. I move on autopilot in a half walk, half jog toward the promenade.

Christ. I'm sick in the head. And not just because I didn't think twice about hopping over the blood splatter on the sidewalk.

'What were you doing out here?'

I glance down at the walkway, and with a sinking feeling, realize Gabriel's shadow is stretching alongside mine. 'Volunteering.'

'Alone?'

'Yes.'

'Are you out of your fucking mind?'

I am now.

Though my feet throb in these heels, I don't dare stop to put on my sneakers. Don't want to risk him picking me up again. So I keep my head down and sheepishly keep moving, warily watching his shadow on the coattails of mine.

His heavy footsteps, my heavy breaths. It's awkward and uncomfortable, so I do what I do best.

I force myself to lighten the mood.

'And what about you? Were you out partying tonight?' The moment the question leaves my lips, I know it's a ridiculous thing to ask. There's no parallel universe in which I can imagine Gabriel Visconti two-stepping on a dance floor, beer in hand, having a good time. But for once, I have no other conversation starters in my locker, so I carry on. 'I bet you get free drinks everywhere. Um, not because you're scary or anything, but because you're a Visconti. Your cousins own most of the bars in Cove, right?'

As expected, there's no reply from behind me. Just frosty silence and a shadow haunting my own. It follows me from one end of Devil's Cove to the other. When the glitzy lights abruptly meet the road leading out of town, my heart lifts an inch with the hopeful thought he'll leave me from here.

A rough tug on my wrist spins me around and snatches my next breath. *No such luck.*

It feels instinctive to yank myself from his grasp, but the fury pulsating from his palm stops me. I must be more tired than I thought, as my gaze has no business dropping to his large hand around the cuff of my glove, and my imagination has no right to run in the direction it does.

I drink in black symbols and wonder what they mean, then scan silver scars and wonder what he did to get them. His busted knuckles, protruding veins, thick, swollen fingers. I wonder if he punches every man who follows women into phone booths. I can't imagine hands like these being anything but weapons, and now I'm wondering what else they do.

If they're capable of a light caress, of skimming along the soft curve of a hip. If they ever slide south, under lacy fabric, and bring pleasure.

A wave of hot jealousy comes out of nowhere.

Jesus. I'm not tired. I'm out of my damn mind.

I move to pull away, but my eyes snag on the rivulet of blood trickling between two of his knuckles. It slowly drips over his thumb, then down the side of his hand. I still don't move when it slithers, hot and wet, over my skittering pulse and into the cuff of my glove.

A tingle of unease and something darker hums through me as the blood trickles along the length of my palm. There's that spark again. He punched a man, for *me*.

My gaze snaps up to meet his. He swallows whatever he turned me around to say and studies me instead, something between curiosity and regret flickering over his face.

He snatches his hand away and balls it into a fist by his side.

With a curt nod over his shoulder, a black car pulls off the curb and crawls toward us, its headlights illuminating the path ahead.

'*Walk.*'

Confused, but not stupid enough to argue, I turn around and start my journey home.

Unfortunately, leaving the bright lights of Cove doesn't mean I get to leave him behind too. He falls in step behind me, his shadow stretching out along the road in the glow from the headlights trailing us.

The sight of it is starting to make me panic.

'You have a weapon?'

Gritting my teeth, I pick up my pace, trying to keep distance between us. 'What, like pepper spray?'

'Like a gun.'

I choke out a laugh. I'd think he was kidding if I thought this man was capable of cracking a joke. 'No,' I state. 'It wouldn't fit in my purse.'

His angry glare bores into my back. 'So you can't fight, can't protect yourself. You wear those ridiculous shoes that you definitely can't run in, and yet, you still insist on walking these streets alone after dark.' He mutters a curse under his breath. 'You know what happens to girls like you?'

'They make it home safe and sound because bad things don't happen on the coast.'

'They end up as a statistic on a Wikipedia page,' he spits back.

My heart flips, and the road ahead jolts. The irony comes out of left field and punches me in the gut, landing too close to home.

Good, I think bitterly. Because nothing else I do seems to finish that goddamn sentence.

His comment has thrown my thoughts off track, and now all I can focus on is the dreaded midnight email waiting for me when I get home. But it's also behind the safety of my *locked* front door, so I force myself to focus on putting one foot in front of the other.

'What, you wanna be kidnapped? Raped? Murdered?' he carries on, voice growing darker by the syllable. 'You're a walking target. A sitting duck. And what the fuck were you thinking, putting your location on Instagram?'

My spine straightens, and I come to an abrupt stop. Curiosity and surprise spin me around. 'You looked at my Instagram?'

He stands in the middle of the road, his looming frame backlit by the car's headlights, and regards me with a look of contempt so violent my wrist burns from the memory of his grip.

I wait for the familiar shiver of trepidation, but it doesn't come. My head is still in the phonebooth, along with the worst part of my soul. I hate that he brought it out of me.

Hate that he just won't go away.

Fueled by frustration, I tilt my chin and return his glare. 'I'm not a damsel in distress, and while I appreciate the concern, I don't need your help. Besides,' I add, fumbling around in my collar for the cord hanging from my neck, 'I have a whistle for emergencies.'

When met with his blank stare, I start to feel all itchy, so I give the whistle a pathetic toot. 'See? More than capable of getting out of sticky situations.'

A dense beat passes. Then another.

His nostrils flare as his eyes fall to my lips and harden to black ice. Rage radiates out of every pore, and when he steps toward me, I wonder, for a heart-stopping second, if those hands I'm still thinking about will find their way to my throat.

It's worse. They find their way to my hips instead, and then I'm balancing over his shoulder, staring at my whistle as it swings in and out of my vision.

'Wait!' I squeal, kicking my legs against the iron-clad grip on my calves. 'Put me down!'

My plea falls on deaf ears, and the ground moves beneath Gabriel's boots in a gray blur. The glow from the headlights spread wider, and so does the knot in my throat. I stuff the whistle back in my mouth and shout for help between loud, desperate blows.

He's rough when he folds me in half. Even rougher when he drops me into the open car trunk.

And when the ink, scar, and *green* disappear behind the falling door, his voice is the roughest thing of all.

'Get out of this sticky situation, then.'

CHAPTER
Fourteen

Gabe

'Jonah was a real man. Six foot, biceps the circumference of my waist. He was fresh meat, straight off a plane from Cape Town. You ever look at someone and just know you'd make beautiful babies? 'Cause I was a smoke show back then too, even after I had a kid. Every time I stepped out to the store, I'd turn more heads than a car crash.' Her laugh breaks into a crackling smokers cough. 'Not that you'd know it from my mugshot, of course.'

She'll rant about her mugshot for the next ten minutes, so I pick up the angle grinder and drown her out with the sound of metal scraping metal. Green sparks fly, and the garage fills with the smell of burned dust.

When I switch it off, set it back down on the workbench, and readjust my earbud, she's still fucking going.

'... hadn't had my roots done in months. Not to mention, the police dragged my ass out of bed in the middle of the night, which is why my eyes are hanging out of my head. And what's up with that lighting? I looked so pale, you'd think I hadn't had a vacation in ten years.'

I headbutt the lip of the tool shelf, impatience fizzing through me. *Come on, Mildred. Get to the good part. I need the good part.*

I'd learned to weaponize secrets in The Middle, but my obsession started back in The Beginning.

The first time my brothers and I squeezed into the crawlspace behind the confessional after Sunday service and listened to Mr Foster admit to blowing his late wife's life insurance on hookers and cocaine was the first time my brain stopped hurting. Because suddenly, I didn't feel so bad about drowning Angelo's best friend in the pool that summer or setting the outhouse on fire to see how quickly the flames would spread.

I'd realized listening to the sins of others had a way of silencing my own.

But I grew older and more depraved and more *addicted*. The highs became weaker, the trips shorter. I needed to find bigger Band-Aids for bigger wounds.

So I began to dig.

First, I dug deep into our bloodline. Then I dug up the whole coast. When that stopped working, I dug up the state, the country, the world.

I dug until my fingers bled. I dug all the way to fucking China. I dug until I was a full-fledged crackhead, desperately chasing the feeling of my first hit.

'. . . and it wasn't even about how handsome he was. We connected on a spiritual level, you know? I'm a Scorpio, he was a Virgo. He loved ramen; I studied Japanese for a semester in school . . .'

Grinding my jaw, I palm the workbench and close my eyes.

And then along came Rafe and his hotline. Another game to him, a gamechanger for me.

Though he'd created Sinners Anonymous to bond us brothers and scratch a nostalgic itch, he'd also unknowingly hooked an addict up to an infinite supply.

Now, all the sins I could ever ask for are in my ear. A constant stream of bad thoughts to distract me from my own.

Granted, most are dog shit.

Few are potent.

And none are Hers.

I snap my eyes back open and turn up the call to max volume.

'... he was smart. Unfortunately for him, it was in a solve-Soduku-puzzles-over-breakfast way, not in a check-that-my-affair-partner-hasn't-left-lipstick-on-my-collar way.' Mildred lets out a wistful sigh. 'But even if she hadn't, the stench of her dollar-store perfume walked through my front door before he did, anyway.'

Mildred Black calls like clockwork. And today, she's called just when my brain hurts the most.

'... so I had his favorite meal cooking on the stove and had lit loads of candles to set the mood. I'd brought his favorite wine too, but it turns out, he hadn't planned to drink that night.' She scoffs. 'I'm sure he regretted that decision when I –'

The side door connecting the garage to the main house crashes open just when Mildred's finally getting to the good part.

My agitation bleeds into amusement when I glance up to find my sister-in-law darkening the doorway.

She's rolling her sleeves up, then throws her curls into a careless bun. When her gaze roves around the garage, I sigh, end the call, and prop my foot up against the wall behind me.

'Gabe.' She pushes over a broom. 'What did you do to Wren?'

Her name rakes down my back like glittery pink nails on a chalkboard. Hearing her name aloud, through someone else's mouth, stings.

But Rory notices these things. So I retrieve the cigarette tucked behind my ear and slide it between my lips to stop them from curling.

'Seems like you already know,' I muse, watching her foot

connect with an empty bucket. It skids across the concrete and clatters against the far side of the wall.

I'm not surprised she snitched – she looks like the snitching type – I'm just surprised it's taken her so long. She kept her mouth shut after she crossed my path three years ago. Said fuck-all when I shoved her house key down her throat in her own hallway.

So what was it about me folding her into my trunk that has her squealing like a little pig?

It could be the accumulation of events, of course. Three-chances-and-you're-out kind of thing. But then I remember her reaction to the last time I'd picked her up and headed toward a waiting car. How she fought and begged and *touched me,* and I can't help but think, that somehow, it all leads back to her secret.

'But *why* ?' Rory topples a box of screws as she passes. 'Why *Wren?* It's Wren, for goose's sake.'

A dark wave of irritation brushes my skin, and not because she's stomping toward my tool cabinet.

I did it because she couldn't tell me what she'd do if someone tried to hurt her.

Because the sound of that fucking whistle snapped my one and only nerve.

Because I didn't force her into my trunk after the explosion, and I needed to prove to myself that I could.

'I let her out, didn't I?'

'Yeah, well –' Rory huffs, reaching for a hammer. 'You made her cry, so now I'm gonna make *you* cry.' She swings it into the wall with so much energy, yet so little strength, that the impact doesn't even crack the bricks.

I'd laugh if She hadn't got me so fucked up.

Last night was a rare moment of weakness.

The silence was too loud. Her voice even louder. No sins coming through the hotline were bad enough to drown out the feeling of her weight in my arms or the sight of her dress sliding up her thigh.

So I did what I've resisted doing every damn day for the last three years: I googled her.

I drag my teeth over my bottom lip, bitterness brewing in my chest.

Turns out, ignorance really is bliss. The only thing worse than finding something is finding nothing.

No news articles. No family tree to climb.

No secret.

There's barely any trace of her on the internet. In fact, typing in her name only brings up one result: Her Instagram profile.

She's lucky I was out of my mind last night. While I was zooming in on cheesy selfies, reading every pun-filled caption, and rolling my eyes at photos of every meal, coffee, and cocktail the girl had ever shoved into her fucking mouth, she'd posted again.

It was yet another picture of herself. On a *public* Instagram profile. And if that wasn't stupid enough, she'd tagged her location.

And clearly, I wasn't the only man with ill-intentions to take advantage of it.

My thoughts shade black at the memory. Standing under a punched-out streetlamp in the alleyway between Moodys bar and the Irish pub, I watched as he fed her an act even a five-year-old could have seen through. Then I watched in disbelief as he led her to a phone booth and slipped in behind her.

I grind my molars and reach for the matchbox on the side shelf to light my cigarette. Then Rory gives up on trying to smash open the padlock to the guns cabinet and upturns a jerry can instead, so I think better of it.

'Oh, sparrow,' she mutters as oil splashes on the cuffs of her joggers. She lifts her gaze to mine and puffs out a breath.

'You done?'

'No, I'm taking a break.' She wipes her arm across her brow and glares at me again. 'You're going to apologize.'

I laugh. Hell will freeze over before an apology of any kind leaves my lips.

'I'm being so serious. You know she's scared of cars, right?'

A familiar itch crawls over me. The fresh scab I'd picked at last night starts to crack. It covers a wound three years deep that just won't go away.

The Google search didn't heal it. Finding her Instagram account only sliced it wider.

No. Can't. Shouldn't.

'Why?'

Fuck's sake. I turn around and adjust the settings on the drill press so Rory doesn't notice the self-loathing tightening my jaw.

'I'm not sure – she won't tell us. She just walks everywhere instead.'

'I'm aware,' I grit out. 'She's asking to get kidnapped.'

'Gabe. It's *Wren*.'

There she goes, saying her fucking name again. And in the same breath as mine. She says it as though her name alone is an explanation. A perfect reason as to why she can walk the streets alone with no consequences.

Behind me, something metal and heavy lands on the floor with a dull thud.

'The girl's a liability,' I grit out, curling my hand around an old rag.

'She's not. She's, like, the nicest person on the planet. It's like an unspoken rule around here, everyone leaves Wren alone.'

'Apart from the man who followed her into the phone booth.'

Rory pauses for a beat too long. I turn around in time to see the surprise flicker over her face.

Interesting. The little angel failed to mention that part when she snitched.

'Oh,' Rory mutters, letting the hammer clatter to the floor. 'She didn't tell me that bit. Well, who was it?'

Some loser who'd gone to Cove on a business trip. Clean record. That's about all I know, because hitting him too hard too soon was the second mistake I made last night. His head bounced off the sidewalk like a tennis ball, and he was a goner before I could drag him into the cave, string him up, and have some fun with him.

Feeding off her distraction, I palm the workbench and stare down at her evenly. 'We're in the middle of a fucking war, Rory. Your little friend's a liability. If Dante or anyone else we've pissed off wanted to get to you, they'd do so by way of her.'

She chews her lip. 'Fair point. Fine, I'll tell her to be more careful.'

'No, you'll tell her to stop walking home late at night. You'll tell her to stop volunteering in Cove.' I dig my fingers into the wood top. 'You'll tell her to stop posting her fucking location on Instagram.'

Rory's eyes find mine, her brows knitting. 'You're stalking her Instagram? How? You can barely use a phone.'

Ignoring the heat brewing under my collar at the word *stalking*, I double down. 'I stalk all of your Instagram accounts. I vet everyone in our outer circle, and she's a weak link.' Then, before I can stop myself, I add, 'Tell me everything you know about her.'

The demand leaves my mouth with the taste of regret, but the longer it stews in the air, the easier it is to justify.

I'm the fucking consigliere. I was put on this bastard earth for one reason – to keep my family safe. Finding out more about her isn't something I can avoid, it's a job requirement.

'Um.' Rory scratches her nose in thought. 'She moved here from Seattle in sixth grade. Lives on Strawberry farm with her Uncle Finn, who used to be a lawyer. She's going to be a lawyer too – eventually.' She glances up at me. 'She's deferred college twice, but she can't defer again, so she has to go next September.'

Nothing she didn't tell me herself on the night of the explosion, except the putting off college part.

I pick up a buffer and get to work polishing my latest contraption. 'And her parents?'

'She never knew her father, but her mom is dead.'

My shoulders tighten. 'How?'

'That's all she'd ever say, and I've never pushed.' She purses her lips. 'I'm not as nosy as you.'

I ignore her not-so-subtle dig, because now my brain is ticking over. Dead mom. I can work with that. 'What's her mom's name?'

Rory shakes her head.

'Last name? Job? Fucking date of birth?'

She shrugs.

'Why doesn't she drink?' I grit out.

She rolls her eyes and saunters over to the workbench. 'I don't know, but I've never known her to drink.'

'And why doesn't she drive?'

Rory's pause is brief, but it crackles on the nape of my neck. She lowers her gaze and traces a finger along the wood grain. 'I don't know.'

My sister-in-law is a psychopath. She'll smile and swear she didn't key your car, or serve you a coffee and not even flinch as she watches you drink her spit.

She's a flawless liar. Until she's not.

'Rory,' I warn.

'I don't know!' she says with an impatient huff, her cheeks reddening. 'One day she was driving, and then the next day she wasn't, okay?'

A chill works its way through my veins. I swallow and force out my next question as calmly as I can muster.

Though I have a creeping suspicion I already know the answer.

'And when was this?'

She lifts her eyes to meet mine, guilt swirling in the brown. 'Just after her eighteenth birthday.'

Her words crawl across the table, push into my chest, and hammer puzzle pieces into place.

She stopped driving just before she met me.

Just before her glossed lips brushed mine, her breath warmer than the wind.

'Can I tell you a secret?'

Though I've always obsessed over her secret, it's always been to satisfy my own fucked-up addiction, not because I've ever thought it'd be anything worth uncovering. I've always been certain it'd be petty. Stealing a nail polish from the mall, or something equally as dumb.

But to suddenly stop driving?

I've given up the pretense of polishing now. Heart thudding and ears burning, I glare at Rory and wait for her to continue.

'It was all a bit strange. She'd gone out of town to celebrate her birthday with her Seattle friends, and when she came back a few days later, she no longer had a car.'

'So she had an accident.'

'She swore up and down she didn't, and she didn't look hurt or anything.' She glances up at me with a sheepish smile. 'I didn't believe her, but I googled car accidents in the whole of the Pacific Northwest, and nothing came up.'

I drag a knuckle over my jaw, my mind racing. 'And now she doesn't get into cars at all.'

'Nope. Sometimes, she'll take the bus, but most of the time, she walks everywhere. But that's not all. When she came back, she was . . . *different*. Not in a bad way,' she hastens to add. 'She was just nicer.'

I run my tongue over my teeth. 'Meaning?'

'She started volunteering in Cove, then at the hospital. At first, I thought it was just so she had something to put on her college application, but she'd already secured her place. And then I thought, maybe she's found God or something.' She lets out a little laugh. 'But that doesn't explain why she suddenly started wearing so much pink.'

My skin is fucking fizzing. The driving, the volunteering, the sudden niceness. There's a linear story there, a *secret*, one more depraved than petty theft, and I'm so close to finding it out I can taste it on her strawberry lip gloss.

'Anyway, shouldn't you know all of this already? Denis found Rafe's banking login for me in ten seconds flat.'

My eyes narrow. 'Why'd you need that?'

'He keeps beating me at blackjack, so I donated a million dollars to the Washington Bird Sanctuary on his behalf,' she says brightly, tugging her keys out of her pocket and jangling them at arm's length. 'And look, they sent me this cute keyring as a thank you!'

But I can barely register her obnoxiously large magpie keyring. Can barely fucking think.

She's right. I could have found out her secret years ago, and in minutes. And if it was anyone else, I'd have ripped it open like a kid with their gifts on Christmas morning.

But it's the Angel in Pink.

I made a vow to myself, for my own *sanity*, that I wouldn't.

Self-loathing runs hot under my shirt. *Why did I fucking ask?*

Rory nods down to the Frankensteined gun between us. 'What are you making?'

I bite on the change of subject and slide it over the table. 'What you asked me to.'

Her demeanor flips one-eighty, and she lights up with a

childlike wonder. 'Oh, my Goose,' she breathes, holding it up to the light with cupped hands, like I've handed her the Holy Grail. 'Does it work?'

'Only one way to find out.'

Her eyes meet mine with a spark of mischief, and despite the tightness at the base of my skull, a reluctant amusement bleeds through me.

This girl, honestly. There's not much of me that's soft, but there's a tiny speck, somewhere between my top and bottom rib, that's a little soft for Vicious's wife.

I knew of her long before she sank her claws into my brother. Long before Uncle Alberto sank his into her, even. She'd been calling the hotline for years, confessing the pettiest shit with the weight of the whole world's guilt in her voice.

If Mildred Black's calls were my drug of choice, Rory's were the sitcoms I'd watch to buffer the blow of the comedown. I'd find amusement in her small acts of revenge – tampering with Alberto's whiskey, cutting the brakes of Dante's car. Then as her wedding to Alberto grew closer, her calls changed genre, and suddenly, I was watching a limited series thriller I couldn't turn off.

I listened to each call as if they were episodes. The show was slow in the beginning, picked up pace in the middle, and ended with the perfect plot twist: she was going to shove Fat Al off a cliff before he could force her to marry him.

Angelo went and spoiled the fucking ending, of course. Popped a cap in his head and wiped out any chance of a second season.

But now that she's my sister-in-law, she entertains me in other ways. Like bringing me moodboards with her latest inventions, and in my spare time, I bring them to life.

'This is so cool,' she exclaims, cocking the gun to the ceiling and posing, like she's one of Charlie's Angels. 'It's like Russian

Roulette but cuter, right? Instead of firing blanks, it shoots off confetti canons?'

I lunge over and snatch it off her when she turns it around and peers down the barrel. *Jesus.* I double-check the safety is on and make a mental note to go over the basic rules of gun safety, *again*, before we get to the range.

'Are we taking the Harley?' She jogs over to the wall and lifts her motorbike helmet from the hook.

Before I can reply, Emile pushes through the door with his shoulder. He smiles at Rory and glances at me before heading over to the sink.

I drag my front teeth over my bottom lip, sensing the air shift. 'Yeah. I'll meet you out front.'

'All right, but hurry up, we've got to get back before Angelo wonders where I am.'

She turns on her heel and hops, skips, and jumps over the destruction she caused moments earlier. As if the puddle of oil and upturned bucket suddenly reminded her of why she stormed in here in the first place, she pauses at the door and turns around, pinning me with a sober expression.

'I'll talk to Wren, but you have to promise me you'll leave her alone,' she says, swallowing hard. 'She's innocent. In fact, she's the only wholesome person I have left. She doesn't know about . . . us.'

I cock a brow. 'Us?'

'The family. She doesn't know what you guys do, and I need to keep it that way. So, no stalking, no vetting. And definitely no shoving her into cars. Just pretend she doesn't exist, okay?'

It takes a beat before the realization hits. She means her little friend has no idea that she's living, breathing, and roaming in *Cosa Nostra* territory.

Heat rushes up my spine. Christ, the girl must be more ignorant than I thought. It doesn't take a genius to see the blacked-out cars and men in suits to realize they're probably the reason this tiny coastline in the ass end of nowhere bleeds with wealth.

But I trap all my questions behind pursed lips. I've asked enough of them for one day.

Instead, I give her a curt nod, and when she leaves, I turn my attention to Emile.

'Denis just got back to me,' he mutters, turning on the tap with his elbow. 'Blake is Griffin's nephew.'

I glare at the water running from clear to red to clear again. 'Does my brother know?'

'I doubt it.' He turns off the water and reaches for a hand towel. 'He's got nothing on record.'

I drag a knuckle through my beard, fighting the unease creeping up my back like graveyard fog.

Something stinks.

I've had my suspicions about Rafe's head honcho, Griffin, for a while. No reason in particular, just a hunch. But now it's come back that he's got family ties to the new hire, I know I'm on to something bigger.

'Track the both of them,' I say through gritted teeth. 'I want to know when they eat, piss, and shit.'

Emile nods and tosses the bloodied towel in the waste bin. 'Anything else?'

The veins on my hand bulge as I curl it into a fist.

I told Rory I'd leave her alone.

Told myself many times too.

'You're with me tonight. I've gotta pay someone a visit.'

Guess the only rules I'm good at sticking to are my father's.

CHAPTER
Fifteen

Wren

Everyone has a claim to fame.

My uncle plays golf with a man who cowrote a Led Zeppelin song. A girl I went to school with has a sister with a YouTube channel; she's got over 100,000 subscribers and counting. Matt has a hockey puck signed by Wayne Gretzky.

Mine isn't a cool anecdote, a humble brag I can pepper on small talk at parties. It's a stain that won't wash out, no matter how hard I scrub.

Scrolling through the camera roll on my cell, I select the new photos added to the album titled 'Wren's Good Deeds' and send them to my laptop. There's one of me sweeping up debris in the port, another where I'm pushing my candy cart through the hospital hallways.

I attach them to a passive-aggressive email, along with a local news article about the explosion, and fire it off. Then I close my laptop and flop back on the bed, the weight of that unfinished sentence pinning me to the mattress.

Sometimes, I wonder why I poke the hornet's nest. Because

sending all this evidence to Damien Asshole Cross isn't me righting a wrong, it's just me finding another way to bury it.

Lungs tightening, I roll over and bury my face between the pillows, waiting for the guilt to pass.

It always comes in waves. They ebb and flow and pull me under. Back to the butterflies, the letters, the bar. Back to the house with the flowers and perfectly striped lawn. Back to *her*.

Her cackling laugh plays down my spine, and I burrow my head deeper, my ragged breaths damp against the sheets. I breathe until it hurts, and when I can no longer stand the pain, I drown out and distract.

I flip over and grab for my laptop again. ABBA on. Google open. My search history is made up of a million variations of 'Incidents in Devil's Cove', but I've found nothing that reveals the fate of the creepy phone booth guy. This time, I have every intention of typing 'Dogs meeting puppies for the first time' into the search bar, but my forefinger has other ideas and strikes the letter G instead.

A. B. R. I. E. L. V. I. S. C. O. N. T. I.

My hands hold a tremble as I tap the *Enter* key.

I scroll through the search results. Raphael's and Angelo's Wikipedia pages are at the top, and below, there's an obituary page for a guy in Italy, another for a man in Australia. I keep scrolling and scrolling, but there's nothing about Gabriel Visconti himself.

I click on the 'images' tab because surely, I'll at least find a mugshot. There's no way in civilized society a man like him can go through life without spending some time behind bars. But it's all smiling pictures of Rafe at fundraisers and scowling paparazzi shots of Angelo leaving shiny buildings. It's like the internet has no idea they even have a brother.

I didn't either until our eyes locked across the dance floor at Rory's bachelorette party, and now I wish I was still blissfully ignorant.

With Google letting me down, I grab my cell off the side table, open the Instagram app, and type his name into the search bar.

Nothing.

So how the hell was he looking at my Instagram page?

Something between frustration and fear prickles behind my eyeballs, and a lump the size of a golf ball forms in my throat.

I *loathe* that man. From his buzzcut to his steel-capped boots and everything between. I hate his stare and how it sours when it touches me. Hate his shadow and how it looks on the edges of mine.

I hate he was the one to save me from the creepy man in the phonebooth, hate the lecture that followed. Hate that he tossed me into his trunk like I was destined for a landfill, just to prove that he *could*, and that he showed no remorse or sympathy when he finally let me out, a crying, blubbery mess.

I hate that his cryptic words – *If it happened in the dark, it didn't happen* – echo around my head when it's quiet. Hate that they fascinate me, and that black hole in the center of my soul swells at the sound of it.

Most of all, I hate myself. Because now he's consuming my thoughts. He floods through my veins and fizzes in places he shouldn't.

It feels all too familiar.

Before I can spiral, I stab the volume key on my laptop and turn 'Does Your Mother Know' up to full blast. Then, before I can stop myself, I go back to Google and type in another name.

The Boogeyman.

My heart pounds in my ears as I wait for the Wikipedia page to load. And when my eyes skim over the first sentence, it slows to a stop.

The Boogeyman is a shadowy, amorphous ghost who hides in dark places to frighten unsuspecting victims.

Unease works its way down my back, chilling every knot on my spine.

His power is neutralized by bright light.

I read the page from top to bottom, back to front. Then I go back and click on all the other search results too, working my way through fables, myths, cautionary tales. I stare at every sketch of ominous figures seeping out of dark corners, until I swear, I see green eyes, ink, and scars within their black mass. Until they leap out of the screen and climb my own walls.

When the 'low battery' sign blinks on the corner of the screen, I glance up to the window for a respite and realize that so much time has passed darkness has swallowed the sun.

Blowing out a trembling breath, I reach for the lamp on the bedside table and turn it on.

Nothing happens.

I click it again, and when it still doesn't work, I roll over to try the one on the opposite side.

Nope.

Muttering under my breath, I get up and try the main switch.

A quiet *click* – no light.

A whisper of fear raises the hair on the back of my neck, but I force it aside. The power cut has nothing to do with my Google search history and everything to do with the fact that the wiring in my house is in shambles. The kitchen light only turns on if I punch it, and the other day, I switched on the stove and the shower upstairs started running.

God bless Uncle Finn, but if he did build this house, he built it with a YouTube tutorial, sticky tape, and good intentions alone.

Shuffling into the hallway, I feel my way along the wall and press every light switch my fingers brush over, to no avail.

Dammit. I consider going back upstairs and grabbing my cell to call Finn but decide I'll walk over to his house instead. I've been horizontal for hours; I could use the exercise.

I descend the stairs and awkwardly hop around on the welcome mat, tugging on my rain boots. As I slide into my puffer jacket, a sense of foreboding crawls up my shoulders and squeezes my nape.

No.

Dread moves through me like a slow-moving tide. I fight against its current to lift my gaze to the door, though in my heart, I already know what's behind it.

Who's behind it.

Gabriel's outline is unmistakable. His broad shoulders spill out beyond the perimeters of the glass panel, and his glare burns through the double glazing like a blow torch.

My head swims and my knees buckle. If my arms weren't stitched to my sides, I'd reach up and smack myself on the head, because Christ, what was I thinking opening my big mouth?

It seemed like a good idea in the cold light of day. I'd woken up stewing after the events of the night before, fueled by anger and the burning need for *justice*, and stomped out of my house and over to Rory's.

I'd knocked on her front door with the intent to tell her everything. From the night three years ago, to the breaking and entering after her bachelorette, but the tongue he threatened to cut out wouldn't work. I found myself skipping over the creepy phone booth guy too, mainly so she wouldn't get distracted, or worse, take Gabriel's side. Instead, I focused on the issue at hand. Between sobs, I regaled how he picked me up and plonked me in his trunk. How he stood there, silently, as I kicked and screamed and begged to be let out. How he didn't even hang around once he freed me; he just disappeared into the woods and had his stone-faced colleague frog-march me home in the beam of his headlights.

But more fool me.

Because the Boogeyman has come back to bite me on the ass.

The air throbs with my terror as we stare at each other through the glass for three restless heartbeats.

He rattles the door handle.

Smirks when he realizes it's locked.

My relief is fleeting and doesn't stick, because without breaking eye contact, he slowly lifts an inked hand into view and slides on a leather glove.

Then he curls it into a fist and draws back his arm.

'Wait!' I yell, bolting forward and unlocking the door before he can smash through the window.

The moment the icy wind slithers through the gap, I regret my haste. It must be all over my face too because Gabriel wedges his boot between the door and the frame, stopping me from slamming it shut again.

Well, then. There's nothing left to do but accept defeat. I drag my gaze up to meet his and side-eye him with trepidation. 'What do you want?' I sniff.

Jeez. It's so easy to forget how large he is when I'm not shriveling in his shadow. He's broader and blacker than the night sky behind him, and though he's part monster, I realize he does an excellent job masquerading as all *man*, and in its rawest, most primal form. It's in his stillness, his strength, his stance. I know his blood runs as hot as his temper, because even with two feet of space between us, I can feel his warmth.

Tonight, he's carved from stone and clad in leather biking gear. When he lazily reaches up to rest his forearm on the top of the doorframe, leather chafes leather, and annoyingly, something primal stirs within me too.

He looks down at me with a steady gaze. 'You ever heard the expression, "Snitches get stitches"?'

A tremor runs through my bottom lip. 'If you don't leave, I'm calling the police.'

Amusement flickers over his features, as though I'm a petulant toddler who's announced they're running away from home.

'Hit me.'

I stare at him, confused at the sudden change of conversation.

Jaw twitching with impatience, he nudges the door all the way open with his foot and fills the frame.

My eyes narrow. 'I'd need to hit you with a frying pan to make us anywhere close to even.'

'Don't think that'd fit in your little purse.' Resentment darkens his gaze. 'Do it.'

The rough edge in his voice controls me like a puppet. It lifts my arm and curls my fist, and I land an uncertain blow on the center of his chest.

When he doesn't even flinch, my cheeks grow hot, and when disdain curls his top lip, they burn.

'Scared you'll break a nail?'

Well, yes, actually, but I'd never give him the satisfaction of telling him that. 'No, I just don't want to break your nose or anything,' I huff back.

A gruff laugh escapes his lips in a curl of frost. 'You couldn't break wind.' He steps backward onto the porch and jerks his chin. 'Come here.'

My hand curls around the edge of the door, and every square inch of my brain screams at me to slam it shut, slide the deadbolt, and get a head start in the game of hide and seek that'd inevitably follow. But my body has other ideas. I'm too nosy, too foolish. I'm a little drunk on the idea of dancing with the Devil too.

And so, with a shaky breath, I step out into the night, following Gabriel's retreat.

'Your first mistake was letting me get so close to you.' His heat shifts around my body as he circles me like a lion sizing up his prey. 'You ever heard of fight or flight'?'

I'm viciously aware of the decking groaning under every footstep. 'Yes?'

He comes to a stop behind me, the tingle of his presence making my back itch. 'You have neither.'

Pursing my lips, I spin around to protest, but only a small breath escapes them when my shoulder grazes his stomach. My coat swishes over leather and the hardness beneath it, and both the feeling and sound are dizzying.

Proving him wrong, I choose flight and take a step back. Then I meet his eyes before my own can wander south to the stomach I came into contact with.

He pins me with a glare. 'Since your punches are pathetic and you insist on letting men get this close to you, you'll want to use your elbows.' Lifting his arm, he connects his own elbow to his palm with a *thawp* so sharp it makes me flinch. 'It's more effective for shorter range and has a higher force-to-surface ratio.'

I frown. 'And in English?'

His jaw tics. 'It'll hurt them more, and you won't break a nail.'

'Well, why didn't you say so?'

Letting my sarcasm slide, he continues. 'Strike in a downward motion and aim for the weak spots. Face, throat, ribs.' I follow his finger as he points to them on his own body. 'And if all else fails, you kick them in the balls.'

Instinctively, I look down at his crotch. Though, I realize my error in less than a heartbeat and quickly glance away, sensing Gabriel stiffen.

'Not *my* balls,' he warns.

Heat floods my face. It touches more-private places too, because now I'm thinking about *his* private places and wondering what they look like under all that leather.

I bet his penis is huge. Like the ones in porn. I wonder if it's tattooed like the rest of him, or even *pierced*, because he seems like the type.

'Got it,' I mutter, raking through my bangs as if it'll brush away the sordid musings going on beneath it.

'Good.' He rolls his shoulders and cracks his neck, then beckons me forward with a gloved hand. 'Hit me.'

His demand drags my mind up out of the gutter and sets me on edge. I regard his blank expression with caution, unable to read it. 'Are you going to hit me back?'

He drags his front teeth over his bottom lip, eyes sparking with something menacing. 'Not to begin with.'

Well, that doesn't sound promising, but knowing this man isn't in the business of asking twice, I reluctantly bend my arm and strike down on his torso. Nylon glides over leather with a frictionless *swish*, and I stumble forward.

Gabriel steadies me with a bitter hiss. His grip is impatient, and it lingers, soaking through my sleeve and into my skin. 'We'll work on that,' he states. But I can barely hear him. Can barely register my embarrassment because he's still holding me. Black-clad fingers sinking into pink fabric, so thick and long I'm sure if I were to turn my arm over, the tips of them would meet his thumb.

I'm still staring with morbid fascination when the tendons in his wrist flex. He suddenly yanks me toward him, ducks, and drives his shoulder into my stomach. The force lifts me up and over his body until I'm looking down the length of his back.

A puff of shock escapes me, though I don't know why I'm surprised; I've been over this man's shoulder so many times I should be used to the view by now.

Then he starts walking. The deck turns into steps which lead into the garden path, and the sight of my front door slipping away from me makes me heavy with dread.

'Where are we going?'

'You ask every man who kidnaps you that question?'

'If I ever get kidnapped, I'll let you know,' I bite back, thumping my fist on his back in frustration.

'Won't be long, I'm sure,' he mutters.

He takes a few more strides, then with a rough tug on the bottom of my jacket, he finally yanks me back down to *terra firma*.

The world is spinning, but his simmering glare remains in focus. 'Your second mistake was letting me pick you up. Once your feet leave the ground, your chances of survival drop to thirty-three percent.'

My back hitches in suspicion. Kidnapped. Survival. All these buzzwords reach down and pull my heart into my mouth, and I don't like the way it tastes.

What's his game plan here, anyway, rocking up to my house after dark and giving me all these tips and tricks? It's not because he feels guilty for shoving me in his trunk, that's for sure. I don't have to climb into his skull to know this man is incapable of feeling anything but anger, irritation, or simply nothing at all.

I study the hard set of his lips and search his eyes for clues too, but of course, his gaze in impenetrable, galvanized by the wall of disdain that, I swear, is built brick by brick with his hatred for me. The girl who saved his life.

My eyes narrow. 'Did you have nothing better to do tonight than pay me a visit? You know, like puppies to slaughter, old ladies to terrorize?'

I regret my quip the moment it leaves my mouth. It tightens the lines of his shoulders and hardens his jaw. Makes him take a step toward me too and fills the gap between us with the threat of danger. 'You think this is a joke?' he asks in a quiet rasp. 'You think your safety is a joke?'

My confidence dissolves into my blood stream, and I frantically shake my head. Though I stop short of saying *sorry* because if he can't say it, why should I?

A friction-filled beat passes. Then he lets out a puff of air through his nostrils and retreats.

He jerks his chin over my shoulder. 'Get in.'

I glance around, squint into the darkness, and freeze.

There's a motorbike parked by the gate but also a car next to it. Trunk open, headlights off. It's a scene all too familiar, and I know all too well what comes next.

Terror whips through me, nearly knocking me off my feet. Curse me and my big fat mouth; I should have known there was no way the Boogeyman would let my snitching slide.

He's carried me halfway to hell, and now he expects me to walk the rest of the way.

Panic seizing my lungs, my gaze darts from left to right, looking for an escape route. Between the trees is his domain, and there's no way I'm fast enough to spin around and run past him to get to Uncle Finn's house. Even if I was, all his lights are off. Maybe he's had his power cut too, though it's far more likely he's at the country club guffawing over a glass of expensive wine.

Welp. My brain is too mushy to come up with anything else.

Running it is.

Twisting on the heel of my boot, I manage a step and half before a hand grabs my wrist and turns me around.

'Stop.'

'Let me *go* –'

His grip flies from my wrist to my face.

I freeze.

Butter-soft leather, all the evil in the world etched into the four fingers and thumb beneath it. He could crack my jaw with the slightest squeeze; snap my neck with the flick of his wrist. And suddenly, I get it: the age-old appeal of bad boys. Just being *touched* by a man like him has me breathless and out of sorts. It feels like I'm riding a motorbike in the rain with no helmet, the roar of the wind louder than the threat of danger.

He lifts my chin and lowers his, and when his gaze touches mine, my heart does a double beat.

'You think I'd hurt you?'

Well, duh. Does the pope go to church every Sunday?

I let out a disbelieving laugh, but it wilts in my throat when his gaze drops to my lips and flickers with a different strain of annoyance. It's softer, with no sharp edges. I don't know why it twists my insides or why I have the sudden urge to reassure him I don't.

He swallows and releases me. Walks toward the car, and pathetically, I follow.

'It's highly likely that your annoying screaming and your pathetic elbow striking would scare a kidnapper off,' he mutters. 'But if it doesn't, here's what you're going to do.'

He grips the lid of the trunk with one hand and reaches out for me with the other.

The weight of unease slows my steps as I move toward him. I take a deep breath and slip my hand into his. As he pulls me closer, panic flashes through me like a lightning bolt, and I curl my fingers around his palm. 'You promise?' I blurt out, growing weak. 'You really promise you won't hurt me? Because I swear if you do, I'll never talk to you again.'

A dry amusement sweeps over his gaze. 'You trying to convince me or deter me?'

Before I can answer, he walks around to the driver's door and dips his head to talk to someone through the window. My ears prick up; obviously, he must have ridden here on his bike, but I hadn't given thought to the fact someone else must have driven the car. Even when I strain my eyes, I can't see who it is.

He comes back just seconds later, holding a set of keys. 'Here,' he says, tossing them at me. 'Hold onto them.'

I look down at the silver in my palm. Not entirely convinced it isn't a trick, I click the fob and the rear lights flash twice.

'Happy?'

'No.' I zip the keys into my coat pocket anyway.

'Good. If you're being kidnapped, you're not meant to be happy.' He raps the trunk lid with his fist. 'Now, hurry up. I've got puppies to slaughter.'

Sighing, I take a step toward him, and despite every fiber of my being screaming in protest, I clamber inside.

'Lay down.'

I'd rather cut my own bangs than lie down in this trunk, but alas, I've already walked through the gates of hell, I might as well make myself comfy.

Shifting sideways, I bend my knees and lower onto the bed, then drop my head with a self-soothing puff. I feel sick, and the musty carpet smell entwined with the faint kick of fuel isn't helping.

The car groans under Gabriel's weight as he drops to his haunches and sits on the rear bumper.

'Good girl.'

What?

I thrive off being called good, but the words are unexpected coming from Gabriel Visconti; my body's reaction even more so. My breath shallows, and the lightest lick of heat sizzles in my core. I've always been a people-pleaser, though his praise feels more pleasing than it should.

'I'm going to shut the lid now, okay?'

If I weren't so distracted by his approval tap dancing on my skin, perhaps I'd have protested, but he's reshuffled my priorities, so all I can do is nod.

The night's sky slides behind a veil of black, and the darkness becomes even darker.

An ominous *click* steals the breath straight from my lungs. Terror lights like a match in my stomach, my nervous system the wick. It tears through my veins, the fire burning me from the inside out.

Gasping, I slam my palms against the lid on instinct, driving my knees upward and bucking my hips.

'I don't like it, let me out!'

'You're going to let yourself out,' he states. 'Most cars have a safety release latch. Take your right hand and feel along the lining.'

In a blind panic, I do as he tells me, skimming my fingertips along the edge of the cage. 'There isn't one!'

'In the middle of the front wall.'

My hand snags on something plastic and protruding. I pull it, and now the *click* is one of dizzying relief.

I kick upward with all my strength until the gap between the lid and the bumper widens. Cold air whooshes in, and I inhale it in large, desperate gulps.

'Oh my God, I'm dying.'

'You're not.'

'I am. Can't breathe.' I sit upright and glance up at him. He's standing a foot away, arms crossed, observing me with a look of indifference.

When my breathing slows, he crouches down and lazily rests his arms on the bumper. 'All new cars have release catches. If they don't' – he reaches inside the trunk and pushes out the left rear light – 'these pop out. Shove your hand through and wave like crazy.'

'And if that doesn't work?'

He shrugs. 'Then you're fucked.'

'Great,' I mutter, unzipping my jacket to let some air circulate around me. 'I'm going to be sick.'

'Not in my car, you won't.'

Yeah, well, he'd deserve it. Though I'm not stupid enough to say that while I'm still cross-legged in his trunk, an arm's reach away from being trapped within it again.

Instead, when he rises and steps aside, I clamber awkwardly out of the vehicle. My boots touch solid grass, and the impact rolls a thrill through me. It's the adrenaline-fueled type you get after staring your fears in the face and realizing they've blinked first.

I look up at the dark house and exhale into the night. I'd almost forgotten about the power outage. I almost forget Gabriel's behind me too until he slams the trunk shut and his voice touches my nape with a rough edge.

'Why don't you drive?'

My lids flutter shut. His question's a hard puff of air to my high.

I curl my hands into my fists at my sides and stare up at my bedroom window. 'Never learned.'

I'm not a liar, I'm a pretender. There's a difference. His frigid silence drifts up my back, and the heat of his gaze chases after it. Swallowing, I turn around to gauge how believable I sounded.

He's leaning against the trunk, one foot crossed over the other. His expression is invasive and gives nothing away. I turn around and lean against the car too, because standing beside him suddenly feels less scary than being in his line of sight.

I was wrong. Because at least I couldn't feel his heat crackling down the right side of my body when I was in front of him. Couldn't feel his arm brush over mine as he slides a cigarette between his lips.

He strikes a match. The sharp *hiss* sizzles through my blood, and I strain my eyes sideways to stare at him as he shields the flame from the wind with a cupped hand.

He blows a tendril of smoke into the night.

Then he extends the cigarette pack to me.

I glance down at it, then up to him. He's still staring straight ahead. I've never smoked a day in my life, though for a second, I'm half tempted. Partly because it'd give me something to do instead of fidget, and partly because there's something dangerously thrilling about sharing a smoke with the Boogeyman.

I shake my head.

'You don't drink, you don't smoke,' he murmurs, snuffing out the match with a snap of his wrist. 'What does the Good Samaritan do for fun?'

It's too dark to tell if he's genuinely curious or if he's trying to belittle me. When I don't answer, a small noise of amusement follows his next exhale and confirms the latter. I watch it dissipate into the dark, my shoulders hitching in defense.

Raking my fingers through my ponytail, I force myself to look up at him.

'They call you the Boogeyman, you know?'

'Good.'

'But you don't scare me.'

It's the blackest of lies told in the most transparent of tones. If he took a half step to the left, my stomach would lurch into my throat.

He studies the stars through another puff of smoke, the corners of his lips lifting. 'And yet, you haven't stuck your tongue out at me since.'

'And yet, here I am, standing in the dark alone with you again.'

At the word *again*, he stills, the cigarette an inch from his mouth. I realize, with a pounding pulse, that I've reached out and touched the taboo. Alluded to the night we've barely spoken of. But now that it's out there, I want to squeeze it, rip it open, and lay its entrails on the grass before us.

Perhaps I'm still riding the high of escaping his trunk, so I press on.

'You never told anyone about that night.'

His eyes are still fixated on the sky, but I'm close enough to see a muscle flex beneath his beard. He flicks the butt on the grass, then runs a hand over his mouth.

'Neither did you.'

My chest concaves with the weight of my next breath.

Of course I didn't. I couldn't. Uncle Finn was still furious with me, and I couldn't go to him with yet another drama, and certainly not so soon after the first.

Silence brews between us, and it's louder than the relentless howl of the wind. I'm fascinated by how Gabriel seems to melt into it, as still as a statue. Unaware of the restlessness in my legs or how hard my heart is beating.

The conversation has died; I know it's time to go, but I also know I don't want to. Standing here, side by side with a man like him in the dark is making my blood hum with excitement. I feel like I'm doing something I shouldn't, like I'm a teenager who's shimmied down the drainpipe in the middle of the night to meet a boy too old and too wrong for her.

I run my palms over my puffer, for once at a loss of what to say. Sure, I have a million questions I want to ask – like how he got that scar and why the cold never bothers him. Why he's here at all. Instead, I glance up at dark house again, and something clicks.

'You're behind the power outage.'

'Tell me why.'

I pause. Then the realization sprouts and *sparks*, lighting up my core. It's the same reason he never told anyone about that night.

'If it happens in the dark, it didn't happen,' I whisper, a tremble in my tone.

The words feel sordid coming from my mouth. Exhilarating. The feeling heightens when Gabriel slowly turns his head and his eyes warm my lips again, as though he likes what came out of them.

'Smart girl,' he murmurs.

Christ.

My pulse is pounding. Other parts of me too. Because Gabriel Visconti wants to keep this a secret. This. *Us*. Here, alone, under the stars. I'd think I were hallucinating if my body wasn't having such a visceral reaction to him staring at me.

I look up at him through my lashes, wrestling with every breath.

'Why'd you teach me how to get out of a trunk?'

'Because you piss me off,' he bites back, too quickly. He swipes the back of his hand over his mouth, as though trying to erase the remark that just shot out of it, and rolls his shoulders back, recalibrating. 'You're too close to my family for comfort. If someone wants to get to Rory, they'd go through you. You need to learn how to defend yourself from these things.'

Oh, right. He's responsible for his family's security, so of course having to rescue Rory's best friend from a creepy guy in a phone booth would get his back up. Him being here in the middle of the night isn't anything strange or secretive in his book, he's just doing his job.

A brick of disappointment wedges itself between my ribs, though I don't know why.

Before I can pick it apart, he shoves a gloved hand out between us. 'Keys.'

With a small tremble, I unzip my pocket and hand them over. He curls them into a tight fist and nods. 'Consider lesson one complete.'

My heart leaps an inch. 'There's going to be another lesson?'

He glances toward the house. 'Your mains switch is outside in the white box on the porch. Just flick it.'

'I know how to do it,' I huff. *Lie.*

Seems like I can't stop telling them around this man.

He smirks like he knows it too, then turns on his heel and stalks over to his motorcycle.

'Wait. When's lesson two?'

The wheels hiss under Gabriel's weight as he throws his leg over the seat. He tugs on his helmet and checks his mirrors.

Then his gaze slowly crawls back to mine, as though answering me is an afterthought.

'When you least expect it.'

He slams down his visor so suddenly that the sound makes me flinch. With a sharp rip on the throttle, the bike's engine roars to life. The vibration rumbles across the grass, surges through the soles of my boots, and trembles every nerve, cell, and bone in my body.

And I'm still trembling, long after the dark swallows his tail lights.

CHAPTER
Sixteen

Wren

The smell of sunscreen and coconuts bake under the heat of the sun. Gentle waves lap the shoreline in a rhythmic lull, and overhead, birds glide across the azure sky. I set my cocktail aside, settling on my pool floatie, and let out a blissful sigh.

Ah, this is the life.

'This is fucking ridiculous.' From behind my heart-shaped sunglasses, I pop an eyelid in time to see Tayce reach for my cell. She stabs *pause* on my 'Relaxing Beach Sounds' playlist and tosses the device onto my bare stomach. 'And it's hotter than hell in here.'

'Then you must feel right at home, honey.' I roll onto my front and turn the playlist back on, turning up the volume to full blast to drown out the sound of the rain beating down on the window. 'Just relax. Close your eyes and imagine you're on a beach in Fiji.'

Her air mattress lets out a loud squeak as she flops back on it. 'I need a *real* vacation.'

'You got back from a real vacation less than twelve hours ago,' Rory tuts, adjusting the side tie on her bikini bottoms. 'I, for one, am having a great time.' She plucks the cocktail umbrella from her piña colada and tucks it behind her ear. 'Who needs a honeymoon when you have friends like you two, hey?'

I beam up at her despite the sadness pressing on my chest.

Rory should be on a real beach, with her new husband. Instead, she's with us, in her guest bedroom, lying on a pool floatie in front of an industrial-strength heater I borrowed from the bar.

As for Angelo, he's down the hall. Every so often, I hear the office door open, and my ears prick up at the sound of hushed Italian words and feet treading floorboards. Then it closes and an unwarranted disappointment rolls through me. Because no voice is deep enough, no footstep dense enough, to soothe this itch beneath my skin.

Gabriel's secret visit left me restless, and I fear it won't go away. It's of the clock-watching, sheet-tangling, appetitestealing variety.

A cocktail that's lethal when mixed into my bloodstream.

I flip back onto my back, unable to get comfortable.

It's nothing in the grand scheme of things, of course, and it's definitely not the same.

It's a phase, like when I went brunette for a week, or the time I got my nose pierced and lost the stud the second I sneezed.

It'll soon drift past, like a cloud on a breezy afternoon. Then one day, I'll look back and laugh at the time I thought I had a crush on Gabriel Visconti.

Jeez. It's a reach to even call it a crush. He's just a man, and I'm just a girl who has never been touched by one. Hell, even *Matt* could have gripped my jaw like that or called me a *good girl*, and my body would have gotten all confused.

Sighing, I shuffle onto my side and pick at a loose thread on my towel.

Lying's bad. Lying to yourself is even worse.

No, but it's really not a crush. I'm not capable of crushes. The more I stew on it, the more I realize it's not actually *him* I'm drawn to but the anticipation he brings with him. I never know where he will be or what he will do next. One day, he's folding me into his trunk, and the next, he's teaching me how to get out of it. 'Lesson one' came out of nowhere, and 'lesson two' will apparently come when I least expect it.

Despite baking under the heat lamp, a cold thrill skates over the curve of my waist.

I won't lie to myself twice: I'm looking forward to it.

A sigh leaves my lips, too loud and wistful. I glance up at the girls to make sure they didn't notice, but Rory's still engrossed in her book, and Tayce is too busy contorting her body to take selfies of her ass.

As I reach for the fruit platter, there's movement in the hall. My heart swells, then deflates when muffled laughter seeps under the door.

Definitely not Gabriel.

While I nibble on a strawberry, my gaze drifts back to Rory. 'How's Angelo holding up?'

Her brow dents over the top of her book. 'He's . . . busy. And stressed. I haven't seen him much, to be honest.'

'I bet. Are they any closer to figuring out who was behind the explosion?'

'Uh-huh. It was a rival shipping company farther south.'

I frown. 'Really?' Now I'm even more surprised it hasn't been picked up by national news. 'What company was it?'

'Oh, none that you'd know,' she says, reading intently.

I reach for my phone. 'Yeah, but I can Google it.'

'Actually, I can't remember the name myself now.' She flicks the page. 'Something beginning with s or a b.'

'I think it was a y,' Tayce drawls, pulling the sides of her thong bikini even higher over her hips and snapping another photo.

I open my mouth with the intent to interrogate further but close it again because I'm steering off track.

'Well, anyway. Angelo seems to be working around the clock, and I'm sure he'll have the port back up and running as soon as possible, what, with all these late-night meetings.' I make a show of looking at my watch before realizing I'm not wearing one. 'Who's he in a meeting with at this time, anyway?'

'Oh, you know,' Rory says, fluttering a dismissive hand toward the door. 'The usual suspects.'

'Uh-huh. Like who?'

'Like Rafe.'

'Of course.' I pick up another strawberry. 'Who else?'

'Cas. Nico's here too, I think.'

'Cool.' I pause. 'And?'

'Maybe Benny?'

'Is that it?'

Rory slowly lowers her book and narrows her eyes at me. 'Is there someone in particular you're looking for, Wren?'

Crap. I guess that wasn't as subtle as I'd hoped.

The shells of my ears grow hot, and my brain can't think of a casual reply quick enough. Before I can blurt out a sniffy comment about just making conversation, Rory sighs.

'Oh, Goose. You're worried about Gabe, aren't you?' She shuts her book, expression softening to something more sympathetic. 'I made him promise he won't go near you again.' She studies me. 'He *hasn't* come near you again, right?'

My nerves hum like a live wire, short-circuiting when they reach my brain.

I barely pause. My breath comes out steady, wrapped around a two-letter lie that has no business leaving my lips so easily. I don't even blink. I don't even feel a twinge of guilt about lying to my best friend. My body is too distracted by the thrill of sharing a secret under the cloak of darkness with the Boogeyman, even if it was just a routine night at work for him.

It happened in the dark.

It didn't happen.

'I'm bored,' Tayce announces. 'Let's watch a movie.' She grabs the controller off the floor and points it at the television. 'Sorry, Wren. I'm vetoing *Mama Mia!* We've watched it twice already this month.'

Heart still thumping, I settle back on the floatie and stare at the screen while she navigates through movie trailers. Tayce wants to watch a low-budget horror, but Rory wants to watch a Christmas movie, so they compromise with The Nightmare Before Christmas.

Halfway through a musical number, Rory starts snoring and Tayce stops complaining, which means she must have fallen asleep too.

I can't sleep though. The restlessness won't let me. My eyes are on the movie, but my ears are on the bedroom door, straining for any hint of slow, heavy footsteps or the deep timbre of a rough command. The mere thought he could be under the same roof as me right now has me on a knife's edge.

Frustration and curiosity are a dangerous combination, and I eventually give in to it. I just need to know. Grabbing my cell, I slowly rise to my feet, slide on a robe and slippers, and creep out into the hall.

Abstract shadows pass through the glow spilling out from beneath Angelo's office door. The possibility that Gabriel is somewhere behind it slows my movement. I imagine he's darkening a corner, his mere presence spilling out of the shadows and charging the particles in the room. I bet he barely speaks, but when he does, the room falls silent, and everyone turns to listen.

I keep walking before I do something stupid, like knock and find out.

As I reach the top of the stairs, I freeze at the sight of a figure climbing them. It's tall and broad but far too smooth around the edges, and when a glint of gold winks beneath the moonbeam coming through the entryway window, my heartbeat resumes its regular pace.

'Ah, it's the lovely Wren.' Rafe's warm voice rises toward me. He retreats to the bottom step and stands aside. 'After you. It's bad luck to cross on the stairs.'

He watches me descend, amusement curving his mouth at the sight of my robe. 'Sleepover?'

'Kind of. We're on a make-believe honeymoon in Fiji.'

'Ah,' he says, glancing at the sheet of rain on the other side of the window. 'I trust you've remembered your sunscreen?'

'Of course. I don't want to look fifty when I'm forty.'

His laugh is sheer silk. 'I've no doubt you'll be the most glamorous fifty-year-old on the beach.'

I beam up at him. 'Oh, and congratulations on the new casino, by the way. I can't believe it's on a yacht!'

He dips his head in acknowledgment. 'Thank you. Stop by anytime, we have the freshest lemonade on the Pacific,' he says, green eyes twinkling.

We bid each other good night, but when he's halfway up the stairs, I remember something else.

'Hey, Rafe. I heard Penny is working for you, right?'

His shoulders form a tight line. After a beat, he slowly turns his head. 'Who?'

'Penelope Price. You know, around my age, pretty short, red hair –'

'I've no idea who you're talking about.'

I blink at the sharpness of his tone.

'Um, I guess you hire hundreds of girls, so . . .' I shift my weight from one foot to the other. 'Well, anyway. If you happen to see her, please tell her –'

My mouth falls slack when he takes the steps two at a time and disappears around a corner, then a door slams shut.

'To stop by The Rusty Anchor for our girls night,' I mutter to myself.

Weird.

I brush it off and continue exploring the house in an aimless drift. I pass locked doors, descend more stairs, and marvel at how Rory navigates this place without a map.

As I move from room to room, flinching at every shadowy corner and feeling mildly disappointed when it's empty, I realize I need to get on the other side of the office door.

I know – I'll make brownies. Everyone answers the door for brownies.

Pumped by my bright idea, I find myself under the bright lights of the kitchen. I poke around in the four-door fridge and peer inside cupboards. I get distracted by the fancy coffee maker sitting on the center island and pull my cell from my robe pocket to Google the price of it.

As I gawp at the five-figure price tag, a notification pops up at the top of the screen. Absentmindedly, I click on it.

Dear User 3569,

Your edit has been rejected.

The kitchen spins in a blur of chrome and marble. My blood heats, and my heart pumps it around my body so fast it *whooshes* in my ears.

The midnight email is always bad, but it's worse on the nights I'm not watching the clock. The nights when it hits me sideways instead of head-on, where I can at least see it coming and brace myself for the impact.

I fear she was right.

She always was, and maybe good deeds and a big heart won't change it. Law school probably won't either. Those five words, twenty-nine characters including spaces, are stitched together with an iron thread, forming a sentence as long as hers. The full stop at the end of it is etched into my DNA, and each midnight email only deepens the scar.

I loosen the tie around my robe and press my palms against the countertop, but it does nothing to cool me down. I need cold air, need to feel the rain sizzle on my skin.

I need to breathe.

A rush of panic drives me to the glass door leading to the garden, but it's locked. So is the one in the living room and the dining hall. I rattle doorknobs and handles along the length of the house with increasing frustration.

Finally, I find one at the back of a laundry room and burst through it.

The rain is louder out here, but it doesn't fall. The air is colder, but there's no bite to it.

Disorientated, I blink, trying to clear the tears blurring my vision. There're stacks of boxes, and tools hanging from a pegboard. The smell of gasoline and burned plastic rise from the damp concrete floor, then I realize I'm in the garage.

And so is Gabriel.

CHAPTER
Seventeen

Wren

Only his head is visible above the propped-up hood of a car, though the lone, naked light bulb hanging from the tin roof spreads his shadow along the breadth of the brickwork behind him. His gaze clashes with mine for a single heart palpitation before narrowing on my mouth.

Probably because of the sob that escaped it.

An awful scraping sound bounces off the walls, and a metal chair skids along the length of the car, stopping by the back tire.

'Sit.'

He ducks back out of view.

Nausea roils through me, my chest tightening with every ragged breath. I should go back out the way I came, but I won't make it that far. It's either faint, vomit, or sit, and the latter seems like the least embarrassing option, so I stagger over and sink down into the chair.

The cold metal burns the backs of my thighs. The sight of my slippers pulsating in and out of focus makes me feel even more nauseous, so I squeeze my eyes shut and silently beg the world to stop spinning.

It doesn't and it's relentlessly loud. The rain pounds down on the roof, and the wind rattles the roll-down door, desperate to be let in.

A voice slices through the chaos, as smooth as butter dripped in sin. 'Hector Fisher owns a cabin on the lake.'

What? Mild annoyance grates my skin. I couldn't care less about the Mayor of Devil's Dip's property portfolio, especially at a time like this. Like, *hello*, I'm dying over here.

'On the last Friday of every month, he kisses his wife and kids goodbye and spends the weekend down at the cabin.' The clanking of metal fills his pause. 'Ask me why.'

I shake my head, choking on my next breath.

'Ask me why,' he repeats, his tone tightening.

'W-why?' I grit.

'To meet escorts.'

My ears prick up, an eye pops open, and my curiosity has me looking over to the shadow shifting along the wall. 'H-he's cheating on his wife?'

'Mm. With men.' An inked hand reaches out from beneath the hood and curls around a wrench on the roller cart beside it. 'He pays them to dress up in his wife's underwear, and then he fucks them.'

A cool breath fills my lungs, and I exhale it in slow disbelief. 'Does she know?'

'Of course not.'

Wow. Hiccupping, I drag my sleeve under my nose and sit back on the chair. The midnight email has loosened its chokehold now that I have fresh gossip to feast on.

Mayor Fisher – who would've thought. He's such a charming family man. I always see him walking along Main Street hand in hand with his beautiful wife.

I guess even the nicest people have secrets.

I ponder why Gabriel's even telling me this, but then he

steps out from behind the car hood and suddenly, it doesn't even matter.

The sight of him wipes my brain clean of thought. Muscle upon muscle carved into a never-ending mass and shrink-wrapped in ink.

Had I known he was behind the unlocked door, I'd have hesitated before crashing through it. Had I known he was also *shirtless*, I'd have run in the opposite direction.

It's rude to stare, especially so brazenly, but *jeez*, what else is a girl to do?

My gaze slides down his chest. To the angel wings spread across his sternum, and the lone square-inch of bare skin between them. Then it slides down his torso, snagging on every symbol, scar, and ab before settling on the taut skin between a prominent V. Heat rises to the surface of my skin and blooms into a fluster.

With a hard swallow, I find just enough sense not to let my gaze drift below the low-slung waistband of his joggers and force my eyes back up to his face. For once, it's the safer place to look.

Gabriel's looking at me too. Though without the slacked jaw and bulging cartoon eyes, of course.

Wiping his hands on a rag, he regards me with indifference, as if I'm just another inanimate object taking up space in his garage.

'You good?'

I'm far from good. My blood is humming at a different frequency around all this skin, but if he's talking about the panic attack, then sure, that's a distant memory now.

I consider nodding and rising to my feet, but then that would mean leaving, which every cell in my body doesn't want to do.

I guess men his size have a stronger gravitational pull than everyone else.

So I let out a weary sigh, press the back of my palm to my

forehead, and puff out my bottom lip. 'I think I'm having another funny turn. I better stay here until it passes.'

Gabriel's mouth pulls taut, as if he finds my distress positively irritating, but then he gives a curt nod and disappears beneath the car hood again.

Running my hands down my thighs, I sit with a straight spine, all too aware of every clink and clunk disturbing the relentless hammer of rain. Though I can't see him, his looming silhouette on the back wall is a constant reminder of his presence. It shortens when he dips his head and expands when he reaches for another tool. Everything shifts and flickers, except for the broad outline of his shoulders, which stays perfectly still.

Time doesn't pass easily. I cross my legs. Uncross them again. Tie my hair up; let it back down and rake my fingers through the kinks. I want to poke him in the ribs, like he's a lion at the zoo. *Come on, do something.*

When a restless shudder gets the best of me, I curl my robe tie around my fist and squeeze it for moral support.

'What cha' doin?'

His reply is dryer than the Sahara. 'What's it look like?'

Sucking in my cheeks, I scan the length of the car. It looks old, but in a rare and collectible way, not a passed-down-from-your-grandma-and-will-probably-leave-you-stranded-on-the-freeway type of way.

'Cute car. Is it yours?'

The silence that follows makes my bones cringe. In an attempt to shake it off, I rise to my feet and pad over to the other side of the garage. Investigating the contents of a toolbox, I try again. 'How'd you find out about Mayor Fisher?'

'I'm nosy.'

Well, that's one thing we have in common, at least.

Gnawing on my bottom lip, I slowly walk the perimeter of the wall, brushing my fingers over the row of different-sized screwdrivers hanging from it. As I near the front of the car, Gabriel's bicep comes into view. Then his forearm, then his hand resting on the engine block.

When I take another step, it curls into a fist, and the shadow behind him stills.

My nerve endings tingle. I reach for the closest thing to busy myself with: a cardboard box wonkily stacked upon a handful of other boxes. I lift the flap and rise onto my tiptoes to peer inside. I couldn't say what's in it because the heat of Gabriel's stare climbing the backs of my thighs makes my vision dim.

'You touch everything that doesn't belong to you?'

My breathing shallows. 'I like touching things,' I mutter.

The last syllable tastes like regret and heats my cheeks. That somehow sounded . . . *sexual*, and I swear, I feel the air grow thicker behind me.

The sound of metal scrapes down my back, and an answer laced with bitterness chases it. 'I've noticed.'

What's that supposed to mean?

I turn around, making the mistake of not bracing myself for the view.

Gabriel's profile is razor sharp and just as lethal. Corded muscles flex and contract; his tattoos dance beneath the light. His bicep must be as thick as my waist, and I can't help but stare at the bulging vein running down the side of it when he tightens something with a wrench.

I clear my throat. In response, Gabriel readjusts the AirPod in his ear, seemingly irritated, before reaching deeper into the hood.

I hover for a moment. No small talk in my locker, not a cohesive thought in my brain. I settle for turning around and looking in the box again, but my hand holds a tremor, and when I tug back the flap, it topples sideways and crashes to the floor.

It's only cable ties. They're made from light plastic, so the deafening clap of metal makes little sense.

No sooner does a breathy 'Oops' leave my lips do large hands grip my waist and drag me backward. A low growl grazes the sensitive spot behind my ear.

'*Stop. Touching. Things.*'

The garage spins in a yellow haze. I fight against the wall of black closing in on me. I'm all elbows and ragged breaths – stuttering heartbeats and heat. I move to strike his ribs like he taught me, but he catches my wrist, then grabs the other as it flies past his face.

With a viselike grip, he holds them above my head in one hand, pulling me so taut a burning sensation spreads between my shoulder blades.

'Get *off* me,' I squeal, my heels rising and the toes of my slippers scraping against the concrete.

In response, his free hand curls around the knot of my robe tie, and he yanks me closer. My chest collides with his bare torso, and the impact ignites something *ungodly* within me. I'm spinning, spiraling, so focused on the pressure of Gabriel's knuckles digging into my stomach that I can't think straight.

He flexes his grip on the knot and flashes me a look of molten resentment.

Then he pulls.

'No –'

It's too late. The tie slides out from my belt loops with a friction-filled sweep, and my robe falls open.

A breath of shock leaves my lips, and I jerk my head back, watching helplessly as Gabriel ties my wrists to a looped chain hanging from the ceiling with my own belt. His jaw clenches from the force he uses to give the knot a final tug.

Taking a step back, he folds his arms across his stomach and glares at me. 'Lesson two: free yourself.'

The rain thrashes on the roof, my heart beats on my ribs, and the two sounds become indistinguishable from one another. But

Gabriel, he's deadly silent. His expression is pulled taut, but his eyes are all flames and no mercy.

It's only a matter of time before I feel their heat on my skin.

Because it's only a matter of time before he realizes I'm not decent.

The air crackles with anticipation; my pulse thrums in my ears. Eventually, his shoulders tighten, his eyes narrow, and bitter regret slithers through them.

He flicks a look of self-loathing to the roof beams. The angel wings on his chest expand and contract, then he carves a reluctant path down the opening of my robe.

Every square inch of my flesh catches fire under his scrutiny, my flimsy bikini doing nothing to protect me from the flames. They burn through the wall of my stomach, sizzle beneath my top, tightening my nipples and heating my breasts.

The side door flies open.

'Boss –'

Gabriel doesn't look up from my chest. He reaches behind him, a slither of silver catches the light, and two *pops* ring out in quick succession.

There's a thud to my right, the sound of shattering glass to my left, and in the middle, a blood-curling scream rips straight from my mouth.

I squeeze my eyes shut and yank at the ties so hard my wrists burn. When I open them again, I'm staring into a black void.

A frigid chill coils around me.

Gabriel shot the lights out.

At the sound of slow-moving footsteps, the ice spreads to my chest, then my pulse begins to thaw when the heat of his body brushes over my bare stomach.

I let out a slow, trembling breath. 'Did you kill him?'

'Would you snitch if I did?' The rough timbre of his voice

grazes my throat and slides south, vibrating every cell on the way down. I hadn't realized he was so *close*.

'Yes,' I breathe out, dizzy on gasoline and gunpowder. The dark shields me like armor, making me brave and reckless. 'It didn't happen in the dark.'

His steady breaths grow ragged; I feel each like a shot of hot adrenaline in my veins. 'And if it did?'

I swallow thickly. 'It didn't happen.'

A deep hum of approval touches my ear. 'Good girl.'

Christ.

Two words, little more than a whisper in an empty room. I've built my entire world around hearing them, but they've never made my fists curl and my back buck like this.

I'm so hyper-aware of my remaining four senses that I can hear the *swish* of soft fabric moving, followed by a light chill fluttering across my waist.

And when I feel a concentrated heat roll up the curve of my hip, I stop breathing.

It feels like a too-close candle. Its flame dances up my rib cage, raising every hair and goosebump in its wake. It must be Gabriel's finger or knuckle, and My God, the mere proximity, the mere *thought* of him touching me, is all-consuming.

As the heat drifts along the band of my bikini top, a cramp of desperation seizes me. I need more than his near-touch or his praise. I need his grip, his friction. I need to feel the scratch of his beard between my inner thighs, the sharp points of his teeth sinking into my flesh. I need to know what it'd feel like to be pinned between his body and a mattress.

I need to hurt every woman who already knows.

The thought slices through my lust-fueled haze. It thumps at the base of my skull and churns my stomach. The rain roars louder, and somewhere beyond it a cackling laugh rings out.

Panic grips me; realization slaps me in the face.

This is a very dangerous game.

'Stop!'

It shoots from my lips like a flare thrown into the dark. Though I can't see I know where it lands, because I sense Gabriel stiffen.

The heat lingers for one heavy breath, two. On the third, it retreats into the unknown.

Sweat cooling on my skin, I blink as hard as I can, trying to recover my bearings. But there's nothing out there to guide me but silence. It stutters over heartbeats, stretches into seconds.

A bead of unease slowly trickles through my core, dragging all my thoughts south.

Oh, God. This is bad. I'm shackled, half-clothed, and at the mercy of a monster I have no business being alone with in a dark garage. I can't see anything – not even his outline, let alone his expression or the weapon he fired just moments ago. I can't study the intent in his eyes or predict his next move.

Curse my stupid habit of romanticizing everything. Darkness isn't freeing. It just makes you vulnerable.

Panic chews away at my edges, and when I can no longer stand its bite, I choke out a desperate breath.

'Y-you're scaring me.'

More silence. More stillness. Fear itches like a rash on my skin. It flares up when the heat returns to my chest and brushes up my arms, and fades to a dull relief when with a sharp tug, my arms drop back down to my sides.

Blood rushes through my veins so fast I feel lightheaded and, strangely, more vulnerable than I did when tied up. The darkness warps around me. I can hear glass crunching underfoot, but I can't tell whether it's coming or going. When it stops and another noise starts, I freeze.

It sounds like bones grinding into dust. Only when a puddle

of light seeps out from the dark do I realize it's the sound of the garage roller door rising.

With every churn of the motor, moonlight creeps across the concrete. It stops just short of my toes, and for a moment, I stare down its narrow path.

Then I step into the light.

I step over broken glass and oil stains. Over the thick stretch of Gabriel's shadow. And when concrete meets grass, I have every intention of stepping out into the rain too.

But the thing about the dark, is that it's never needed chains to trap me.

A monster's attention is leash enough.

Pausing at the door, I peer over my shoulder for one last look. Gabriel's standing just outside of the moonlight's reach, though when his hand drags across his mouth, it cuts into its path.

And maybe it's my eyes playing tricks on me, or maybe it's just delusion.

But I swear, it holds a tremble.

CHAPTER
Eighteen

Gabe

Three years.

I lasted three fucking years.

I'd folded her into a box that only rattled on the quietest of nights. Now all that self-restraint has come undone with a short temper and a tug.

Ripping back the throttle, I lean into my Harley and drive into the blizzard head-on. Can't see for shit, but it doesn't matter. I know the winding ribbon of these mountain roads like the back of my hand, and even if I didn't, I'd still take the risk just to get away from the coast. From *Her*.

'Skip,' I mutter. The sinner in my ear cuts off mid-sentence, and the next call plays. I know it's Raj the Gambler within the first two seconds by the self-pitying sigh that fills my helmet.

Gritting my teeth, I skid around a deep bend and snap at Siri to skip again. I'm not in the mood for Raj's monthly woe-is-me ramble that comes every time he wastes his paycheck on the races.

I need something darker. Something that breaks the loop of her breathy voice fizzing in the black.

You're scaring me.

Of course I scared her. Scared my-fucking-self too when she burst into my garage mid-panic attack and my gut twisted into a shape it's never made before.

I wanted to make it stop and strangle whoever started it.

The next call is from a new sinner. She's chained her husband to a water pipe in the basement and won't let him out until he admits he's fucking the new girl at work. I turn up the volume to max when she mentions she'll give him until the weekend to come clean before she shoots him point blank in the dick with his own hunting rifle.

Her confession. The howling wind. The deep purr of the engine beneath me. They blur into white noise, but it's not long before it darkens to pink.

Those two flimsy triangles covering her tits are etched into my fucking eyelids. Forget the look in her eye when she begged me to take her secret to the grave, or the fact she doesn't drink, or that she suddenly stopped driving yet told me she never learned in the first place.

The girl's a confirmed sinner based on that body alone.

'Siri, play my favorites,' I grit. This caller has started crying, and I'd rather turn left off the mountain ridge than listen to it.

There's a beep in my ear, followed by a robotic voice.

'This is a prepaid call from –'

Mildred Black states her name.

'– an inmate from the Washington Corrections Center for Women . . .'

The voice goes through the usual spiel about the call being recorded and monitored before Mildred's smokers cough rattles down the line.

'I really thought Danny was The One. He looked like Brad Pitt in his hey-day, just a few inches shorter, and unfortunately, not as rich.'

The sound of her voice makes my thoughts slow down and my shoulders drop a few inches.

Mad Milly calls like clockwork because she calls from prison. Hers are the only calls I answer in real time because inmates can't leave voicemails. Every Thursday at noon, I pick up, mute my microphone, and listen. I'll press record too if it's worth it.

Though with Milly, it's always fucking worth it.

By the time the ghostly outline of the gates emerges from behind the haze, my brain is so full of her psychotic ramblings there's barely any room left for my own.

I park between a Lambo and a beat-up truck, shake the snow from my leathers, and head into the house.

The gentle sound of music drifts down the hall, and the ice in my bones begins to thaw. Tucking my helmet under my arm, I follow it to the family room, then lean against the door.

Luan's at the piano, spine curved, scars dancing down his back in the firelight. He plays to the storm battering the far window, and though his fingers barely move, they strike chords that could haunt a house.

He was born to play. But he was also born to Petrit Dritan, the head of the largest human trafficking ring in Albania, so his talent stays within the walls of this chalet.

Leaving him to it, I continue down the hall. I nod at Kwame through the window of the therapy studio – he'll be walking again within the month at this rate – and pass through the kitchen, where Jason is cooking up Sinigang on the stove. It's his mama's secret recipe, and even Arben has given up trying to beat it out of him.

I find Denis in his usual haunt and in his usual stance: crouched over the snooker table in the games room. His shoulders tighten as I approach, and when I click the door shut behind me, his gaze slides along the length of the cue and flicks up to mine.

'You killed Seb.'

My lungs clench, and I run a hand down my throat. 'Fuck.'

'I'm kidding.' He taps the white ball and straightens to watch it connect with the green. 'But you blew out his knee and he hit his head pretty bad on the way down.'

I let out a tense breath. On any other day, he'd eat my knuckles for that joke. 'Where is he?'

He jerks his chin to the ceiling. 'Sulking in bed and watching *Netflix*.' Raking an eye over me, he asks, 'Why the friendly fire?'

I walk over to the drinks fridge and grab a beer. 'It was a warning shot.'

'Warning him about what?'

About taking another fucking step into the garage.

I'd fired the first shot because the thought of another man seeing what I was seeing made me feel violent. The second shot was at the light because I wasn't worthy of seeing it myself.

But I need to work on my damn reflexes because I was too late. I'd already seen the soft dip of her hips and the curve of her chest. Had already committed the outline of her nipples to memory. I could even look at a color wheel and pick out the exact shade of pink that flushed her skin when she caught me staring.

Plunging us into darkness was the worst thing I could have done. Because then the temptation to touch her like she'd touched me was too great. It eliminated the ability to see the fear in her eyes and her seeing the Devil take over mine.

You're scaring me.

I scare every woman, and I'm perfectly fucking fine with that, but there's something about scaring her that makes me do stupid shit. Like rocking up to her house again to teach her how to get out of the trunk I folded her into. Like cutting her out of her restraints before I could even show her how to free herself.

Self-loathing bubbles through my blood and heats to boiling point. I take it out on the closest inanimate object, the *PacMan* machine, and drive my fist through its screen.

'Oh no, my high score,' Denis drawls, chalking his cue tip.

The rage in my veins simmers, and I let out a breath of amusement.

Fucking Denis. Nothing fazes him. Then again, compared to the shit he deals with in this house daily, my little outburst is child's play.

He's my right-hand man, left side of my brain, and the heartbeat of our army. He works behind the scenes making sure my men are fed, watered, healthy, and sane before shoving them back over the front line to me. Need stitches? You go to Denis. A good beating? Denis. Passports, translators, tech support. He does anything and everything to keep the organization ticking over.

Heir to the largest illegal timber logging company in Gabon, Africa, he was born into this life too, but he wasn't built for it. Not physically, with his lean runner's build, pressed shirts, and glasses as thick as a bible. Not mentally either – when I first met him on our first day in Hell, he'd brought only a Rubik's cube and a book of crossword puzzles with him. Right then and there, I knew his heart was too big, his conscious too heavy.

There were three of us once.

The last gulp of beer tastes bitter. I grab another and sink down on the sofa to watch him play.

The roar of the storm whipping through the mountain ridges. The occasional *clunk* of balls dropping into pockets. The soft melody drifting out from under Luan's fingertips and down the hall. The chalet's soundtrack usually has a way of dulling the constant ache between my ribs, but not tonight. Tonight, I'm too distracted by the words brewing at the base of my throat and the fight to stop them spilling out into the room.

I let out a hot breath through my nostrils, rest my elbows on my knees, and glare down at the carpet; I can't fucking look at Denis while he leans on his pool cue and studies me.

'This isn't about Rafe's men, is it?'

I give a tight shake of my head.

He sighs. 'Her.'

He knows better than to say her name.

A ball rolls into a pocket; I feel the thud in the pit of my stomach. Silence follows, all the heat trapped in Denis's glare.

'It'd take me five minutes to find –'

'*No*.'

No.

Three years.

I've lasted three fucking years.

She's perfect, in her little box. My little angel with wings from *Amazon*. With a touch too warm for my skin; with a name too sweet to ever pass my lips. I want to keep her there forever. A reminder of all the good in the world, of everything I've never had or deserved.

I swore I wouldn't dig, though now I've seen her fucking body, it's getting harder to resist finding out what she's hiding beneath it. And maybe if I found out she isn't so *perfect* after all, I could set her free.

But that's the problem. The Devil himself couldn't claw Her from me.

I grit my teeth and drag my gaze up to meet Denis's.

'Fine,' he mutters, his shoulders sagging. He cracks his neck, runs a hand over his short braids and tightens his grip on the snooker cue. 'Buckle up; this is going to hurt.'

Good.

I close my eyes and brace for the blow.

CHAPTER
Nineteen

Wren

Welcome to The Rusty Anchor, where the fire roars, the roof leaks, and the bar gives you a splinter every time you slide your money across it.

Uncle Finn hates that I work here. He says the place should have been shut down years ago, because there's no way it turns a profit selling chicken wings and cheap beer to the same twenty port workers. He also says not to get him *started* on the health and safety issues that come with welding two decaying shipping containers together, balancing them on the side of a cliff, and filling them with fat drunk men.

It turns out, The Rusty Anchor is some sort of architectural miracle; it survived the port explosion with little more than a few busted windows. With my boss, Eddie, not being one for sensitivity or tact, it was business as usual a mere few days after it happened.

Only, it isn't business as usual at all. People are dead, everyone else is laid off. A handful of locals have turned up, probably with nowhere else to go, and are drowning their sorrows in the bar's darkest corners. It'd be an unbearably slow shift tonight if it weren't for Tayce and Rory propping up the end of the bar, and the gaggle of out-of-towners who stormed through the front door ten minutes after opening.

Businessmen and rich tourists heading for the bright lights of Devil's Cove end up in the drowsy town of Devil's Dip all the time, especially during the festive period. The signs on the highway are confusing, and if you take an exit too early, the next sign you'll see is the flickering neon one slapped on the side of this bar.

They usually just duck in and ask for directions, all while keeping one eye on their belongings and the other on the suspicious stain on the rug. Not these guys, though. They strolled in, shook the rain off their suits, and didn't stop for a second to read the somber mood in the room.

As soon as one of them snapped their fingers in my direction and ordered a cocktail I had to Google, I knew I'd be running off my feet tonight, especially since I'm flying solo. Dan called in sick, and though I feel sick for a different reason, one with rough hands and inked skin, I don't have the luxury to do that. I need the money too bad.

Sweeping Tayce's beer bottle off the bar and replacing it with a fresh one, I turn my attention back to Rory. She's holding a fan of playing cards, and the frown denting her brow tells me she's not happy with her suit.

'Okay, but like, what does he actually *do*?'

Tayce tosses down the Four of Clubs, and Rory bites out a bird pun. 'He's head of security,' she snaps, taking her irritation out on me. 'He makes sure my husband doesn't get murdered.'

'But *how*?'

'By looking like that,' Tayce murmurs, studying her hand.

Rory stabs a thumb over her shoulder to the man in a suit standing behind the Christmas tree. If he's trying to hide, he's not doing a very good job. Partly because Eddie bought the cheapest, skinniest tree on sale, but mainly because he's *huge*. 'By having loads of scary-looking men like Gio hanging around.'

'Does he carry a gun?'

'Gabe?' she tuts. 'Of course not.'

Heat flames my cheeks.

Well, he certainly had a damn gun last night.

I snatch up Rory's wineglass though it's still half full. Ignoring her protests, I pour the contents down the sink and scrub it clean with trembling hands.

Gabriel's touch was non-existent, but it's gotten under my skin and grown roots. They've tangled around my lungs and made it hard to breathe. They've wrapped around my wrists too, so every time I look down at them, I'm reminded of being strung up and restrained.

A white-hot heat rolls through my core for the millionth time today. A bead of sweat trickles down the small of my back. Guilt mixed with pleasure is a foul-tasting cocktail.

I hate that man in daylight.

But in the dark . . .

'Why's a girl like you working in a dive like this?'

From the end of the bar, I hear Tayce scoff. I drop the glass, it shatters in the sink, and my sigh follows the shards down the drain. Eddie is the biggest penny-pincher on the planet, so no doubt he'll dock the cost of it from my wages.

Although I'm on a knife's edge – and every time the door opens, the ghost of gasoline and leather blows in – it won't stop me from spinning around with a sunny smile and a chirpy *what can I get ya* ? Because I'm nothing if not *nice*.

I sweep the broken glass into the trash and turn around. My smile loses its plastic edges, and I stand up a little straighter.

It's him.

The quiet guy with the neat hair and the kind brown eyes that have been following me around since he and his fellow out-of-towners walked in. I know because my eyes have been following him around too. That's also how I know he has dimples. I watched them deepen when I told his buddy the cocktail he ordered – an Aperol Spritz – sounded like a dollarstore perfume.

With a light laugh, I wipe my soapy hands on the back of my miniskirt and rack my brain for a witty response. Telling him I need the cash before heading off to college next fall is too boring, and it simply won't do.

I ball a dishrag in my hand and grin up at him. 'If I had a dollar for every time someone asked me that, I wouldn't *have* to work in a dive like this.'

His shoulders shake with amusement. It was a good answer. As his gaze leaves mine and sweeps the room, I rake my fingers through my bangs and gawp up at him from underneath them.

Tayce will tell me off for staring, but I can't help it. I've decided this man isn't just cute, he's *handsome*, and it's making my skin all warm. I like the cut of his suit, how perfectly the pink of his tie matches the color of my cropped fluffy sweater. I like that he brought his empty wineglass back to the bar. I like that he drinks wine.

His eyes follow mine down to the glass. 'That tasted like vinegar, by the way.'

I lean against the bar, fluttering my lash extensions. 'And if I had a dollar for every time someone told me that, I wouldn't have to work at all.'

Tayce groans, but I ignore it because *he* laughs.

Now I like that about him too.

Our eyes lock for a beat too long, and the warmth seeps through my pores and into my stomach. I squeeze the dishrag tighter, ignoring the burn in my wrists, and take stock of the situation.

Eyes locking, butterflies dancing, laughter floating.

Ladies and gentleman, this might be it. I'm finally getting my meet-cute.

My heart beats faster. I mean, I'm not a waitress working in a cocktail bar, but a bartender working in a dump that sells two beers for five dollars is close enough, right?

'Well, you're far too cute to be working here.'

'Believe me, she knows,' Tayce grunts, glugging from her beer.

'Shut *up*, Tayce,' I hiss through my smile. 'Let him tell me.'

Kind Eyes glances over at her in amusement, then looks to the wonky Christmas tree. He nods to the bare branches at the top of it. 'I thought the angel was supposed to go on top of the tree, not work behind a bar?'

Flushing red, I stifle a squeal of delight, reach over, and playfully push him on the chest. 'Oh, stop that.'

He laughs. 'What's your name?'

I squint up at him, suddenly shy. 'Wren Harlow. What's yours?'

'I'm David. It's a pleasure to meet you, Wren.'

'David,' I repeat, saying his name slowly, thoughtfully. Toying with the idea of saying it for the rest of my life and saving it in my cellphone contact list with a little love heart emoji. Moaning it in his ear as we make love on our wedding night.

Wren and David, David and Wren.

And just like that, the warmth in my stomach cools to tepid, and the view beyond my rose-tinted glasses dims to gray.

I nod, smile, and mutter something about it being a nice name. That's just what you do when someone tells you what they're called. And it is, I suppose. It's just not the name of The One.

Doesn't have the same ring as *Wren and Gabe*, either.

A shock zaps through me, and I silently scold myself for daring to even think it.

David asks for another wine. I pour it with a polite laugh and some small talk, but my heart is already over it. My head too preoccupied with veins on biceps and gruff commands.

The conversation soon dies, and when he retreats to his friends, the night's soundtrack takes over. Drunken anecdotes ebb and flow; rain fights through the crack in the roof and sloshes into the bucket in the corner. 'Top of the World' by Carpenters fizzes out of the jukebox for the millionth time. It's a hunk of a machine as old as the bar itself. A few months ago, one of the locals punched it in a liquor-fueled rage, and it's only ever played this song since. It's not in Eddie's budget to replace it.

'You're still here. I thought you'd be riding into the sunset by now.' Tayce smirks when I approach, giving the playing cards a lazy shuffle. 'What happened?'

Lesson two happened. But instead, I say, 'His name is David.'

'Oh gosh, what a travesty.'

I brush off her sarcasm. 'Oh well. I'm used to the disappointment.' I let out a dramatic sigh and put the dishrag in my hand to work, wiping away water rings and my stupid daydreams. 'It wasn't explosive enough to be my meet-cute anyway. If The One doesn't crash into me at a coffee shop and spill his Americano down my dress and then awkwardly scrub at my boobs with a napkin, I don't want it.'

'Wren.' Rory puts down her cards. 'What I'm about to say comes from a place of love.' She takes a deep breath. 'You need to start dating.'

I roll my eyes. *Not this crap again.* I swear, we've had this conversation more times than I've curled my hair. 'And I will start dating. When I meet The One.'

She places a warm hand over mine. 'But to meet The One, you've got to wade through The Many.'

Tayce nods in agreement, for once not a single slither of

sarcasm on her face. My gaze narrows on Rory's wedding ring. It winks back at me purely to taunt me.

'Well, you didn't do that. You met Angelo, and that was that. Your fingers brushed, sparks flew, and now you're living happily ever after with your Prince Charming.' I sniff, suddenly feeling defensive. 'Now you live in a house so huge you need a compass to navigate it.'

Rory steals a shifty glance at Tayce, who grabs my other hand and takes over. 'Yes, but Rory is a peasant. Hers is a rags-to-riches story. But you, you're already a princess! And you know what princesses do?'

'Hang around in an ivory tower brushing their long blonde hair, waiting for their Knight in Shining Armor to rescue them?'

Rory laughs. 'No, not that princess. The other one. The one who had to kiss all those frogs before she met her prince.'

I chew on my bottom lip, my stomach twisting. I know they're right, of course. Though they couldn't torture me into admitting it. I must be the only twenty-one-year-old on the planet who's never been on a date, let alone been kissed.

They don't understand I can't go around kissing frogs to find my prince.

Because I learned the hard way: I'm hardwired to be incapable of telling the difference.

Instead of biting, I ignore them. I ignore the 'out of use' sign Eddie slapped on the dishwasher too and load it up with beer glasses, then bump it shut with my hip.

Dammit. Speaking of signs. I forgot to check that these out-of-towners are adhering to the rules of my own.

Chest tightening, I glance up at my 'No More Than Two Drinks If You're Driving' sign above the bar to make sure it's still there, then spin around and frantically count the empty glasses scattered around on tables.

Okay, so the guy fiddling with a cigar has barely made a dent in his first beer, probably because it tastes like dishwater. The one who snapped at me is only halfway through his fancy cocktail – probably because I made it wrong – and David and the two others are all just starting their second drinks.

Phew.

I grab my notepad and pen and head outside.

It's the kind of blistery December night that makes you want to cancel all plans. The rain has slowed but the wind hasn't, and the moment the door swings shut behind me, it whips at my ponytail and scorches my ears. I curse myself for not tugging on my coat.

Hugging my notepad to my chest for warmth, my gaze slides over to the gravel where the harsh glow of the neon sign bleeds into black. The parking lot isn't usually this dark, but last week, all the streetlamps shattered. Eddie said it must have been from the explosion, but I think it's more likely to have something to do with his rant about rising electricity prices and the sledgehammer I saw in the back office.

I step into the abyss. When the ground transitions from slippery cement to rough gravel under my heels, I know I've reached the start of the parking lot, so I use the flashlight on my cell to see. The light washes over shiny cars with fancy logos and leather seats, and I quickly scribble down the license plates. Having worked here for nearly a year, I've come to be real good at guessing what vehicle belongs to which out-of-towner. The Bentley has cigar man all over it, and the Aperol Spritz dude definitely has the gumption to park his four-wheeler across two disabled bays. When I write down the plate for the Toyota, a sad smile tugs at my lips. I just know it belongs to Kind Eyes, which is nice, because this model was voted the safest in the US last year.

Such a green flag.

And such a shame his name is David.

I'm crossing over to the sleek sedan parked in the farthest corner of the lot when my torch cuts out.

I frown. Tap my cell screen.

Nothing.

What the hell? The battery can't be dead, I've had it on charge behind the bar for the last thirty minutes. But now that I think about it, the plug sockets probably use too much electricity for Eddie's liking too.

The night swallows my sigh. As it snatches the tendrils of my icy breath too, my shoulders stiffen. I scan the horizon and strain my eyes, waiting with bated breath for the prickle of awareness or the glimpse of a shadow shifting within a shadow. Even the mere thought the Boogeyman is out there *watching me*, makes my pulse throb and my breasts ache.

Christ. I've never been afraid of the dark, but now I'm afraid I'm looking forward to encountering the monster that lurks within it.

Disappointment and self-loathing hang bitter in my chest. I finish scribbling down license plates with a tremble in my hand and head back to the bar.

As I step onto the patio, the door opens and Kind Eyes appears. He doesn't fill the doorframe like Gabriel does. Doesn't fill me with the same *heat* either.

He feels safe.

He makes me feel nothing at all.

Which is why I bite down on my pen, rip the cap off, and grab his hand. 'You're going to take me on a date,' I say, writing my cell number on his skin. 'Somewhere romantic. Got it?'

When I look up at him, an amused smirk plays on his lips. 'Yes ma'am.' He admires the number on the back of his hand as I brush past him and stomp back inside.

The dark follows me in too.

I fear all the frogs in the damn world couldn't drag it away from me.

***

I slide a fresh beer over the bar. 'So, what's it like working for Rafe?'

Penny scrunches up her nose. 'It's like stepping on Legos repeatedly for eight hours a day, then having to wake up at the ass-crack of dawn to do it all again.'

I bite back a smile. The flush creeping up her neck at the mere mention of his name tells a different story.

I'm not being dramatic when I say Penelope Price is the coolest girl I've ever met.

She's wedged between Rory and Tayce, flipping through the deck of cards with one hand and twirling her beer bottle with the other. She's moved on from bad-mouthing her new boss to showing Rory how she can beat him at Visconti Blackjack, and though I'm too stupid to know what card counting means, I can't help but hang onto every word that slides out of her mouth.

'All right.' Penny shuffles the cards with the finesse of a magician. 'Don't worry about being subtle, because chances are, your brother-in-law will be too busy staring at himself in the closest shiny surface to notice what you're doing . . .'

Her arrival tonight was unexpected. Sure, I invited her when I'd bumped into her at the hospital after the port explosion, but I never thought she'd actually come. I assumed she'd have way more important things to do, like hang out with the likes of Nico Visconti at one of those invite-only bars in Devil's Hollow or something.

She grew up on the coast too, but went to the other, less *desirable* school in Devil's Dip. The one filled with girls who hiked up their skirts and hung out with older boys until way past curfew. Even back then, I remember being in awe of her anytime we crossed paths. With her flame-red hair and an attitude just as fiery, it was like she jumped right over the awkward ugly-duckling phase and straight into being a full-blown woman with opinions and boundaries and perfect skin.

It's no wonder she skipped town when she was eighteen. No doubt her return is just a pit stop before she heads back out to somewhere cooler than the coast.

The rest of the shift flies by in a blur of watered-down beer and complicated math sums. Thirty minutes before closing, I start my usual wind-down routine, which includes yawning loudly, glancing at my invisible watch, and nudging at stubborn feet with a soaking-wet mop.

Thankfully, even the drunkest of locals take the hint, and by the time Angelo Visconti strolls through the door with ten minutes to go, my friends are the only patrons left, and I'm already counting the cash in the register.

I stop and watch as his gaze finds Rory in half a heartbeat. He's behind her in less than three, his hand around her throat, and his mouth nestled in the top of her bun. I don't hear what he whispers in her hair, but it doesn't matter, because when Rory turns as pink as my sweater, I *feel* it burning through my veins in the way only jealousy can.

I know I'm staring, but I can't look away. And not just because the PDA is a fascinating glimpse into a foreign world, but because now I've seen how Gabriel commands the dark, I'm looking at his brother in a new light.

It doesn't make sense. Gabriel, Angelo, and Rafe were born to the same parents, they lived the same childhood. They're woven from the same DNA, and yet, somewhere, somehow, Gabriel's strand frayed and veered off path into the shadows.

I can't understand why he's scarred while his brothers are

suited. How they're smooth small talkers, yet Gabriel doesn't even crack a smile.

I only tear my eyes away when Penny shrugs on her coat and scoops up her purse.

'Same time next week?'

'If my asshole boss doesn't schedule me for a shift, sure.' She glances at Angelo and grimaces. 'Oops, don't tell him I said that.'

'Nothing he doesn't already know,' he states with dry amusement.

She dismisses his offer of a ride home and saves her number in my cell before heading out into the night.

'And what about my ride?' Tayce slugs the dregs of her beer and slams it on the bar. 'Is it the same hottie who drove me home last week?'

It's not, but she reapplies her lipstick anyway, just in case her new driver is cute too. As the door slams shut behind her, Angelo reaches for Rory's hand, but she snatches it away.

'And what about *my* ride?' She mocks sweetly. 'Is Gio driving me home? Is he going to brush my teeth and tuck me into bed too?'

Angelo frowns. 'Gio?'

'Uh-huh.' She glares at the shadowy figure by the tree and sniffs. 'He's been following me around all day. Your orders, according to Gabe.'

Now Angelo's glaring at Gio too. Then he slowly turns, and suddenly, he's glaring at me.

I freeze, a fistful of fives in my hand, then glance over my shoulder at the liquor wall. Surely, he can't be looking at *me* like that. Like I've done something wrong. Like I've pissed him off.

Like he's his brother.

I swallow the lump in my throat and flash him a nervous smile. He doesn't return it and instead jerks his chin to the door, his eyes still latched onto mine. 'Gio, escort my wife to the car. I'll be right out.'

'Okay, bye Wren,' Rory chimes, oblivious to the shift in the air. 'Love you. Text me when you get home.'

The slam of the door rattles through me. I stare after her, a desperate hole burning in my chest before the silence becomes too uncomfortable to ignore.

I drag my gaze back to Angelo, wide-eyed and waiting.

The floorboards groan under leather loafers as he approaches the bar. He palms it and pins me with an even stare.

'Stay away from my brother.'

His words reach over and steal the breath from my lungs. It's an order, not a threat, but my body can't tell the difference. A dim spark at the base of my skull tells me to protest, to scoff, to ask him what on earth he's talking about, but when he raises an expectant brow, I'm too stunned to do anything but nod.

'Good.' His shoulders drop with the release of a breath, and relief softens the hard lines of his face. 'Can I drive you home?'

'No, thank you,' I whisper.

He nods. 'Stay safe, Wren.'

I stand there, paralyzed, tracking his every step toward the exit. I find a voice when he reaches for the door, though I'm not entirely sure it belongs to me.

'I thought he wasn't as scary as he looks?'

Angelo pauses, then turns his head just enough to reveal the hard set of his jaw.

'He's worse.'

The door swings shut just as another raindrop plops into the bucket.

CHAPTER
Twenty

Gabe

The sun rose too early. The sky's the color of bruised fruit, and beneath it, the birds circle low, eerily quiet. No cawing or squawking, just the soft hiss of their feathers ruffling as they glide over the ocean.

It's the type of morning that doesn't belong to a mid-December day. There's no bite. No sharp air or stiff joints. No sting of salt in the wind.

I lean against the helm of the speedboat and crack my neck.

'You ever get the feeling something bad's gonna happen?'

No reply.

I glance down at the man staring up at me and let out a breath of amusement. 'Stupid question.'

Stooping to zip up the body bag, I wince at the tenderness flaring between my ribs. Then I limp down to the stern and start the engine.

Even the fucking water is out of sorts today. The surface is calm, as though the entire Pacific Ocean is holding its breath. The waves feel sluggish and dense, sloshing against the hull as I make a beeline for the gaudy boat in the distance.

Irritation fissures through me at the sight of Rafe's yacht. It's as flashy and as obnoxious as he is, bobbing against the horizon like a twenty-million-dollar iceberg. I hate the fucking thing and hate myself too for not beating the stupid idea of opening a floating casino a mile from the shoreline out of him before he'd dropped the anchor.

Not only is it a disgusting show of wealth, it's also a floating target. Even counting Dante out, simply being a Visconti has put a bullseye on my brother's back, and now every man he's ever pissed off knows where to aim. The fact he has his own security doesn't put me at ease either, because they're just a bunch of pussies in suits. They'd probably jump overboard at the first sign of a threat.

As I line up the tender with the back platform, Rory comes into view. She's standing with her arms crossed on the swim deck, scowling at me. Her gaze grows hotter the closer I get, and it burns like the look of a girl who found out I tied her up her bikini-clad friend and got trigger happy.

Gritting my teeth, I kill the engine half a second too late and throw my weight behind the wheel, just to make sure I put a noticeable dent in the paintwork.

'I have a question.'

I glance up at her, stone-faced. *Here we fucking go.*

'Can you beat Rafe up for me?'

Relief marred with amusement touches my chest. 'You lose at Blackjack again?'

'No. Well, yes, but I'm working on that.' She throws her hands out dramatically, like Jesus on the cross. 'Anyway, look at the size of this thing! Did you know that running a yacht for just a week emits more carbon than most people do all year?'

I rake an eye over her flight suit. 'How much carbon does flying emit?'

She frowns at me, confused. 'I don't know. Why?'

Shaking my head, I secure the tender instead of pointing out that you can't be an eco-warrior and take flying lessons three times a week in a bid to get your pilot's license. She steps aside as I climb the ladder and follows me across the decking.

'What've I missed?'

'Hmm, let's see. Well, I've put the Christmas decor up, but I'm going to need your help with the roof lights.'

I cock a brow. 'Your husband can't climb a ladder?'

'He can, he just doesn't know I've bought more lights. Oh, and I've been hanging out with Penny, Rafe's new employee. I think he's a bit obsessed with her, but he won't admit it. Anyway, she taught me how to card count, so don't worry about beating him up, actually; I'm going to shake him down for all he's got instead.'

A smirk lifts my lips. Penelope Price – she's my new neighbor and definitely my brother's new obsession. I'm getting sick of hearing about the girl and *from* the girl. She's been using the hotline as a diary for fucking years.

'Anything else?'

'Yes.' Rory shoves her cell screen under my nose. I stop, tug off my aviators, and squint to figure out what I'm looking at. 'Is that a dog?'

'Uh-huh, it's Maggie. Look at her little curls!'

'I've only been gone three days. When did you get a dog?'

'Well, she's not technically mine yet. She's a Christmas gift from Angelo. She's been staying at the outhouse with the housekeeper, but I sniffed her out.' She grins up at me, then her face falls when her eyes touch the welt on my cheek. She cocks her head and studies me like she's seeing me for the first time. I fucking hate when she does that; it always brings a lump to my throat. At least she never asks questions. Guess that's why I can tolerate her more than I do most people.

We reach the door to the lounge, but before I can slide it open, something glints up at me from the shoe rack.

Pink. Sparkly. A heel so high it'd make a stripper jealous.

My gaze narrows. 'Who's here?'

'The usual. Angelo, Rafe, Dan . . .' She follows my glare. 'Oh, and Wren.'

Her name lights up the bruises on my back and tightens a noose around my neck.

The last time I saw her was days ago, strung up and indecent in my garage. My shot at the light was like a camera flash, burning my last glimpse of her into my retinas. She was all bikini body and Bambi eyes, and I couldn't get the image out of my fucking head even if I blew my brains out. I see it in the dark. Behind every blink.

And now she's here. The irony isn't lost on me: I can't escape the girl, even in the middle of the fucking ocean.

I drag my knuckles over my mouth to hide my grimace. Rory's gone back to the subject of her new dog, showing me a whole camera's worth of pink tongues, floppy ears, and tiny paws. I nod in all the right places, but I'm barely listening. Too busy straining my ears for any sign of *Her* on the other side of the door. Like her fairylike laugh, or worse, the damp, heavy pants that grazed my nose as my hand considered exploring the curve of her bare hip.

Fucking Denis. Though he made good on our pact and cracked me around the head with a pool cue, he didn't hit hard enough to shake her out of it.

Rory's moved on to showing me videos. When her phone speaker crackles with the sound of her cooing behind the camera, I make my excuses, plus a promise not to tell my brother about her snooping, and take the long way round to the sky lounge.

If I weren't already on edge, stepping inside the lounge shoves me closer to it.

Nineties hip-hop thumps out of the surround-sound speakers. Empty beer bottles litter the coffee table, and behind it, are my idiot brothers sitting side by side on the sofa, controllers in hand.

'You drive like your wife,' Rafe muses, not taking his eyes off his mushroom-shaped avatar on the screen.

Angelo's dinosaur thing skids around a bend, knocking the mushroom off the road. 'One more comment about my wife, and I'll shove this controller up your ass sideways.'

'According to your wife, ass play is more *your* thing –'

As Angelo's fist clenches, I snatch up a beer bottle and hurl it at the television. It was either that or throw it at their fucking heads.

The screen shatters the Mario Kart track into a thousand pieces, and both pairs of eyes slide up to me.

'Well, that was a bit dramatic,' Rafe tuts, tossing the controller on the couch beside him. 'You got Bud Light all over my rug too.'

I let out an acidic hiss. 'Where are your men?'

Rafe shrugs. 'Probably hiding from you after you shot out Leo's kneecap last week.'

Angelo smirks. 'What did Leo do?'

'Looked at him too long, apparently.'

'They shouldn't be hiding from anything,' I grit. 'You've got three points of entry, and none of them are covered.' I nod to the sea beyond the glass. 'Even a one-armed sniper on a paddle board could have taken both of you out by now.'

My blood heats up with every security flaw I notice, and unease runs through me like an undercurrent. Something about Rafe's men, especially his head honcho, Griffin, has never sat right with me. Though my background checks always come up clean, the fact he's just hired his nephew . . . I don't know, something stinks.

Maybe it's just another bad feeling, like the one I have today.

Rafe calls for one of his slaves to clean up the mess, and I sink down into an armchair. The sharp pain in my thigh must have shot right up to my face because Angelo's gaze thins on me.

'Christ. What the fuck is wrong with you?'

Bitter amusement rolls through me.

That question used to be paired with another: *Where have you been?*

The first time I heard it was when I graduated from Hell and limped into the dining room just in time for dinner. I'd been gone for three years, and the world I returned to was different to how I left it. It was darker.

And so was I.

I had a new scar running from my eyebrow down to my chin and a look in my eye that reflected all the fucked-up things I'd done to get it.

They could have found the answer if they'd looked hard enough. It doesn't matter now, anyway, they've grown so used to me disappearing on a whim that the second question disappeared and the first became rhetorical.

Which is exactly why I don't bother answering it.

'Let's get on with it. I've got shit to do.'

Angelo purses his lips, gives me a final once over, then drops it. 'How's it going with eliminating Dante's men?'

'Fine.'

Rafe studies me, rolling a poker chip between his thumb and forefinger. 'And you're sticking to the plan? Making them quietly disappear without Dante noticing?'

Well, two are hog-tied in my cave, and another is wriggling about in a body bag on the tender, but I did cut out one of their tongues the other day because their screams were pissing me off, so I guess that counts as being quiet. 'Yep.'

Then again, I left said tongue on Dante's pillow during my last nighttime visit, so maybe not.

Angelo releases a tense breath. 'Good. The stupid fuck is going to be the last man standing soon enough. Then we'll figure out what we're going to do with him.'

A spark of adrenaline lights up my chest. There's no *we*, and there's no figuring it out. I already know what I will do with him.

Been planning it for the last three years. Been fucking with his head for the last three years too.

The day I finally look Dante Visconti in the eye and cut him from cunt to chin with his own knife, is a day I've been looking forward to.

As the dutiful employee sweeps up shards of glass, Rafe launches into a tirade about his latest misfortunes. I took care of the kids who raided his casino in Vegas, but there's more. His investments are down; he lost a six-figure bet to our cousin Benny because he beat him at an arm wrestle. I'm normally the first to point out the irony of him moaning about losing a fraction of his fortune while wearing a Brioni suit aboard one of his several multi-million-dollar yachts, but today, his first-world problems seem to weigh heavier on his shoulders than usual.

He's agitated. Gray half moons underline his eyes, which keep darting toward the door as if he's also waiting for something bad to happen.

When he tops off his rant by mentioning he dropped his iPhone in the downstairs bar and cracked the screen, my shortlived curiosity reverts to annoyance.

'I'm going,' I grunt, shoving myself to my feet. I nod to Angelo. 'You coming?'

He shakes his head. 'We've got a meeting.'

'With who?'

He glances at Rafe, who's suddenly preoccupied with tightening his cufflinks. 'O'Hare.'

The hairs on the back of my neck rise at the mention of the Irish. 'Martin?'

'Kelly.'

'Then I'm staying.'

'No,' Rafe snaps. 'It's just a quick catch up. No reason for you to stay and scowl in the corner.'

Unease tightens its grip on me. Rafe co-owns a few

establishments in Vegas with Kelly, and I've never fucking liked it. Never liked him either, and not just because he's Irish. The man's unpredictable, always jacked up on pills that his doctor stopped prescribing him years ago. All it'd take is an ill-timed joke from my brother, and shit would hit the fan.

Sensing my hesitation, Angelo's gaze lifts to mine. 'I've got it covered. I'm packed and loaded, and I haven't missed a shot since ninety-two.'

I let out a wry breath. 'Yeah. I'm more concerned that Rafe hasn't shot a gun since ninety-two, though.'

But Angelo's words are reassuring. He's right, he never misses, and with the temper of a toddler, he never pauses before he shoots either. Besides, I've got bodies to dump and lackeys to torture.

'Fine. Call me if shit turns south.' I glare at Rafe. 'Not Griffin. *Me*.'

I move to leave, but Angelo's question stops me. 'Gabe. Why have you got Gio stalking my wife?'

I run my tongue over my teeth and consider letting a lie filter through the gaps. The truth's complicated, and is less about my sister-in-law's protection, and more about who she's always hanging out with.

I settle on no answer at all.

I leave them bickering over who technically won at Mario Kart before I put an end to their game and slide open the external doors.

I have every intention of turning left toward the tender. Every intention, until the sea breeze drifts up over the railing and brings that fairylike laugh with it.

The sound knots my shoulder blades.

Between my brothers acting like they're on vacation and Rafe's self-pitying monologue, I'd almost forgotten she was here.

With a sudden weight in my jaw and a thump in my chest, I grip the railing and glare out to sea.

Turn left.

Turn. Left.

Then another laugh rises from the deck below and blisters my skin, igniting a violent spark beneath my ribs – who the *fuck* has her laughing like that?

I turn right without thinking, then stomp down the stairs and through every room.

I pause in the entryway of the downstairs lounge.

Rory's perched on one end of the bar. She gives a lazy wave before turning back to her deck of cards and a calculator. And on the other end is *Her*.

Head back, eyes closed, her hand resting on her chest. My next breath catches when I suddenly realize why the sun is shining on a cold mid-December day. It's shining for her. Like a personal spotlight, it pours through the window and surfs down her golden waves, catching the sparkle of her lip gloss and the shimmer of her eye shadow.

The light loves her.

And clearly, so does the cunt standing in front of her.

She has her other hand on his chest, *touching him*, while he stares at her like she put the fucking sun in the sky herself.

I know how her hand feels. I know the exact number of seconds it takes for her heat to bleed through my shirt and warm my skin. I could pick out her fingerprint on its texture alone because it's etched onto my bicep, the hollows of my cheeks, the scar on my face.

Jealousy swells into impulse in my stomach. It twitches my muscles and makes my vision hazy. I'm all too aware of the gun in my waistband and the knife strapped to my ankle, and now I'm wondering how I can use both at the same time to do as much damage as possible.

A soft sigh slips through her parted lips and pulls me off the edge. She opens her eyes and slides her hand off his chest.

'I was right, I'm afraid. We're totally out of sync.'

Her gaze shifts to the right and lands on mine. His follows, and when the realization hits, he jumps back like he's been shocked.

'I –'

'If I didn't have places to be, I'd take you to the top deck, tie a brick to your ankle, and make you jump off,' I say quietly. 'Get back to work.'

He scrambles out of the nearest door – which I'm sure leads to the supply closet and not the hall – putting his earpiece back in as he goes.

Guess I now know why Rafe's men are nowhere to be seen. They're too busy trying their fucking luck with women twenty tiers above their league.

I glare at the door rattling from the impact of his slam, still tempted to follow him through it and make good on my threat. Filing the thought away for later, I look to Rory, because I can't look at Her. Her gaze is too heavy, and that fucking skirt she's wearing is too short.

'Need a ride?' I ask through gritted teeth.

Rory waves a dismissive hand, engrossed in her calculations. 'No thanks, I'm waiting for Penny.'

I nod and stride toward the French doors leading out to the deck. I have a grip on the handle and can almost taste the sea air when a breathless voice touches my back and brings me to a stop.

'I do!'

My jaw clenches. I muster up the will to turn around, and find her staring at me with a shy, goofy grin on her lips.

Rory looks up, frowning. 'What? Why? You're not waiting around to see Penny?'

Her eyes hold a sparkle, glued to mine. 'Would love to, but I've got to get ready.'

'For what?'

'The poker night, silly.'

'You know that's tomorrow, right?'

'Of course I know. But to have cute hair tomorrow, I've gotta wash it tonight.'

'True,' Rory says. 'Okay, make sure to send me a photo of your dress.

Agitation slithers through me as I realize she means *the* poker night in Devil's Hollow. Rafe holds it every year, and unfortunately, I'm going too.

Temples throbbing, I watch as she collects her coat and purse – both ridiculously fluffy and pink – and hold open the door for her, glaring at the space above her head as she passes, before reluctantly following her outside.

Leaning against the wall while she tugs on her stupid shoes, I stare out to sea in silence, fists clenched at my side. I last all of two seconds before my eyeballs get itchy and slide down to her.

No surprise, she's head-to-toe in pink. Skirt shorter than my patience and a top that shows a slither of her midriff. There's something written across the chest in rhinestones, and I narrow my gaze to read it.

Cuddle me, I'm cute.

There's that violent feeling again. It bubbles at the base of my throat and foams in the form of a bitter question. I turn my eyes back to the sea. 'You touch every man like that?'

She doesn't miss a beat. 'Only when they ask me out.'

My lungs squeeze. 'What?'

'Only when they ask me out,' she repeats slowly, as if I'm hard of hearing.

I suck in a breath and clamp my jaw shut, tensing every muscle in my body. If I move, it'll be to go back inside and slit that scrawny asshole's throat.

'My mother used to always say that your soulmate's heart will beat exactly in time with your own. That's how you know they're The One,' she continues, straightening. I make the mistake of looking at her again. She returns my glare through her long lashes, doe-eyed and innocent. 'Ours were *way* out of sync. So, no date for him.'

My blood is fucking fizzing. I'm breathing so hard steam would be coming out of my nostrils if it were cold enough. 'You believe that shit?'

'Uh-huh.'

She's so quick to invade my space, I don't expect it. There's no time to sidestep or bark at her either, so I just stand there, frozen, as she closes her eyes and places her hand on my chest.

Now I'm not breathing at all. Every muscle in my stomach tenses. It'll take only one, two, *three* seconds until the heat of her palm soaks through my T-Shirt.

I knew it'd get under my skin too; she already lives there. It poisons my nervous system and works its way south, stirring up shit it shouldn't.

I glare at her long lashes resting on her cheeks, self-loathing chasing the spark, like thunder after lightning. And yet, I still don't fucking move – can't. She's too still, too perfect.

Her touch doesn't belong to a man like me.

I'll be damned if it belongs to another man either.

'Huh.' She frowns, opens her eyes, and steps back. 'That's strange.'

My heart beats even faster. 'What?' I snap.

'You don't have a heart at all.'

She flashes me a cavity-inducing smile and flounces toward the tender.

I let out a bitter laugh, a tremble in my hand as I drag it over my jaw.

This will be the longest boat ride in history.

CHAPTER
Twenty-One

Gabe

I tug the zipper down just enough to see the panic in his eyes. 'Move a muscle or say a word, and I'll drag this out for another week,' I growl. 'Got it?'

I zip the bag back up on his frantic nod and kick the body bag down the tender until its hidden deep beneath the back bench. He's one of Dante's more vocal lackeys, and two layers of duct tape doesn't muffle his cries well enough. I'd tack on a few more strips, but there's no time. I told Her to give me a couple minutes to start the tender, but clearly, she can't count, because after thirty seconds, she's on the swim platform, gazing down at me. That goofy smile hasn't left her lips, and it has me even more on edge than the ghost of her hand on my chest. Something about her . . . is different. She's brighter, sunnier. If that's even possible. Her eyes follow me around like she knows something I don't. I don't know what that look is, but I know it doesn't match the shaky *you're scaring me* that rushed out of her mouth the night I strung her up in my garage.

Great. Now I'm thinking about her body again.

Blood rushes to my dick, and I turn my back to her, because

even with mirrored sunglasses on, I don't want to risk looking at her legs in that skirt again.

'Get in,' I grit, stabbing the key in the ignition.

'Ah-*hem*.'

I turn my head and find her fingers wiggling in front of my face, nail polish sparkling in the sun.

I lift my gaze. 'What?'

'It's very ungentlemanly not to help a lady onboard, you know?'

For fuck's sake.

I flex my hand, then grab her by the elbow like I'm helping an old lady cross the road. Resisting the urge to tug her onboard and then throw her over it, I let her go the second she finds her footing.

'Sit.'

But she's not listening. Instead, she tugs out her cell and flashes me her palm. 'Uh-huh. Give me a sec.'

She zones in on her cell screen, fingers flying, sparkly pink 'W' phone charm swinging. My eyes narrow into slits on her smirk and glassy eyes, and my disbelief hardens into something hotter.

Who the *fuck* is she texting?

Before I can act on the impulse to snatch her cell from her hand, she locks it, drops it into her purse, and glances up at me.

'Sorry!' She huffs out an exaggerated breath. 'Okay, I'm ready when you are.'

It takes every ounce of self-restraint to keep my mouth shut and turn around. Doesn't fucking help when she joins me at the helm, like the little space invader she is.

I bite my tongue and white-knuckle the wheel, trying to concentrate on steering away from the yacht and not the fluff of her coat tickling my arm.

With a clear path, I yank the throttle, partly in the hope she'll fall back and out of my orbit, and partly to get back to shore and get her off the boat as soon as possible. But no jolt or jerk disturbs her. She simply stares over the windscreen, the wind ruffling her hair, that stupid smile still dancing on her lips.

'You won't get in a car, but you'll get on a boat.' I take a sharp turn, for no reason other than to try and throw her off balance. Doesn't work. 'Make it make sense.'

'Did you kill him?'

I squint. 'What?'

Her gaze lifts to mine under a cupped hand. 'You heard me the first time, Gabriel. Did you kill him?'

My full name on her tongue, and in that *tone*, slides under my skin and chills. Her brazenness both unnerves me and pisses me off, and it takes a few seconds for me to realize she's not talking about the dude in the body bag behind us, or the guy from the phone booth, but Seb.

I glare back out to sea. 'No.'

The silence hums louder than the engine. I feel the memory of that night crackling between us, and shit, I feel almost . . . *embarrassed*. Like a teen caught jerking off to his father's porn mags in the garage.

The sun beats down on the back of my neck. 'Forget about that,' I mutter.

'Forget about what?'

I let out a hiss through my nostrils. This chick's really going to make me say it.

'That night,' I grit.

'I don't know what you're talking about.'

What? I turn as she lifts her face to the sun and closes her eyes as if she said nothing at all.

I study her for a moment and suddenly realize what she's playing at.

'If it happened in the dark, it didn't happen.'

Fuck.

That's why she never told Rory about the incident in the garage or the night I showed up at her house and taught her how to get out of the trunk.

The girl's taken my father's rule and spun it into a whole new meaning. And – dare I even let myself think it – she's into the fucking idea.

Is she?

Electricity laced with ill intent zaps through my core and swells in my groin.

No. *Christ*.

I resist the urge to slam my head against the dash to knock the ungodly thoughts out of it so they can't come back to haunt me later. Or to reach over and finally cut out her tongue like I threatened to. Because her saying that is the last thing I need. It's too ambiguous, too bad for me. And no sin, even Mildred's, will ever be good enough to drown out my imagination when it festers on all the bad things I could now get away with doing to her in the dark.

My right hand is going to have a field day.

'Have you ever killed anyone?'

I'm barely listening. I run a clammy hand down my throat and consider strangling myself with it. 'No.'

'Then why do you carry a gun?'

'It looks cool.'

'Oh. And why do you always wear black?'

'Hides the blood stains.'

'Wait – I thought you'd never killed anyone?'

As I turn to pin her with a blistering glare, the wind whips her hair and a strand hits the corner of my mouth like a stray bullet.

A faint taste of her sweet shampoo snaps my last nerve.

I kill the engine so fast the boat lurches forward. Yanking

the key from the ignition, I palm the dash, painting it with heavy breaths.

I'm rigid from my shoulders down to my boots.

Whatever she's doing, it's pissing me off. I scared the shit out of her, and now she's making small talk?

I glare down at her shadow on the dash and contemplate my next move.

I don't even need to ask Denis to pry; I could just choke the secret out of her. Scratch the itch and breathe a sigh of relief as her body breaks the water's surface.

I know I'm bluffing myself just even thinking about it. Her shadow alone makes my chest feel too tight in my shirt. It's tiny and five shades lighter than mine, and the mere sight reminds me of the foreign flicker of guilt I felt slamming down the lid of my trunk on her screams.

A second option is hard to come by; I'm too distracted by the sound of her heavy breaths in my ear. Then her shadow shifts toward mine, just an inch, and my mouth moves without consulting my brain.

'We never finished lesson two.'

Her breaths cease. 'What?'

With a sharp inhale, I slowly return to my full height, glance up at the sky, and curse the sun for shining and myself for being born with the Devil on my back.

Then I stoop to grab the moor line.

'Lesson two.' My voice is as rough as sandpaper. 'We never finished it.'

She freezes. Her eyes slide down to my hand and grow wide. It's an expression that'd make any man with a heart stop.

But she was right: I don't have one.

'Was it the questions? I can totally stop with the questions.'

I take another step.

'Wait,' she yelps, throwing her palms up. 'I'll sit down and be quiet, I swear! You won't even know I'm here!'

She hurdles backward over the front bench, and I follow her retreat. I'd be impressed she cleared it in those ridiculously high shoes if my vision wasn't red at the edges.

I catch her wrist, then the other, and her muscles grow limp as I wrap the rope around them in a tight and unforgiving knot.

Annoyance sparks hot in my chest. She doesn't put up a fight. No elbow striking, no annoying squeaking. She just stares like she's catatonic, only moving when I tell her to.

'Lay down.'

She obeys.

She fucking obeys.

I crack my knuckles and lower myself to the bench, my hands still burning from the contrast of rough, weather-worn rope and delicate skin.

I clear my throat and rest my elbows on my knees. 'Get out of it.'

Wrists clenched to her stomach, she gazes up at me, chest heaving under every breath. 'I don't know how,' she whispers.

'You haven't even tried,' I bark.

As if brought back to life by my tone, she wriggles and squirms like a fish on a hook. Tugging at the binds, shoulders rolling, hips shifting. Her skirt rides up her thighs, inch by inch, as she bucks.

A flash of pink, and I'm on my knees before I can stop myself.

Awareness prickles the nape of my neck, and I grow rigid. Regret churns through me as I force myself to look down and take stock of what I've done.

I've pinned her beneath me. Knees pressed against her thighs, a hand by her head. My gaze climbs over golden hair fanned out like a halo, down her slogan tee and the chest heaving beneath it. Across the inch of tanned stomach and her clenched fists, down to my other hand, yanking down the hem of her skirt.

She looks down at my hand and swallows. 'What are you doing?'

Good question.

I saw bare skin.

I saw pink lace.

I saw *red*.

I acted on instinct, and it wasn't a gentlemanly one. There's only one other man on this boat, and he's halfway dead already, but he's not the fucking problem.

I am.

I let go of her skirt and glare over the side of the boat out to sea, trying to compose myself, but it's fucking impossible. I'm too aware of every inch of her beneath me. Soft, warm, bleeding through my clothes and burning low in my gut.

Seconds drip by. A bead of sweat glides down my back.

'Um,' she mutters. My jaw clenches as she shifts her hips an inch. 'So is there a trick or something? L-like, do I need a hairpin or . . . Hey, what happened to your face? It looks painful.'

I look down as her bound hands rise to my cheek. She moves slowly, watching me as though I might bite, before spreading her fingers like a flower in bloom and brushing them over the welt.

Every muscle in my body seizes. Her touch is as light as a whisper; soft enough to hurt. I don't stop her. Can't.

Instead, I stare at her and wonder if her gaze would soften like that if she knew why I have it. If she knew she is behind every slash, bruise, and ache in my body right now. If she knew how sick I am, how *desperate* I am to know her secret.

If she knew she is lying five feet from a man in a fucking body bag.

The lump in my throat swells as her fingers trail south over my cheekbone. When she reaches the corner of my lip and slides her thumb across it, my cock twitches, and something within me snaps.

I catch her finger between my teeth. A rough warning bite – not hard enough to hurt, just enough to make it *stop*.

She blinks up at me and lets out a puff of air.

'Do you bite every woman that touches you?'

I don't reply. Mainly because my brain's spinning too fast to think of one, but partly because I wouldn't know. In my thirty-two years on this earth, she's the only girl I've met who's been brave enough to touch me with such a gentle caress.

I hold her finger between my teeth longer than I should, deciding what to do with it. Half tempted to bite harder to wipe the warmth from her face, half tempted to suck it and taste her skin and the sweetness underneath.

Instead, I use every ounce of restraint I have and pull back with a low grunt. I grab the knife at my ankle, and with a clean slice between her wrists, the moor line falls away.

Arms dropping to the deck, she's all flushed cheeks and parted lips, hazy gaze and ragged breaths. Lying there like I've just fucked her into oblivion.

My stare lingers a beat too long. Just enough to etch the image into my brain for later before I stagger back to the helm.

I book it back to the coast, my balls tight. She sits behind me in perfect silence, like she should have fucking done in the first place.

Once I cut the engine and moor up at the dock, I turn my back to her and glare out to sea. Not just to hide my hard-on, but because now that I've seen her hurdle a bench like an Olympic athlete, I know she can very well disembark without me having to touch her again.

The boat dipping and the deck groaning brings a slither of relief through me. It's gone as quickly as it arrived when her sweet voice floats over and prickles my nape.

'You know, if I didn't know any better, I'd say you have a crush on me.'

My shoulders snap into a tight line, and I run my tongue over my teeth, still tasting her.

'Good thing you know better, then.'

She pauses. 'Phew. Well, thanks for the ride.'

The sound of her heels clicking down the dock fade, but a final question strains against the base of my throat.

I shouldn't ask; I know I won't like the answer.

But fuck, I was born bad, but I was born a nosy bastard too.

I turn my head. 'Who were you just texting?'

She stops and glances at me over her shoulder. 'Oh, just some guy I'm going on a date with.'

My body turns to stone.

I was right: something bad is about to happen.

Just not to me.

CHAPTER
Twenty-Two

Wren

When Uncle Finn bought Strawberry Farm, he hired a Mom-and-Pop construction company to renovate the dilapidated cottage at the heart of it. But then the 'pop' cheated on the 'mom' somewhere between drawing up the blueprints and breaking ground, and now Finn's house stands as a testament to their bitter divorce.

The welcome mat on the front porch is a battle line. South of it, the cottage exterior is storybook-cute – whitewashed stone, periwinkle-blue shutters, and a chimney that coughs up smoke on winter evenings. Cross over into enemy territory, and you'll find yourself in the lobby of a high-end hotel: loveless, clean lines, cold marble, and sofas you're not allowed to eat snacks on.

Usually, Finn wouldn't tolerate such a farce from the construction company, but it turns out, the couple's inability to communicate worked in his favor. His home is the brick-and-mortar version of him: a big-city hotshot wrapped in a smalltown disguise.

His voice shoots down the stairs the moment I click the door shut behind me.

'Wren? Is that you?'

I roll my eyes. 'No, it's a burglar who just happens to have a key.'

'Very funny. Come upstairs, please. I want to show you something.'

Sitting on the bottom step, I tug off my boots, check the soles for dirt, and place them neatly beside the umbrella stand. Then I climb the stairs on my hands and knees, because I wouldn't trust a staircase with floating steps and no handrail at the best of times – let alone one built by a man distracted by the prospect of losing half of everything he owns.

I find Finn in his office, sitting rigid in the Herman Miller chair behind his desk. His eyes rise over the rim of his glasses, then fall down the length of me in a measured sweep.

'You were meant to come by last night. Everything okay?'

No, nothing's okay.

Though I'd ridden out of Gabriel's garage on my high horse, the darkness had followed me out. And as a sleepless night in Rory's spare bedroom bled into day, the guilt and disgust wore off like cheap temporary tattoos.

He'd taken up every square inch of my brain, as though he were paying rent to live there. I'd replayed what had happened in the garage over and over, until my version of events distorted. Excitement replaced the fear and the dark had a rose-tinted hue.

By the time I climbed aboard Rafe's yacht yesterday, I couldn't remember why he'd ever scared me in the first place.

He hadn't even touched my skin and yet, he lingered beneath it like a hot fever. I didn't want it to cool. I guess that's the only explanation I have for why I forced myself onto his tender boat. Why I probed him with questions, and tried to get under his skin too.

I learned real quick I was in over my head.

I learned how his touch felt, and even worse, I learned I

liked it. The weight of his body on mine, the friction burning my wrists. The sharpness of his teeth and the heat of his glare as he stared down at me, like he didn't know whether to kill me or kiss me.

It was everything I've never had nor wanted, and still, his touch chased me home and through the front door, where I barely made it to my bedroom before my hand was between my thighs and my ragged breaths were dampening my pillow.

Finn's question is a simple one, but it twists my gut into knots. We're close, sure, but his coldness is a direct result of the only other time I felt like this, so I flash him a weak smile instead.

'I'm a busy bee, honey. What's up?'

If he notices my tone is tighter than usual, he doesn't mention it. Instead, he ducks out of view, then reappears holding a stack of books.

He drops them on the desk with a deft thud. 'I've dug out some of my old textbooks from my pre-law days at Silvercrest. They're a little dated, but I've spoken to Professor Barton, and he's confirmed the syllabus hasn't changed all that much. I thought it'd be good for you to get a head start on the reading material before the fall.' He looks up at me, expression hardening. 'What do you think?'

The silence crackles between the paper skyscrapers and sagging brown boxes. I see his chest tighten beneath his cableknit sweater. I know he's readying himself to jump down my throat the moment my usual excuses start pouring out of it – I can't say that I blame him.

Despite having deferred my place at Silvercrest for two years in a row, following my uncle's footsteps into law was actually my idea. Initially, I just wanted to live out my Elle Woods fantasy, but when the midnight emails started coming in, I realized being a defense lawyer for the voiceless is the ultimate good deed. It would shatter that one sentence, five words, and twenty-nine characters, including spaces, into a million pieces, and finally make the emails stop.

Though my GPA was good and I took part in every extracurricular that didn't involve sweating, I was far from an Ivy League candidate. It took a little discretion and a whole lot of nepotism to secure me my place. Uncle Finn pulled strings like a master puppeteer. He called in a favor from his golf buddy on the Silvercrest admissions team, and another from a former classmate who works on the American Bar Association's scholarship committee.

Finn has put everything on the line for me, and more times than I deserve.

I can't let him down again.

He's still staring at me across the office, his jaw locked and loaded for a fight. So I swallow the familiar knot in my throat and grind down the rising panic between my back teeth.

'I think that's a great idea, thank you.'

As his face spreads into a broad grin, emotion prickles at the back of my eyes. I love it when Finn smiles.

After the incident, he didn't smile at me for months.

'Phew.' He leans back in his chair and puffs out a breath, blowing away all the tension between us. 'I'll drop these off on your porch in the morning, then.'

I nod and move farther into the room, straightening piles of paperwork and picking up empty coffee cups. The modern, minimalist design throughout the rest of the cottage stops sharply at his office door. Behind it, it's forever September. It smells like the first day of school, like sharpened pencils, leather-bound books, and dust.

'Speaking of things showing up on my porch.' I shut a cabinet drawer with the bump of my hip. 'Why'd you leave your boots on my porch this morning? I hope you weren't expecting me to clean them.'

He frowns. 'What boots?'

'Those hideous black lace-ups.' I screw up my nose at the memory. 'I mean, honestly. Do you really need steel toes to hammer a few shelves together?'

He lets out a dismissive laugh, opens his MacBook, and lazily scrolls through a document on the screen. 'I've no idea what you're talking about, Wren.'

I open my mouth to call him a liar, but a sudden realization severs my vocal cords.

The boots waiting on my front porch this morning aren't Finn's.

My heart kicks my sternum, and a cheap high rushes through my bloodstream.

Of course they belonged to Gabriel. But why? Was it some sort of threat? Part of another lesson? A cryptic game I didn't know we were playing?

It doesn't make sense, but then again, nothing about Gabriel Visconti makes sense.

Gosh. Maybe I was right – this man really *does* have a crush on me.

I feel like I'm floating, delirious at the mere thought. Catching my breath, I concentrate on the bookshelf behind Finn's desk to stop my thoughts from spiraling. I read the title on every book spine and the looping signatures on every certificate. I scan from left to right, and when I reach the end of the middle shelf, I freeze.

My mother's staring back at me.

I set down the coffee cups and reach for the photograph with a trembling hand.

She and Finn are sitting on the front steps of a Georgian house. Her head rests against his and her arm is tightly wrapped around his shoulder, as though she'd yanked him into frame.

It must have been taken in the nineties. A lazy summer memory, shot on film and sealed in glass.

If we were a normal family, I'd have picked it up and smiled. Poked fun of my mother's over-plucked eyebrows and Finn's spiky boy-band hair, before asking a million questions about when it was taken and why. But I don't want to peel back the bark on our family tree; I want to chop it down. Cut it into logs and burn it.

Because looking at this photo of my mother hurts.

Finn's chair groans beneath him, and the heat of his stare brushes up my back.

I turn around. 'I thought you got rid of all the photos of her?'

He stares at the frame in my hands, running two fingers across his lips. 'I did. Every photo except that one,' he murmurs, a sadness creeping in behind his glasses. 'I had to keep that one.'

Emotion clogs my throat. 'But why?'

He releases a slow breath and cocks his head, as if thinking of the best way to answer.

'Because,' he eventually says, 'she reminds me to be the good in the world.'

My gaze falls back down to my mother. Calypso-blue eyes warm enough to light bonfires, a grin broad enough to bridge two oceans together.

As I put her back on the shelf, my comedown is violent.

Once upon a time, I made a vow to be the good in the world too.

If only it came naturally.

* * *

An hour later, I'm in my robe, cocooned in one of Finn's Hermès blankets, being bad again. Though my morals have never extended to adhering to his strict rule about eating snacks on his cream sofas, anyway.

I shift, and the chip bag crinkles in my pocket.

Finn doesn't look away from the TV, but his brows draw together, just like they do when he's reviewing a contract he already suspects is dodgy.

'Do you want to tell me what that noise is,' he asks evenly, 'or should I start cataloging evidence?'

I pretend I haven't heard him, keeping my eyes firmly fixed on Elle Woods introducing herself to the Harvard admissions committee in a pink sequin bikini.

'Ridiculous,' he mutters, smoothing down the front of his slacks. 'Harvard doesn't even accept multimedia applications.'

I roll my eyes. Finn watches every movie like he's crossexamining it for inconsistencies. Spine rigid, ears pricked. All he's missing is his notebook.

'*Legally Blonde* is the greatest law film of all time.' I pop another chip into my mouth and gulp it down whole. The sharp edges catch the back of my throat, and I try not to cough. 'So just shut up and enjoy it.'

The sound of my cell buzzing cuts his protest short. It buzzes again, and again, until the whole sofa is vibrating beneath me.

I flip it over on the armrest without looking at the screen and snuggle deeper beneath the blanket. I knew it was coming, because there's no way Tayce would have read my vague text bailing on tonight's plans and not put up a fight.

It's Rafe Visconti's poker party tonight. He holds it in Devil's Hollow every year, deep within the caves beneath the town. Everyone on the Coast knows about it, and they'd pry the invite out of your cold, dead hands, given half the chance. Not that it'd be much use though, because rumor has it, the buy-in alone could clear a mortgage.

All the stories I've ever heard about it have been

hand-me-downs. It's always someone who knows someone who knows someone else, that's worked at the event in some minor capacity. It's the first time I've ever been invited, of course. And for free, at that. I guess there have to be some perks to your best friend marrying a Visconti.

I've been excited about it for weeks. I bought a new dress I couldn't afford. Practiced my poker face in the mirror. I've daydreamed about locking eyes with a handsome gentleman across a velvet roulette table, and my arm brushing against his when he slides up to me later at the bar.

But recently, the suave man in my fantasy has distorted. Now he's rougher, darker. He lurks in the shadows instead of sitting across the table. Locking eyes with him cuts, and if I were brave enough to brush against him, I've no doubt it would burn.

An electric shudder zaps through me. I pull the blanket over my mouth, and bite into a chip with a decisive chomp.

I told myself I'd be extra good from now on. I don't know what that looks like anymore, only that it doesn't look like spending an evening anywhere near the Boogeyman.

Another buzz. I ignore it again, but Finn doesn't bother hiding his irritation this time. 'You kids and your cell phones. If this were a movie theater, you'd be kicked out.'

'If this were a movie theater, I'd be allowed to eat popcorn –'

A heavy knock lands on the front door, slicing my sarcastic comment in half. I bolt upright, my stomach flipping, because for one dizzying second, I think it's *him*.

Finn tuts, twitches the curtain, then turns his attention back to the screen. 'Tell Tayce if she breaks my door, she's paying for a new one.'

Oh jeez. Not Tayce. Suddenly, finding Gabriel haunting Finn's front porch seems like a less scary alternative.

I pad down the hall, collecting my excuses as I go. When I

crack the door open, Tayce is standing beneath the porch light, her arms crossed and her eyebrow hitched up to her hairline.

'Tayce?' I whisper, squinting out into the night. 'Is that really you? My fever's so high, I think I'm hallucinating.'

Her gaze narrows. 'Stop it.'

'Don't come any closer,' I croak, holding up a feeble hand. 'I'm contagious.'

'If bullshit were contagious, you'd wipe out the entire Coast.'

'Honestly, I'm sick.'

'And I'm sick of *you*.'

Pressing the back of my hand against my forehead, I let out a weary sigh. But she's still standing there, stone-faced, so I launch into a coughing fit instead.

I peek up at her. Nope. Zero sympathy.

She purses her lips. 'You done?'

'For now,' I whimper, clutching my chest.

'Good. Now, do your makeup, put on a cute dress, and –'

'I'm not going and you can't make me!'

The words shoot out harsher than intended, all desperation and no croak.

Tayce blinks. Cocks her head to the side, and sweeps a wary eye down my crumb-flecked robe.

'What's really going on, Wren?'

The sudden softness in her tone makes my throat feel all tight. Guess the age-old warning to be careful what you wish for is true. I wanted Tayce's sympathy, but now I realize I'm too weak to handle it.

I fiddle with the door's safety chain and try to stop my bottom lip from trembling. 'Nothing's going on.'

'Well, you've been acting weird all day. You haven't been answering your phone or replying to my texts. Not even when I sent you that video of the puppy having a spa day.'

My lips tilt. 'That was cute.'

She lets out a breath of a laugh. 'Looked more like animal cruelty to me, but hey, I knew you'd like it.'

For a moment, neither of us say anything. Tayce studies me like she'll find the truth if she looks hard enough. I look down at the fresh manicure I had done especially for tonight instead.

Eventually, she breaks the silence. 'Sure you don't want to talk about it?'

I open my mouth, then close it again. Because it's not even a question of where to start, but where to end. If I told her about the incident in the garage or on the tender boat, I'd have to tell her about the lessons. Why they exist in the first place. It'd lead to the night we met, and the lessons, and the dark.

It's a whole can of worms not worth opening.

I shake my head, small and tight.

Her eyes search mine for another beat, then she gives a decisive nod. 'Fine. Have you got any pajamas I can borrow?'

'Um, yeah?'

'That aren't pink and frilly?'

'Oh. Then, no.' I watch as she pops off her earrings and slips them into her coat pocket. 'What are you doing?'

'If you're bailing, I'm bailing too.' She jerks her thumb over her shoulder, in the direction of my house. 'We can put on face masks and oil our hair and watch *TikTok* videos.' Her nose scrunches. 'I'll even let you put on a musical. Not '*Grease*!', though,' she adds with a shudder. 'It reminds me of Benny.'

Though it sounds like the perfect evening, I dismiss the idea with a flap of my hand. 'You've got to go, the dress you bought looks amazing on you.'

She shrugs. 'So, what's new? Everything looks amazing on me.'

'Well, what about Rory?'

'She'll be fine. Penny's going, and the two of them have got this whole scam thing going on.'

My ears prick up. 'Penny's going to the poker night?'

'Of course. She'll be so bummed you're not going, though.'

'You think so?'

'Oh, I know so,' she says, flicking her long, black hair over her shoulder. 'I bumped into her in Cove the other night. She said you're the kindest girl she's ever met.'

I straighten up. 'Did she really?'

'Uh-huh. She said you're so pretty too, and that she couldn't wait to see what you were going to wear, because you always have the cutest outfits on.'

'Yeah?' I'm grinning now, my cheeks hot with pride. 'What else did she say?'

Tayce rolls her eyes. 'That you're the biggest compliment fisher on the planet.'

'Well, I did buy the cutest dress,' I muse, ignoring her dig. 'It'd be a shame to waste it.' I strum my fingers on the door frame and chew on my bottom lip. 'Besides, I'd hate to let Penny down. I really want us to be friends with her, you know?'

A smirk stretches across Tayce's face, like she knows she's already won.

I let out a long, dramatic sigh. 'Well, I suppose I'm feeling a bit better.'

As I sit on the bottom step, tug on my boots, and shout my goodbyes down the hall to Finn, I try to ignore the screaming voice at the base of my skull. It's begging me not to go, but I drown it out with water-thin reasoning and empty promises, like Gabriel will be easy to avoid.

Besides, my dress was *really* expensive.

CHAPTER
Twenty-Three

Gabe

On my first night in Hell, I was tortured by the Devil himself.

He strapped me to a chair in an eight-by-eight cell, stripped me naked, shaved every square inch of my body, then stuck electrodes on my temples, chest, and groin. Someone wheeled in an old tape player and pressed 'play'. *Roxanne* by The Police crackled out of the speakers, and every time the name 'Roxanne' was sung, he ran a current through me.

That bitch is mentioned twenty-six times.

He played it for eighteen hours straight.

For years, I thought it was the worst form of torture a man could ever endure.

But then Rafe started throwing parties.

'I'm telling you dude – I had a dream.'

The vocal fry sizzles on my back like hot oil. The man at the roulette table behind me isn't Martin Luther King, but a California tech bro who invented a rideshare app and thinks he too changed the world.

'Come on, man,' his co-founder groans. 'An acid trip isn't the same as a dream.'

'All right. It was a prophecy, then.'

'Jesus.'

'Yeah, man. I saw him too. He also said you should go all in on red.'

There's a heavy pause, the type that brews bad decisions, then:

'Fine. Fuck it.'

A chorus of cheers ripples around the table, followed by the swish of chips gliding over velvet. The ball drops and rattles, like teeth in a glass jar. It skips and clinks, growing slower and slower and slower, before dropping into a slot with a dull, final, thunk.

Silence.

'Fuck. My wife is going to kill me.'

I drag a hand down my face. Consider clawing my eyeballs out while I'm at it, because *fuck*, I hate these fucking parties.

We're in Whiskey Under the Rocks, in Devil's Hollow. It's one of the many cave bars buried deep beneath the ground, and for the life of me, I'll never understand why Rafe insists on holding his annual poker night here. The ceiling drips, the walls sweat, and the acoustics amplify every liquor-fueled laugh and coked-up conversation.

Tonight, it's dressed up like an aging hooker working the holiday season. Christmas trees sprout from every corner, their branches sagging under gaudy baubles and lights. There's tinsel wound around stalactites and fake snow jutting from limestone. The whole joint flashes red and green, and to top it all off, some annoying cunt is bashing piano keys in one of the alcoves.

He ran out of Christmas classics to play an hour ago, so now he's working through commercial-jingle versions of mainstream songs instead – not that anyone here is sober enough to notice.

Grinding my teeth, I flip over the next card in the deck and toss it on the table. I don't bother glancing down to see what I've dealt – I'm far too on edge to care.

It's the law of probability: shove three or more Viscontis in a room together and at least one of the bastards is going to set it on fire, then look to me to put out the flame.

I never come to these parties to play cards; I come to babysit. I've fine-tuned my order of observation over the years, always looking for the biggest fire-starting dickhead in the family first – Benny, obviously – then working my way down the list. But tonight, there's a tense undercurrent running beneath the festivities. It's stitched into suits, poisons the drinks. The floor is wet with gasoline, and even if I were a betting man, I couldn't say for sure who's going to strike a match first.

Cracking my knuckles, I glance over at Benny out of habit. He's running the poker game opposite, a spaced-out smirk on his face and a blonde draped across his lap. He catches my eye and winks before blocking a nostril, dipping his head, and snorting a line off her thigh.

Fucking idiot. Of all the girls he could trick into opening their legs tonight, he had to choose the one who arrived with a Turkish arms dealer.

But it's typical Benny behavior. Nothing Emile can't handle. No, tonight I'm more concerned with the fire hazard sitting to my left.

'Deal.'

My attention cuts over to Rafe. 'What?'

'You deaf now?'

My fist clenches. 'The last card was an ace.'

'I have eyes,' Rafe snaps back. 'Deal a fucking card.'

As I flip over another card in the deck, Rory flashes me a shit-eating grin from behind her hand.

A mild amusement prickles my chest. Yeah, and if Rafe's eyes weren't permanently glued to the elevator doors, he'd probably notice that our sister-in-law is taking him for a ride.

He takes after our mama: superstitious as fuck, only he's too embarrassed to admit it. Usually, he's only wary of the stupid stuff. He'll avoid walking under road signs and make sure to salute a passing magpie. But recently, his bad omen has the shape of a short redhead with a smart mouth and sticky fingers.

Penelope Price has got him fucked up. He's convinced she's the reason that his fortune is bleeding out of his asshole. I don't know about that, but I do know she's the reason he's taken first place on my fire-starting dickhead list tonight.

She's also the reason Angelo's sitting three tables over, sulking.

Raking my teeth across my bottom lip, I find our older brother. He's spent more time glaring at Rafe over the top of his cards than playing them, because as expected, the meeting with Kelly O'Hare went south. His eye wandered too far for Rafe's liking, so he blew the dust off his gun, fired a bullet and triggered a war with the Irish.

I hadn't even moored the tender when I got the call asking if I could return to the yacht and clean up the blood before it seeped too deep into the teak.

Bringing my watch to my mouth, I grind out a command over the radio in tonight's language: German.

I need more eyes on Vicious, because I learned a long time ago that his sulking usually leads to shooting.

A crackling confirmation comes through my earpiece, but I'm not done with my sweep. I skip over Nico at the craps table – he just comes to these parties to pick up chicks and watch everyone else embarrass themselves – and find his older brother, Cas.

Cas. Christ, I can't remember the last time he ranked so high on my fire-starting dickhead list, or even when he last broke the top five. He's usually too busy lubing up his fist to fuck investors, or bidding on junk found in a dead grandma's attic, to cause me any problems.

But then again, he doesn't usually let his fiancée, Alyona, out of the house. So, instead of working the room, he's propping himself up against the bar, five drinks down and antsy. He'd surgically detach his last name from his first, if he thought it'd get him out of marrying the Russian vodka distillery heiress, but that hasn't stopped him from glaring at Alyona's hand resting on Rafe's business partner's thigh.

Knowing where everyone is and who they're glaring at marginally softens the tension in my jaw. Everything's under control, for now.

I grab my beer and go back to watching Rory's attempt at card counting.

A bastardized rendition of a Marvin Gaye love song fissures through the club, drowning out her math-related mutterings Behind me, California Tech Bro is trying to convince his buddy that the third time is always the luckiest, and to my right, Cas rips out a booming laugh, too loud and forced to be real.

I gulp my beer. Glance at the vein ticking in Rafe's temple. Hell, I even smirk when Rory drops her cards and declares another victory.

But the thing about my thoughts is that they're just like my fucking family. Never quiet for long.

The next swig of beer burns as it passes through my throat. The base of my skull throbs, and I squeeze my eyes shut so hard I see flashes of pink.

When I open them again, I'm glaring in the same direction as Rafe.

'Who else is coming tonight?'

'Tayce,' he grunts back.

'And?'

'Whoever she's currently fucking, probably.'

'Mm.' I cut a knuckle through my beard. 'Who else?'

'Not Tor, that's for sure,' he says bitterly, checking his watch.

Irritation squeezes my chest like a cramp. 'Anyone else?'

Still staring at the elevator, Rafe lets out a hard puff of air. 'A big spender from Vegas is supposed to be flying in. He better not bail – I could use the cash injection.' He flicks a distracted glance to the pile of cards. 'Deal.'

I slam down a card so hard the table shakes. Rory yelps, someone in my peripheral vision flinches, and Rafe stops spinning his poker chip.

His gaze locks on mine, bloodshot and suspicious.

I clench my jaw. 'Who. Else?'

'You and your circus freaks have vetted everyone I even considered inviting,' he murmurs. 'So why are you asking?'

Rafe isn't expecting an answer, and even if he was, he couldn't waterboard one out of me.

My gaze shifts to the rock wall behind his head. I clench my jaw to an even beat, as if it'll pump the pink out of my brain.

She said she was coming, and yet she isn't here. She doesn't strike me as the type to show up late, so I guess she's not coming after all.

Good.

Good.

My next gulp of beer tastes like lukewarm disappointment, so I flag down a passing server and order something stronger. I turn over cards. Crack my neck. Even strum my fingers on the table to the beat of a 90's one-hit-wonder.

But then a murderous thought grips me.

She's not coming tonight.

So what else is she fucking doing?

The worst-case scenario flashes against the rock wall like a festive montage.

Red: her hand sliding down another man's bicep.

Green: her panties sliding down her thighs.

Venom shoots up my spine and explodes at the base of my

skull. The thought of another man seeing her panties turns my blood acidic.

My fingers grapple for the earbud in the right pocket of my jeans, then change course for the left pocket to snatch up my cell and check her Instagram profile for the millionth time today.

I swear, if she's gone on that *date*, I'll fucking –

Ding.

It's barely audible. The type of sound only mad dogs and me can hear, but it shoots through the cave on the back of a silver bullet.

My eyes snap to the elevator.

Red.

Green.

Pink.

It's only a glimpse. An inch of space between two sliding doors, filled with blonde, sparkles, and heels. But it turns out, I'm no better than my brother, because an inch is all it takes for my spine to jerk straight.

Self-disgust wraps around my neck like a noose. I'd rather be stabbed in the groin ten times over than in the same boat as Rafe, but just like him, I can't look away.

The doors slide all the way open. A pool of gold light spills out onto the concrete, and when she steps into it, my muscles harden to stone, because –

That. Fucking. Dress.

It's the first thing I notice and the only thing I see. Not that there's much of it *to* see. I've used more fabric to polish a damn gun.

My blood heats and my gaze thins, carving a line of fire down the length of her. The neckline is as low as the hemline is high, and what little there is in between clings to every curve and dip like it's been vacuum-sealed to her body.

A hot hiss escapes my nostrils. Christ. She's poured into that thing like hot honey.

I glare until the sparkles make my eyes sore, then palm my jaw and look up at the craggy ceiling for relief. Of all the fucking things to curse, I choose my father's name.

Ten rules, yet none of them were relevant to civilized society. I never learned how to share, say sorry, or play fairly. Every lesson revolved around anger, and though I learned how to channel it into my fist or trigger finger, I never learned what to do with it when it didn't fit the crime.

I was taught that unwarranted anger is as good as any. But despite my fucked-up childhood, somehow my prefrontal cortex developed just enough to recognize the difference.

Did I know it was unwarranted when I caught Rafe's lackey undress Her with his eyes? Yes.

Did it stop me from clawing said eyes out with my car key and tossing his body, heart still beating, into the same body bag as Kelly O'Hare?

Of course not.

Guess I've never cared for the distinction.

My gaze drifts back down to locate her. She's still hovering in the entryway, flanked only by Tayce and Penny – thank fuck. But even though she's not hanging off some cunt's arm tonight, the mere idea of her hanging off anyone at all makes my skin burn.

The memory of yesterday's tender ride sparks behind my eyeballs like a blown fuse. Her drunken grin, her fingers flying across her cell screen in earnest. There's no doubt about it – the girl was drugged up on another man's attention. Side effects must have included a heavy case of delusion. It's the only explanation for why she had the nerve to suggest I had a crush on her.

The thought curdles in my chest. *Me*, of all people. A *crush* of all things.

If she wasn't as high as a kite when she said it, then I'd love to know what I've ever done to give her that idea. Couldn't have been because I threatened to cut out her tongue or because I strung her up in my garage like a freshly slaughtered lamb.

And if it was, then, fuck, guess she's more of a psychopath than I am.

I take a sip of whiskey to give my hands something to do. I glare at her over the rim of the glass, watching as she peers around the room with a wide-eyed curiosity. She runs a hand along the length of her ponytail, then smacks her lips together. The piano is loud, the laughter louder; I can't hear the *pop* her lips make, but I feel it like a bullet to the groin.

Another gulp of liquor, just to numb the pain.

Fucking *crush*. Sure, she's objectively beautiful; anyone with eyes and a shred of mental capacity can see that. She's got that all-American girl-next-door thing going on. You know, if the girl next door was of the curtain twitching variety and always knew whether you were coming or going. She'd probably slip passive-aggressive notes about the state of your lawn under your door too, signed with a smiley-face and a kiss.

She trails Tayce and Penny through the club, and because the girl's a magnet, my eyes move with her. Arms stiff at her sides, she weaves between tables, careful to keep a wide berth, as if she's read in a gossip magazine or something that gambling addictions are contagious.

But watching her brings this weird lump to my throat and turns my whiskey sour. Only when a drunken cheer shoots across the room and she clutches her heart-shaped purse to her chest do I reluctantly realize what it stems from.

She doesn't belong here. Hell, she doesn't belong in the dark at all. She looks like cotton candy dunked into an ashtray. An angel who took a wrong turn on the way to heaven. She looks like she knows it too.

Something primal and protective stirs beneath my skin. It's making me consider dragging her out of here by her silk ponytail and flinging her far away to some distant sunny place, where darkness and panic attacks and *other men* can't touch her. I'd keep her as happy and as perfect as the day I met her.

My gaze slides down to the top of her thighs.

I'd keep her dressed in rags, too.

Christ. I slam down my whiskey glass and give it a rough shove so it's out of my reach. No more of that crap tonight; it's turning me batshit crazy.

Aware that my glaring will only feed into her stupid 'crush' idea, I busy myself with loading cards back into the automatic shuffler. But I don't have to look to know she's closing in, because I can feel it. She's like a lit match, her heat licking up the side of my neck, flames crawling higher with every click of her heels.

Maybe if I weren't so tuned in, or maybe if it wasn't so out of place in this cave bar, I wouldn't catch the sound of her laugh.

For the second time tonight, my eyes snap up. They lock on a hand wrapped around her upper arm. It flashes red, green, red again. I trail along a suited limb to find its owner – a server. The drinks on his tray are trembling, and she's inspecting her dress. He must have bumped into her.

It's not a threatening grip, more of a steadying one. And maybe if I were in a better mood, I'd consider letting it slide. But as he walks away, he makes the mistake of stopping. He glances over his shoulder, and runs an eye from her bare back right down to her ass.

With an odd sense of calm, I finally understand why Rafe blew O'Hare's brains out, and why Cas is thirty seconds away from going nuclear.

Visconti men don't need to love something to hate seeing it in someone else's hands.

Guess it's just not what we were born to do.

CHAPTER
Twenty-Four

Wren

I burst into the restroom, stumble into the nearest cubicle, and trap the door shut with my back. Germs be damned; nothing in this cootie-infested stall could possibly be filthier than the heat rolling beneath my skin.

Jesus Christ. I knew I shouldn't have come tonight because deep down, I knew this would happen.

And down even deeper, I'd hoped it would.

The moment I stepped out of the elevator, my heart slid south and thumped where it shouldn't. Gabriel Visconti was exactly where I didn't want him: bang center in the middle of the cave, wedged between Rory and Rafe. In other words, impossible to avoid.

He sure did a good job of avoiding me though. If he'd noticed I'd slipped into the seat opposite him, he didn't show it. He didn't toss me so much as a glance over the table, let alone say a word. He sat there, carved from the damn rock itself, his only movement a lazy turn of his inked hand to deal another card.

Squeezing my eyes shut, I let out a groan wrapped in fire.

I'm burning up and breathless, and replaying what just happened only adds fuel to the flames.

I'd smiled and ordered a lemonade.

The server grinned and asked if I was sure I didn't want anything stronger.

Aside from nearly spilling a tray of drinks on me when I arrived, his only crime was being annoying and yet Gabriel went from zero to one hundred with no stops in between.

'*She* said, *she'll have a lemonade.*'

Under the flashing holiday lights, he rose like sin in stop-motion. A human in green, a monster in red, and as his shadow bled across the felt and swallowed me whole, I discovered what it felt like to be both terrified and turned on.

It wasn't that Gabriel had lost his temper.

It was that he'd lost it because of *me*.

A lick of fire shoots up my core. I'd made such a flippant comment about him having a crush on me on the tender yacht, but Christ, the thought of it potentially being true . . .

The restroom door flies open.

'Wren?'

I mutter a silent curse at the sound of Tayce's voice.

'Wren!' She barks again, hammering on the door so hard my bones rattle.

'I'm busy,' I grit back. I brace myself against the cold metal, too, because I've seen her kick through doors with sturdier locks and in higher heels.

'No, you're not. You've never used a club toilet in your life.'

'Yeah, well,' I sniff. 'Desperate times call for desperate measures.'

The door opens again, and I know better than to hope it's her leaving.

'Hi, babe,' she chirps to someone else, sugar in her tone. 'You might want to use the other restroom. My friend, *Wren Harlow*, is in there, currently doing the biggest, stinkiest –'

A jolt of panic rockets through me. I wrench at the lock and bolt out of the cubicle. 'I am *not* !' I squeal, cheeks burning.

The girl freezes mid-step, eyes flicking from Tayce to me and back again. Her mouth opens and shuts, then she throws her hands up like I'm holding her at gunpoint.

'My bad . . .' she mutters, backing up toward the door. 'I'll just, uh – yeah.'

'I swear, I was just fixing my dress –'

The door thumps shut on my protest. Huffing out a breath of annoyance, I spin around and glare at Tayce. She's grinning like a Cheshire cat, but when her gaze flickers across my face and down to the flush on my chest, it fades.

'What the hell was that?'

'I told you I was sick,' I mutter.

Her eyes track me as I move to the sink and slam my purse on the counter. I nudge the tap with my elbow and glare down at the water spitting out of it. Anything to avoid her stare burning into my reflection in the mirror.

The faucet hisses. Pipes gurgle. Heels click across the tiles, then Tayce is beside me.

'Wren . . .' Her hips knock against the counter as she leans back on her palms. 'Are you fucking Gabe?'

Her question catches me off guard and my laugh is loud and manic. It echoes off the walls and raises Tayce's brows. 'Me? *Gabe* ? That's the most ridiculous thing I've heard all year.'

'I mean, it's totally okay if you are.'

My eyes slide sideways, suspicion crackling through me. 'What?'

She gives a careless shrug, her face showing no traces of humor. 'Eh. He's fucking hot. I've tattooed him a million times and I still forget my own name when he takes his shirt off.' Pushing off the sink, she turns around and studies her red lipstick in the mirror. 'That body is criminal, honestly.'

Unfortunately, I've seen him shirtless too. Only once, then many times over, every time I close my damn eyes.

A pinch of something ugly twists low in my stomach. I can't stop it. The jealousy is sharp and sour, and I know it's ridiculous, because Tayce has seen half of the coast naked. And Gabriel Visconti isn't *mine* to react over. He's not even mine to look at. But the thought still coils tight around my ribs.

I pump soap into my hands and scrub them if only to hide my tremor.

She doesn't look like she's leaving anytime soon, so I reach for the soap again and set the record straight. 'I am not sleeping with him,' I say quietly.

'But you want to?'

'No –'

'But you totally would, right?'

'No, I –'

'Because I'll be honest, Wren, that David dude is a drip.'

I scowl up at her. 'Are you kidding me? You told me I needed to kiss frogs!'

She rolls her eyes. 'Yeah, *frogs*. David's more of a tadpole. He's . . .' She gestures around the restroom, looking for the right insult. 'Weird and slimy.'

'But Gabriel's not a frog either. He's a whole-ass dragon,' I snap back, before hastening to add: '*Not* that I've ever even thought about kissing him.'

Her gaze sparks. 'Uh-huh.'

Ears burning from embarrassment, I turn away and shove my hands under the dryer. I glare at the crude graffiti on the wall behind it, wrestling with the confession itching at the back of my throat.

But Uncle Finn once told me that the worst thing a guilty person can do is confess to a lesser crime. Piercing the conscience leads to open wounds. If I admitted I had a sick, twisted crush on Gabriel, who knows what I'd admit to next.

No. Instead, I steel my spine, spin around, and put up my best defense.

'First you tell me that he's not as scary as he looks, then Rory insists he doesn't carry a gun. But I'm not as naive as you think I am, Tayce. I know he's a dangerous man. Jeez.' I fold my arms across my chest. 'If you weren't my best friend, I'd think you'd want me dead or something.'

A hollow beat passes; she doesn't shoot down my dramatic claim. Instead, she palms the sink, her fingers tracing the cracked porcelain. When her gaze finally lifts to meet mine in the mirror, she looks a decade older.

'There are two types of dangerous men in this world, Wren. The ones you run from, and the ones you run toward to escape the first kind.' She lets out a breath halfway between a laugh and a sigh, then straightens up. 'Trust me: I didn't need to witness Gabe's outburst tonight to know which camp he falls into.'

Her words hang in the silence, light as steam, yet dense enough to punch me in the gut.

I'm so busy wrestling with my own demons, I forget Tayce is fighting with her own. The only difference between us is that she wraps hers in black and one-night stands, and I bury mine under pink and good deeds.

Guilt tugs on my heartstrings and stings the backs of my eyes. 'Tayce –'

She cuts me off. 'Anyway, I've gotta get out of here before I catch an STD,' she says, screwing up her nose at the suspicious brown smear on the paper towel dispenser. 'You coming?'

Glancing at the door, I hesitate. I'm not sane enough to deal with what's behind it yet, so I shake my head. 'I'll be out in a minute.'

She studies me for a moment, before giving a decisive nod. 'Fine, but if I don't see you in five minutes, I'm sending out a search party.'

She blows me a kiss and then she's gone, leaving me alone with nothing but the ghost of Gabriel's outburst echoing off the tiles.

She said, *she'll have a lemonade.*

They crackle down my core and light a spark between my thighs. When it fizzles out, it leaves me with this hollow, desperate ache. I guess I'm not your conventional addict, but the withdrawals hit hard and fast all the same.

I drift back over to the sink and stare at myself in the mirror.

This is that really unrealistic part in movies where the heroine splashes their face with cold water. Though I'm spinning out of my damn mind, I don't think I'll ever be crazy enough to do *that*.

Instead, I dig out my makeup and touch up my eyeshadow and reapply my blush. I coat on two layers of lipgloss too many. When I drop the tube back into my purse, my cell vibrates against my knuckles.

Three years. Every day, for three years.

And for the first time in those three years, the panic brings relief.

CHAPTER
Twenty-Five

Wren

Stairs, more stairs, two left turns and a door. The sign says 'Staff Only,' but the glowing green one above it says 'Exit,' so I push through it anyway and find myself outside.

Rain falls in a barely-there mist. Icy air slithers down the front of my dress and wraps around my ribs like a lover with cold hands. When I steady myself against the wall, something digs into my lower back.

I fumble behind me and push a button for a heat lamp.

A red glow floods over my shoulders and heat slowly follows. As the timer *tick, tick, ticks* quietly above me, my eyes adjust in the weak light.

I'm in some sort of courtyard, little more than a pocket of air trapped between four rock walls. They jut out just above my head to form a shelter, then climb all the way up to the sky and frame a shaving of the moon. Soggy cigarette butts litter the concrete; a rusty lawn chair darkens a corner, and beside it, half a plastic cup of beer.

Guess I'm having a meltdown in the staff smoking area.

A sob escapes me, chased by a strangled gulp to fill my lungs back up. The lump in my throat feels different tonight. It tastes like despair, and for the first night in three years, there's no fire behind it.

I've never been a quitter, but everyone knows that doing the same thing over and over and expecting a different outcome is a sign of madness. There's only so many nights I can shiver on a street corner, only so many shifts I can pick up at the hospital, only so many rompers I can knit.

That one sentence, five words, and twenty-nine characters has ground me down to my bones.

Being good is tiring, and when it's not in your nature, it's goddamn *exhausting*.

A sudden burst of light to my left makes me flinch. A red glow spills out from beneath a leather boot like a bloodstain. My gaze crawls up to find another boot resting against the wall, then inches over black clothes, black ink, and a black heart, until it sparks on green.

I freeze.

Gabriel's stare reaches out from beneath his heat lamp, cuts through the mist, and lazily probes mine. Then it falls to my lips, runs down the curve of my throat and across my thighs. By the time it touches my heels, my skin's raw.

I let out a breath coiled in a shiver. How long has he been standing there, in the dark, watching me? It feels invasive, like I've just caught him lurking in my closet while I change. But my embarrassment barely has time to rise before a dangerous thought drags it down deep.

Here I am, again. Alone in the dark, with the Boogeyman.

I can do nothing but stare as he tugs a crumpled cigarette from behind his ear and tucks it into his mouth. He strikes a match against the wall, lights it, and blows out a red-tinted tendril of smoke.

His gaze shifts to the sky, voice worn smooth with disinterest. 'You cry often?'

I can't find the strength to lie. 'Every night,' I mutter, dragging a tear around my cheek. Can't find the strength to care about my makeup, either.

His jaw tightens, like my self-pity offends him. Another drag on his cigarette, then he disappears behind a cloud of smoke. When it dissipates, he's looking right at me.

'You know the bakery on Dip's main street?'

I nod.

'Money laundering front.'

I've never really been sure what 'money laundering' means, only that the bad guys do it in movies. Still, I let out a little puff of shock, because it feels like the right response. And I'm glad I do because I like the way his eyes brush over my lips again, and how amusement twitches his own.

'You're kidding.'

'Nope.' He scratches his beard before adding, 'And their "homemade" carrot cake is from Costco.'

This time, my shock is genuine. My mouth falls open, and a laugh of disbelief slips out of it. 'Okay, now you're definitely kidding. They charge like five dollars a slice. Goodness, someone should report them.'

He cocks a brow. 'To who?'

'The police, obviously.'

He wipes the back of his hand over his mouth. The people-pleaser in me hopes it's to hide a smirk. The thought of making the Boogeyman smile, or dare I say it – *laugh*, injects a dose of delirium into my bloodstream.

Silence bubbles in the thin strip of dark separating our lights. The tip of his cigarette crackles with every inhale; the timers of our respective heaters tick over, out-of-sync. I scrape at the wall and fuss over the sequins stitched to my dress. Trying to do something, anything, to make it less obvious that I'm gawping at him sideways.

Eventually, he flicks the butt toward the pile of others, and when he looks up at me again, his eyes are rimmed with that familiar cold disdain.

'You really are the Good Samaritan, huh?'

It sounds like an insult, but before I can feel the sting, his heat lamp clicks off and plunges him into darkness.

My stomach plummets, but my pulse climbs. Silence crackles in each second that passes, and I hold my breath, the sickest, darkest part of me hoping he doesn't turn the lamp back on.

Fists clenched, I stare into the void from beneath the safety of my own lamp. There's nothing but the hiss of rain and the tremble of my heartbeat.

Taking a step sideways would be a terrible mistake.

I do it anyway.

Another step brings me into the path of the night's chill. Another, and the darkness swallows the tips of my heels, my legs, and then the whole of me.

Even the icy rain sizzling on my bare back couldn't make me cold; the heat licking up my chest is too hot. It radiates from his body, the tension, the *thrill* of it all.

When he finally speaks, his voice drags through the void, rougher than gravel.

'Do you invade every man's space?'

'Do you want to hear it's just you?'

That slipped from my lips like melted butter and I don't regret a single word. Being in the dark with this man is like drinking liquor. It loosens my tongue, strips me of my inhibitions.

Silence. It sends me spinning. It rushes straight to my head, steals all my oxygen, and any ounce of decorum I have left.

'I knew you had a crush on me.' It comes out in a breathless, frantic whisper. 'Oh, my God. I *knew* it.'

'Do I look like the type of man who'd have a crush on a girl who has a lip gloss for every day of the week?' he grunts.

My laugh is warped and manic. 'What kind of girl only has seven lip glosses?'

A dry huff of amusement dances down my sternum and coils between my breasts. There's no insult on this earth, thinly veiled or not, that could rip this high away. It's too late: his silence was too long and too loud, I've already snatched it up and saved it to obsess over later.

A lick of heat brushes over my cheek. It skims across my jaw and hardens into a touch on the corner of my mouth.

Every nerve ending in my body turns toward that single point of contact. They vibrate as his finger carves a line of fire along my bottom lip.

Oh, God. My jaw falls slack, and I let out a desperate, ragged breath. I'd fear I was hallucinating if it weren't for the faint taste of tobacco on his fingerprint. I've never had a craving for nicotine, but *Christ*, the taste of secondhand smoke is enough to turn me into an addict.

His question comes out thick, dripping with restraint and something darker. 'When's your date?'

What?

Oh, right. David the tadpole. I forget his existence on the best of nights, let alone when I'm five inches from Gabriel Visconti's six-pack and precisely zero inches from his touch. He's the last person I want to think about right now. Hell, I don't want to think about anything else at all.

In the light, I'd never be brave enough to act like this. I don't recognize this version of me: I'm all heat and hedonism instead of self-preservation and common sense.

Maybe that's why I tilt forward, just enough to feel my next breath clash with his own.

'Why? Trying to figure out when I have space in my schedule?'

He tugs on my bottom lip so hard my thighs clench. 'So I know when to free up my own.'

Adrenaline bursts through me like a blown-out fuse. The smoke is *hot*, burning through my veins and warping every moral I have.

That sounded like a threat, but it isn't enough. A bead of sweat trickles down the nape of my neck, and though I can't see farther than my nose, my vision tunnels into a tight line. All I can think about is digging deeper, ripping the jealousy from him with my claws. I need *more*.

'Don't worry,' I breathe. 'You'll find out when I post about it on my Instagram page.'

The air tightens before the *click*. A half-second warning before the dark shatters.

Light, in the most violent shade of red, floods over us. My pupils shrink and I recoil. When I find my bearings, I realize Gabriel has turned the heat lamp back on.

He's stone-still, dead silent, and far too close for comfort. His glare could scorch wet earth.

A cold realization grips my neck and tugs me backward.

The dark doesn't just hide all sins; it makes you forget what fear is supposed to feel like. Standing there, dripping in the color of blood, Gabriel Visconti embodies it.

His glare burns with every bad deed he's ever done and doesn't regret. Every fight he's ever won is set into the hard lines of his jaw, throat, and shoulders. That scar on his face is the only fault line in something otherwise indestructible.

Light or dark, I must be out of my damn mind.

The only part of him that moves is his eyes as they track my shaky retreat.

My back thumps against the door; I turn to open it.

But two quiet words bring me to a stop.

'Cancel it.'

They drag up my spine like a match, threatening to reignite everything the light just extinguished.

'And if I don't?' I croak.

His pause is dense.

'Then I guess I'll see you there.'

CHAPTER
Twenty-Six

Wren

Salon Privé sits on the beachfront at the far end of Devil's Cove. It's the type of place with a strict dress code and a menu with no prices. I've passed its unassuming door plenty of times but have never had the need nor the budget to see what's on the other side.

I step inside and hover in the entryway, trying to gawp without looking like a spectator at the zoo.

It smells like lemon and old money boxed in by dark wood walls. The sconces lining them are too far apart, creating more shadows than they do light. The tables are spaced far apart too, draped in white linen and plated with the kind of silverware siblings fight over in their grandmother's will.

Jeez. I say a little prayer that I don't need to reach for my wallet when the check comes, because I doubt I could afford a glass of tap water in a place like this, let alone a full meal.

A polished brunette holding a tablet approaches. 'Good evening, ma'am. Do you have a reservation?'

I smile up at her, tugging at my dress, saying another silent prayer that she won't notice my Chanel flap purse is a knockoff. 'Um, yes. It's under the name David, for eight p.m.'

The screen lights up her frown as she scrolls through a list. 'And the last name?'

I pause. Well, crap, I've no idea. David and I have been texting back and forth over the last few days, and I thought I'd covered all the important questions. What he does for work – something to do with computers; what his favorite movie is – the third one in that boring franchise about the Fast and Furious cars; does he have an Instagram account I can stalk – no.

But I'd forgotten to ask his last name.

'Um.' I sweep the restaurant, hoping to spot a friendly smile and a wave. But there's barely anyone here, aside from a handful of men scattered around in corner booths, and even in the low lighting, I can tell none of them are David.

Irritation pulses beneath my ribs. I can't believe he's late. I know I'm late too, but that's beside the point.

I glance toward the bar in a last-ditch effort to find him, but my eyes snag on another familiar figure instead.

I grow cold. Then clammy.

No. Surely not.

Gabriel's resting easy against the bar. Black jeans, black T-shirt covering the black hole where his heart should sit. He's got one boot casually hooked around the other, but when his gaze locks onto mine and sparks *hot*, I realize there's nothing casual about him at all.

A fever drifts through me.

This can't be happening. He can't be *real*.

'Um.' This woman must think that's the only word I know. 'Excuse me for a moment. I've just got to . . .'

Never mind, there's no time for pleasantries.

Gabriel lazily tracks my approach, his gaze peeling off silk and skin. I weave through tables, narrowly dodging a passing server. I'm barely looking where I'm going – too focused on getting to the bar and getting him *out* of it.

He turns around and rests his elbows on the bar as I slide up beside him, as though he weren't watching me at all.

Holding my glare in the reflection of the mirrored wall, he rakes his teeth over his bottom lip. 'Do you know why so many joints have mirrors behind the bars?'

What ? 'What are you doing here?'

He slowly raises his whiskey glass and takes a sip. 'Go on, guess.'

Panic laced with irritation fissures through my blood. Knowing he won't answer my question until I answer his, I bite back, 'I don't *know*. So the barmaid can touch up her makeup probably.'

He releases a dry breath of amusement. 'No. It's a tradition that dates back to the Old West. Saloons would put them up so punters drinking at the bar could see if anyone was approaching them from behind.'

Distracted, I throw a cautionary glance over my shoulder at the door. 'Cool. Awesome fact. Can you leave, please?'

I'm practically begging, but he continues as though he hasn't heard me.

'Because if anyone were to approach them from behind, it'd usually mean they're about to catch a bullet to the back of the head.'

My stomach turns to lead. His tone is sunny-day calm, but when he lifts his chin to look at me in the reflection again, the overhead light catches the slither of dark amusement in his eye.

I can't breathe. Can't think. My throat dries out, and now I can't talk either.

Swirling the liquor in his glass, he turns to face me, the movement slow and deliberate. His gaze is objective, yet it feels like a rough scrape as he takes in my outfit.

'Why do you always wear pink?'

I stare at him.

Oh, my God.

He's here because I'm here.

Guess I'll see you there. It wasn't an empty threat, it was a promise.

Oh, Jesus. I'd clawed the jealousy out of his black soul to feed my own ego. I was out of my mind last night, tossing my remarks into the dark like matches, thinking they'd never land near the light.

But they did. He caught one.

Now he's going to teach me a lesson by setting my evening on fire.

I swallow the dread and try to gulp in a full breath. Gritting my teeth, I fold my hands together and force myself to smile.

'It hides the bloodstains,' I say weakly, mocking his answer to me when I asked why he always wears black.

Something dangerous simmers in his gaze.

He nods once. 'Good.'

'Good.'

We stare at each other, tension hanging between us like smoke, growing thicker with every second.

I don't dare blink.

Not when my eyes start to water, nor when the restaurant door opens, and icy air brushes up my spine.

Not even when David calls out my name.

'Enjoy your date,' Gabriel murmurs. His voice is smooth, but there's an edge to it, sharp and surgical.

Though my insides turn in on themselves, I refuse to flinch. 'Oh, I will,' I say as sweetly as I can muster. 'It's going to be a *blast*.'

I turn on my heel and stalk toward David, trepidation vibrating in my knees. He lights up when he sees me, grin broad and eyes roaming.

'Wren! Wow, you look . . .' He shakes his head so hard the flowers in his hand tremble. 'Just, wow.'

I plaster on my widest smile. 'Thank you, David. It's *so* nice to see you again,' I chime, too jittery and loud for such a fancy restaurant. 'You look just as handsome as I remember.'

It's not a lie, it's a polite stretching of the truth. I'm sure he looks fine, but I can barely see him through the searing heat on my back.

He presses the bouquet into my hand, mumbling through an apology about being late. Then we follow the hostess to our table, under Gabriel's watchful eye.

Something stubborn suddenly knots between my shoulder blades.

You know what? If he wants a first-row seat to the show, I'll give him an Oscar-worthy performance.

Sliding into the chair feels like I'm stepping on stage without knowing my lines. My spine's rigid, my skin's blistering, but my smile is unwavering. How hard can flirting be? I've watched enough rom-coms in my time to figure it out.

I rest my chin on my hand and gaze up at David, trying to ignore the ominous shadow bleeding out from behind his shoulders.

'You know, I've been looking forward to this all week.'

He blinks up from the menu. 'Really?'

'Uh-huh. I even bought a new outfit.' I bite my lip and rake my fingers through my hair, like Meg Ryan in *When Harry Met Sally*. 'Do you like it?'

He glances down at my dress, which has been stuffed in the back of my closet for over a year. 'Sure, it's beautiful. It's very . . .' He licks his lips, searching for the appropriate adjective. 'Pink.'

I throw my head back and laugh like Julia Robert's in *Pretty Woman* when Richard Gere snaps the jewelry box on her fingers. 'Oh, David. I'd forgotten how funny you are.'

He flashes me a look of concern. 'Are you okay?'

Dragging the napkin into my lap with a tight fist, I smile so hard it hurts. 'You know what, David? I've never been better.'

We order drinks. He says me drinking lemonade makes me a cheap date.

I giggle like I understand the joke.

Then he tells me about his job. His Sunday soccer league. I nearly burn my wrist on the candle, reaching over to stroke his arm when he tells me, with a rueful look in his eye, that if it weren't for his knee injury, he would have gone pro.

I nod, smile, and laugh in all the right places. Bat my eyelashes and twirl my hair. I even try to speak in a breathy Marilyn Monroe voice at one point but drop it after the fifth time he asks me to repeat myself.

Because if he can't hear me, then Gabriel definitely can't.

Gabriel. I've avoided looking up to keep him out of sight, but he's never out of mind. He sits beneath my skin, heavy and constant, pumping each of my heartbeats, squeezing each breath from my lungs. I feel his glare on my throat every time I lean back in my chair. I hear the *pop* of his gun every time I lean forward over the table.

He's there, watching me.

And I have an awful feeling that he's not just watching but *waiting*.

Appetizers arrive. I toy with my salad, moving greens and stabbing tomatoes.

David's telling me about the time he almost made it onto national television when the server appears balancing two drinks on a silver platter.

'Lemonade for the lady, whiskey for the gentleman,' he says, placing them on the table.

David glances up. 'Thanks, but we didn't order these.'

The server offers a polite smile. 'They're from the gentleman at the bar. The whiskey is a sixty-year-old Smuggler's Club. Only ten bottles were ever produced.'

My shoulders hitch to my ears.

David throws a look behind him. 'From the guy you were talking to when I arrived? Do you know him?'

'Kind of,' I mutter, suddenly feeling faint.

Unease tap dances down my spine as I watch him take a greedy gulp. Then annoyance climbs back up the way because what the hell is he playing at, sending over a drink that probably costs more than my college tuition?

I get it; he's a Visconti. Though he wears the same black top and pants, like every day, I don't doubt he's loaded. But flashing his cash sure as hell isn't going to impress me.

I look over David's head as he takes a second swig, to find Gabriel doing exactly what I thought he would be.

Staring at me.

Without a word, he raises his glass in a mock toast.

'Bless him,' I say to David, loud enough for Gabriel to hear. 'He's been stood up by his own date. Apparently, she took one look at him and turned right back around.' I drop my voice to a stage whisper. 'I suppose you run that risk when you use ten-year-old pictures on your online dating profile.'

I swear, out of the corner of my eye, I see Gabriel's lips curl upward behind his low-ball glass.

Ten minutes later, David's halfway through a story about his college roommate's dog when he coughs.

It's short, dry. But the second one is harsher.

I give him a sympathetic smile, mutter something about the steak being chewy, and push his water glass toward him.

He moves to lift it, then his hand changes course and flies to his throat.

My eyes narrow. 'Are you okay?'

When he opens his mouth to reply, a gurgle bubbles out of it. First, ew. Second, what the *hell?*

My voice sharpens. 'David?'

I palm the table, but before I can leap to my feet, an awful scraping sound cuts through the air.

My pulse skids to a stop.

Black boots, lazy strides. Gabriel emerges from the shadows, dragging a chair behind him, and saunters up to our table. He spins it around with a lazy flick of his wrist, hitches up his slacks, and sinks into it.

I stare at him, frozen in shock. 'What have you done?'

He settles against the backrest, like a man taking the weight off his feet after a long day working the yard.

'Lesson three,' he says, sounding bored. 'Never accept a drink from a stranger.'

David makes a horrible, wet sound. His eyes are wide now, red creeping into the whites.

My heartbeat spikes so fast I taste it in the back of my throat. 'Make it stop,' I whimper. 'Please. I'm sorry. I'll do anything. Just . . . *stop*.'

He casts a disinterested look at my lips before slowly reaching into his pocket as though he has all the time in the world. As though the man to his right isn't running out of it.

'You make it stop.'

I stare numbly at the syringe he places on the table. 'What does that mean?'

'Say you won't go on another date.'

I stare up at him like he's lost his mind.

'What? What do you care if I date?'

He returns my look with an even glare. 'You're a safety risk to my family. Anyone who wants to get to Rory, would go through you.' He flicks a look of disgust down at my half-eaten salad. 'All because you can't resist the chance to talk about yourself over a free dinner.'

A beat passes before it hits me like a freight train.

He's lying.

It's in the heat behind his eyes. In the way his jaw tightens beneath his beard.

I breathe out so hard the room spins. 'Oh, my God. You really *do* have a crush on me.'

His eyes narrow. 'What?'

'Gabriel Visconti,' I announce, loud enough for the entire restaurant to hear. 'You have a crush on me.'

He barks out a laugh laced with unease. 'You're out of your fucking mind.'

But it's too late; the realization has seeded in my bones and is growing roots.

'It all makes sense now. Why you carried me through the forest after the port explosion instead of bundling me into that trunk. And then when you *did* bundle me into a trunk, you felt so guilty that you took time out of your night to teach me how to get out of it. You also snapped at that poor sever for literally no reason. Oh – and then there was my panic attack in your garage, you talked me down from that too.' My gaze lifts to his. 'And we both know what happened after that . . .' I trail off, leaving bruised wrists and gunshots burning over candles and white linen.

If looks could kill, I'd be dead ten times over. 'Say it,' he growls. 'Say you won't date.'

'Say you're jealous.'

David lets out a strangled sound, his face now alarmingly pale, lips tinged gray. He slumps over, grappling at crumbs and silverware and nothing that can help him.

Gabriel doesn't even flinch. He just looks at me.

'Time's running out.'

I inhale once, slow and deep, and lean back in my chair. I'm trembling, but I force stillness into my limbs, fold my arms across my chest and tilt my chin up, calling his bluff.

'Admit it.'

'*No.*'

'No, you don't have a crush on me, or no, you won't admit it?'

Frustration curls his lips. 'You're really going to let a man die because of your ego?'

'No, you're going to let him die because of yours.'

David gurgles again. My body twitches on instinct, a plea on my tongue. All the good in me wants to help – knows I should help – but something low and ugly and stubborn inside of me slithers up from where I buried it years ago and stitches my arms to my side.

It's not like I've never seen a man die before.

Besides, his name is David.

And David is the king of boring anecdotes.

Gabriel and I stare at each other as though we're the only ones in the restaurant. His gaze is inflamed, but he sits as still as stone, watching my every blink.

I'm sick in mind, body, and spirit.

My date is dying, and I'm too ugly to care. Too distracted, too *captivated* by the monster beside him. His attention is addicting. It burns through my veins, settles in cells of my DNA, and brings the world to rights.

Gabriel Visconti has just poisoned a man for me.

Me.

A river of calm trickles through me.

I wouldn't cave for love or money.

It's not what I was born to do.

David lets out a final breath, slow and stuttered.

I flash Gabriel a halfhearted smile. 'Oops.'

His gaze mars with uncertainty. He opens his mouth, but another voice from the shadows cuts him off.

'Um, Boss?'

He turns his eyes to the ceiling and runs a hand down his throat, then swallows.

Seconds etch by before he barks out a curse. Then he reaches for the syringe on the table, and with one swift, reluctant motion, he stabs it into David's neck.

His eyes spark to mine, all the hatred in the world fanning the flames. 'Happy?'

I hitch a shoulder. 'Indifferent.'

We both look down at David's lifeless body. A beat passes. Then another. Then suddenly, he inhales a violent breath. His chest jerks and a cough rips from his throat, messy and wet.

The restaurant leaps into action. Chairs scrape, suits appear. Large hands fist fabric.

Every head in the restaurant turns to watch David's withering body as two men drag him through the maze of tables and toward the kitchen.

I hear the hum of murmurs like they're coming from another room. See hands clamp over mouths and rest over hearts but only in my peripheral.

A roomful of Good Samaritans. None of them are me.

With my spine rigid and too few breaths, I slowly drag my napkin from my lap and lay it gently on the table.

I stare down at the candlelight dancing on the walls of David's empty glass. 'I guess it's time to call it a night.'

The words trickle from my lips, void of feeling. They sound as empty as I am.

Carefully, I rise from the table, pushing back my chair with more steadiness than I feel.

I don't say another word. Neither does he, but it doesn't matter. Because I notice the tight jaw and the sharp lines of his shoulders. I see the tremble in his palms spread flat against the table. I feel his gaze, murderously cold, follow me across the restaurant and out of the door.

The night air hits me like a punch, more violent than a midnight email ever could. I stagger forward toward the light of a streetlamp, but I don't make it that far before I double over, grip my thighs, and throw up all the rot within.

The burn of bile lingering at the back of my throat, I wipe a shaky hand over my mouth and force myself to straighten up.

He wants me.

Gabriel Visconti *wants* me.

It never left his lips, but I saw it between the cracks of his galvanized demeanor, and catching sight of it was the worst, most dangerous, irreversible, soul-ruining thing I could have ever done.

Because no matter how much pink I wear or how many good deeds I do, that one sentence – five words, twenty-nine characters, including spaces – is set in stone.

Mildred Black has a daughter.

And she is exactly like her.

ACKNOWLEDGEMENTS

It's often said that writing is a lonely process, but that couldn't be further from the truth. There were so many people involved in the creation of the Sinners Anonymous series—family, friends, and four-legged procrastination partners.

I want to thank Sonnie, the love of my life, for the endless cups of tea, the egg sandwiches, and for forcing me to see sunlight every now and again. And our dog, Knuckles, for all the cuddles and kisses between Pomodoro sprints.

I want to thank my family. Mum and Dad—you've always believed I could do it. You're my biggest cheerleaders, and I love you. Thank you for still loving me back even when I cancel plans to write. I'm also sorry for all the sex scenes and the swearwords.

To my sisters, Lauren and Taylor: I'd never hear the end of it if I got soppy about you two, so I won't. You're all right, I guess.

To my author friends—I'm so lucky to have you. Mallory Fox, Autumn Woods, Lily Gold, Gabrielle Sands, Olivia Hayle, and Lola King. I can't put into words how much your support means to me. Long live the group chat!

A huge thank you to Katie, my business manager and, most importantly, my best friend. You've been my ride or die for seventeen (!) years. We always swore we'd work together one day—and look, we made it!

A massive thank you to my agent, Kimberly, for always advocating for me, and to the amazing team at evermore, who have believed in the Sinners series from the very beginning.

And last, but certainly not least, thank *you*, my darling reader. Ironically, I'm not articulate enough to describe how much you mean to me—and I'm definitely not concise enough to tell you in a single paragraph. Instead, I'll show my gratitude by continuing to write the stories you love, forever and always.

All my love,
Somme x

Binge the Sinners Series

evermore

Love, spice and sleepless nights.

The hottest new romance publisher at Penguin Random House UK.

Prepare for excessive swooning, devouring love stories and dangerously high standards for your own happily-ever-afters.

Proceed with caution... and an open heart.

FOLLOW US ON SOCIALS:

 @evermorebooksuk

On a station platform, with nothing to read,
and a four-hour train journey stretching ahead of him...

That's where the story began for Penguin founder Allen Lane.
With only 'shabby reprints of shoddy novels' on offer,
he resolved to make better books for readers everywhere.

By the time his train pulled into London, the idea was formed.
He would bring the best writing, in stylish and affordable
formats, to everyone. His books would be sold in bookstores,
stationers and tobacconists, for no more than the price
of a ten-pack of cigarettes.

And on every book would be a Penguin, a bird with a certain
'dignified flippancy', and a friendly invitation to anyone who
wished to spend their time reading.

In 1935, the first ten Penguin paperbacks were published.
Just a year later, three million Penguins had made their
way onto our shelves.

Reading was changed forever.

—

A lot has changed since 1935, including Penguin, but in the
most important ways we're still the same. We still believe that
books and reading are for everyone. And we still believe that
whether you're seeking an afternoon's escape, a vigorous debate
or a soothing bedtime story, all possibilities open with a book.

Whoever you are, whatever you're looking for,
you can find it with Penguin.